THE
Two Week
STAND

NEW YORK TIMES BEST SELLING AUTHOR
SAMANTHA TOWLE

Charlie Matthews, you are officially the bravest woman I know. You fought the Big C and kicked its butt. I feel privileged to know you and lucky that I get to call you my friend.

one

DILLON

I'M THE FIRST TO step off the seaplane and onto the jetty, saying hello to the staff member waiting to greet us all.

Moving aside so the other passengers can get off, I stretch my back out.

Eleven hours on a flight from Manchester to the Maldives and then a forty-five-minute flight on a cramped seaplane to the island, and I'm finally here.

Alone.

Nope. I'm not going to get upset.

I'm not gonna think about him.

Or her.

I've spent enough time crying over what they did to me. No more.

I'm literally in paradise, surrounded by beauty. I cannot be sad here.

Even though I tell myself this, I still feel my throat start to burn, the hurt wanting to climb its way into my eyes.

I get my sunglasses from my bag and slip them on.

Swallowing back my emotions, I take a deep breath.

The air is heavy. The heat here is like nothing I've ever known.

I've been abroad before but only to Spain with my girlfriends. I thought it was warm when I was there. It's nothing compared to the heat here.

When I landed at Malé airport, I began to seriously regret the leggings and long-sleeved shirt I wore to travel here. It had been freezing when I left home to head to the airport. Thought I was being smart, wearing something comfy to travel in.

But being here now, on the island, I can feel the sweat starting to gather around the nape of my neck and my armpits.

I need to shower and change ASAP. Then, eat something and fall into bed.

I'm knackered after all the traveling.

Retrieving a scrunchie from my bag, I gather my long hair up off my neck and tie it up in a haphazard bun. I know for a fact that it looks like shit. I'm not one of those girls who can put her hair in a messy bun and it come off looking amazing. I usually end up looking like I lost a fight with a bush.

But I'm not here to impress anyone, and I'm fucking melting, so shit hair bun it is.

I press my hand to the back of my neck to remove the sweat there, and then I surreptitiously wipe my hand on my leggings.

I look to my left, and the woman standing there, who was on the seaplane ride here, is watching me, a judgy look on her face, like I'm the grossest thing she's ever seen.

Of course she's totally put together.

We can't all look amazing after a long-ass flight. Some of us are smelly and gross.

Deal with it, lady.

I give her a pointed look—through my dark glasses, of course—and she looks away.

The guy she's traveling with comes over and kisses her. She lifts her hand to his cheek.

My eyes catch on the massive rock and gold band on her finger.

An ache deep inside of my chest tries to claw its way out.

What the hell was I thinking, coming here?

It's going to be full of couples and happy newlyweds, who are going to make me want to poke my eyes out.

Come on your honeymoon alone, Dillon. It'll be fine, Dillon.

Note to Dillon: you're a fucking idiot.

The greeter guy asks us all to follow him down the jetty to the island.

I let everyone else go first.

All fucking couples.

I am the only solo person here.

What did I expect, coming here?

The Maldives is couples central. Not sad, pathetic, single women central.

I should have stayed home.

And lost thousands of pounds on this trip.

I couldn't get a refund.

Apparently, my fiancé fucking … I can't even say it without wanting to throw up.

Basically, *cheating fiancé* wasn't listed on my travel insurance as a reason for cancellation.

And the travel company wouldn't let me change to a different destination. It was literally two weeks before I was due to get married when I found out the truth. And a week before I could even bring myself to contact the travel company.

So, it was either stay home and drink myself into a coma. Or come to paradise and drink myself into a coma.

I chose the latter.

I just didn't take into consideration the happy couples I'd be surrounded by.

Looking at these blissful bastards in front of me makes me wish I were back in my home with a few bottles of Prosecco in front of me and a serial killer documentary on TV for company.

I hear my phone ding in my bag, and I pull it out.

Text from my aunt Jenny. I texted her when I landed in Malé airport to let her know I'd arrived.

How is it? Send pics ASAP! Love you. xxx

I smile at her message even though I blame her for me coming here too. She was the one who first suggested it. I asked her to come with me, take Tim's place, but she couldn't get the time off work with such short notice. Neither could any of my girlfriends.

But Aunt Jen encouraged me to come alone. Said the time away would do me good.

I'm seriously doubting it now. But here I am.

I'm just gonna have to suck it up for the next two weeks.

Doing as Jenny asked, I lift my phone and take a few pics of the island that will be my home for fourteen days.

It's the first time I've actually paid attention to the island since I landed here, which says a lot about my mental state at the moment, but this place is absolutely stunning. I've never seen anything like it before.

It actually slows my steps.

There were some gorgeous sights on the seaplane flight here, but being here on the island and seeing it in all its beauty is something else.

I feel something shift in my chest as I stare at the lush greenery in front of me, the clear blue water lapping against the soft white sand, the water bungalows that sit off to the right and left side of the island.

I'm staying in a water bungalow.

The water bungalows are a little more expensive than the beach villas, but Tim was paying for the whole wedding, so I wanted to contribute something more.

I felt so guilty that he was paying for the wedding, but he had insisted.

Still, I spent a frigging fortune on this honeymoon. Maldivian holidays don't come cheap.

And considering I don't have a job that pays a lot of money and I don't come from a wealthy family, like he does, and that he fucked me over in the worst possible way, I'm glad he stumped up the cash and lost it all. The wedding venue wouldn't refund at such short notice. The rings had been bought. The cars booked. My dress all paid for …

It's still sitting at the store. I never did pick it up.

There was no reason to.

Fuck, I hate him.

And I hate her more.

Stop, Dillon. Don't think of either of them.

Pushing all thoughts of the hell I've endured over the past two weeks, I snap a few photos of the island, beach, and the bungalows and send them to Jenny. Then, I put my phone away just as my feet hit the sand and we're under the shade of palm trees.

Unfortunately, I'm wearing my favorite pair of Converse, so I can't feel if the sand is as soft as it looks.

But I will later.

That can be my something to look forward to.

That, and shower, food, and sleep.

I follow the group into the main reception area.

And there is air-conditioning.

Thank you, gods!

The greeter guy tells us all to take a seat and that someone will be over to check us in.

I grab a single comfy-looking chair on its own in the corner, leaving the two-seaters for all the lovebirds.

God, I'm such a loser.

A waiter appears in front of me with a glass of bubbly, which I happily accept.

I down it in two swigs.

Christ. I needed that. I only wish there were more.

I set the empty glass on the table in front of me just as a super-pretty Maldivian woman takes a seat across from me, a tablet in her hand.

"Hi, I'm Najam. I will be checking you in today. Can I take your name, please?"

"Dillon Dawson."

I booked the honeymoon in my name, thankfully. I was going to have a double-barreled surname. I didn't want to give up my dad's surname. It's the only thing I have left of him.

That, and the fact that Tim's surname is shit. *Prickett.*

Apt really because he is a prick.

She taps on her tablet. "Yes, of course. Miss Dawson and Mr. Prickett. You are on honeymoon. Congratulations!" She beams at me. "Mr. Prickett is here, yes?" She glances around, looking for him.

My heart sinks. I can feel my face reddening.

I'm thankful I'm still wearing my sunglasses, so she can't see my eyes, which are definitely watering. I take a breath before speaking, "Um ... no, it's just me," I say in a quiet voice. "No Mr. Prickett. Just me."

Her expression drops. Eyes pitying. "Oh. I am sorry."

"Don't be. You didn't cheat on me."

Her eyes widen in shock. Clearly, she doesn't get my stupid brand of humor.

I always use jokes as an attempt at deflection. They fail ninety-nine percent of the time. Like this one. Obviously, I've never learned to stop.

"Sorry. I was, um, it was a lame attempt at humor. Ignore me." I wave my hand, like I can somehow erase the last minute.

"Oh, okay." She sounds all awkward now. About as awkward as I'm feeling.

I just need to get the key to my bungalow and get the hell out of here.

She glances down at her tablet. "You are staying in one of our most wonderful senior water villas. Number seventy-eight. Very lovely and private. The views are stunning. Please wait while I go and get your key."

She quickly disappears. Don't blame her. Wish I could disappear too.

Needing something to do, I get my phone from my bag and check the screen.

A message from Jenny is waiting for me.

> *OMG! It's gorgeous. Wish I were there with you!*
> *Call me once you get settled in. Love you.*

I wish she were here too.

Or maybe Chris Hemsworth … or Liam. Both are divine. Also '90s Jon Bon Jovi. And 2000s Brad Pitt, circa *Troy*. Actually, I'd take 2021 Brad Pitt, to be honest. Dude is still hot as sin.

Yeah, in your dreams, Dillon. They'd probably only cheat on you anyway.

Jesus, I'm maudlin.

I don't reply back to Jenny's text. I'll just call her later, like she asked.

I slip my phone back into my bag just as the check-in woman reappears.

"Here is your key. Number seventy-eight. If you follow the signs just outside to the senior water villas, yours is at the very end of the jetty. Your luggage is already waiting for you in your room. Dinner is at eight p.m. Your bed will be turned down every night and made every morning while you are at breakfast."

I take the key from her. Standing, I pick up my bag and hang it on my shoulder. "That's great. Thank you"—my eyes quickly drop to her name tag. I'm shockingly bad at remembering names. Well, my memory is pretty bad overall—"Najam."

"You are very welcome. I very much hope you enjoy your stay here. Anything you need, please call reception or come in to see us. And, Miss Dawson, I hope this is okay to say … and does not offend you … but Mr. Prickett is a very stupid man."

That raises a smile, and not much does nowadays.

"It's more than okay. Thank you, Najam," I tell her again with sincerity.

She nods at me and heads back to the reception area while I make my way out of here, past the happy frigging couples who are still checking in.

I step out of the lovely, cool, air-conditioned reception into the stifling heat. Glancing around, I look for the sign that Najam mentioned, which will direct me to my bungalow.

I spot the sign for senior water villas and follow the direction it's pointing in.

I somehow make it to the jetty leading to the villas without getting lost, which is a miracle for me. Directions are not my strong point.

Much like my ability to pick fiancés.

I step onto the jetty, reveling in the absolute peace. The only sound is the water lapping the legs of the jetty.

I walk along, paying attention to the numbers on the bungalows as I pass them.

Finally, I reach number seventy-eight, which is at the end of the jetty, just as Najam said it would be. I cast a glance at my neighbor, number seventy-nine, and send up a silent prayer that whoever is staying in there aren't newlyweds.

Who am I kidding? They'll most definitely be newlyweds, and they'll have loud sex every night. Because this is me, and my luck pretty much sucks at the moment.

I let myself inside the bungalow. My luggage is waiting just inside the door.

There's air-conditioning in here too. Heaven.

Shutting the door behind me, I slip my sunglasses off and see just how light and airy this place is. I step in a little farther and see the bathroom off to my left. I wander in and see it opens out onto a private area, and there's a bath outside.

A frigging outside bath! I don't remember seeing that in the description when I was booking this place.

I can't wait to get a bath in there. Relax with a glass of bubbly and a good book. Crime book, of course. Normally, I love a good romance book. But I'm not in the mood to read about fictional people's happily ever afters.

Murder … now, that I can get on board with.

No romance is allowed in this bungalow.

It's a romance-free zone.

Leaving the bathroom, I wander into the main room. Plenty of closet space for my clothes. Not that I brought loads.

Mostly bikinis, shorts, and tank tops. Some summer dresses and outfits to wear to my solo dinners.

Nothing fancy.

Although I did bring a pair of heels with me, I can't see them getting much use. Walking on sand in heels is a definite no-no.

Thankfully, I brought some wedges and nice flip-flops, the kind with a bit of bling on them, in case I have to dress up.

I honestly don't know what the dinner dress code is here.

I'm imagining it to be quite relaxed.

And I'm seriously overthinking this.

When I reach the bed, my bag slips off my shoulder and thuds to the floor, right along with my stomach.

The bed is all laid out with a sprinkling of rose petals and some towels arranged into the shape of a heart.

At the end of the bed, there's a small table with a bucket of champagne and two glasses. A fruit basket and a card.

I walk toward it and pick up the card. Removing it from the envelope, I read it.

I don't realize I'm crying until a tear hits the card, smudging the ink.

Fuck this.

I dry my face with my hand. Toss the card onto the floor and grab the champagne from the bucket. Unwrapping it, I pop the cork with proficiency that I didn't know I had, and I take a long swig from the bottle. Fuck the glass. It's not like I'm sharing it with anyone.

Grabbing a banana from the fruit basket, I walk out onto the terrace, into the heat, and sit down on one of the two loungers.

Two loungers and only one of me.

I glare at the empty lounger, like it's somehow its fault that my life went to shit in the span of a few seconds.

A few seconds … walking in and seeing something no person ever wants to see … was all it took for my life and future dreams to dissolve into pieces before me.

Honestly, I'd toss that sun lounger into the ocean, but I don't want to have to stump up the cash to replace it.

That, and the sea life doesn't deserve to have its home invaded by my anger.

Still, I put my foot up against the side of the lounger and push it as far away from me as I can.

God, look at me. I should change my name to Eeyore. I'm like a sad fucking donkey.

I need to sort my shit out. Cheer the hell up.

But first, I need something to eat; otherwise, I'll be a cheap date tonight.

Putting the bottle down on the floor beside the lounger, I peel open the banana.

It's actually a hella big banana. Bigger than my ex's dick—that's for sure. Probably has more potential to fill me as well.

I snort a laugh.

Tim used to hate it when I snorted, so I used to try not to do it.

See, there is an upside to all this. I can snort a laugh without the prick complaining.

I snort again and then a couple more times, just for the hell of it. Then, I take a big bite of banana. Chew and swallow and then chase it down with some more champagne.

I might be alone and miserable. But I'm in paradise. In the most gorgeous bungalow, looking out over the water. I have an outside bath and alcohol, and that always helps dull the pain, making me feel less alone and sad.

I'm a happy drunk, always have been, so I'll just keep drinking this champagne until I'm feeling happy.

Or as happy as I can.

I get my phone and open up the Music app, and then I select a song that never fails to lift my spirits and pump a bit of strength into me—Christina Aguilera's "Fighter." I hit play, and then I put the champagne bottle to my lips and take another drink.

two

WEST

I NOTICE HER THE moment she walks in the bar. She's hard to miss for a few reasons. One, she's clearly drunk and trying to act like she's sober. It shows in the rigidness of her walk. Two, she's wearing a hell of a lot of clothes for this kind of heat. Even at night, it's hot as balls here, and this chick is wearing black leggings and a long-sleeved black shirt, like we're in for a cold flash. And three, which probably should have been the first thing I listed … she's hot as fuck. She reminds me a little of Selena Gomez. Long, dark, wavy hair. She's tiny, but compared to me, a lot of women are. At a distance, I'd say she's five-three, max. For a short chick, she has surprisingly longish legs that would fit nicely around my waist. I have a mental flash of her pressed against a wall with me up against her, my cock buried deep inside her, those legs of hers tightly hugging my hips.

My dick twitches. I bat the image aside. Every woman on this island is either married or has a boyfriend, and attached women are not my thing. Neither are drunk ones.

Taking a sip of my cold beer, I watch her navigate her way toward the bar, where I'm perched on a stool. It's cute, seeing her try to walk in a straight line. She's already stumbled twice—over thin air.

Reaching the bar a few feet away from me, she leans her stomach against it, and I get a side shot of her chest. She has decent-sized tits.

"Bartender." She slaps her hand down on the bar top. "Drink me." She's English.

There are quite a few Brits on the island. As an American, I'm a rarity here. The flight here from the States is an absolute fucker, so it's not the first vacation destination on our list, which is exactly why I chose to come here.

And if I didn't already know that the little Brit over there was drunk, I'd know from that little word fuckup and the slight slur to her voice.

I share an amused look with the bartender, who is already making a drink at my end of the bar for the couple seated outside.

Yes, I've been that bored. Even though this was the perfect place to come for some privacy and quiet time, I didn't take into account the lack of shit to actually do here.

Well, I say I'm bored. But I'm not now that the gorgeous little drunk Brit showed up.

"Pretty sure he's supposed to serve you, not drink you." I put my bottle to my lips and tip it back.

The *bluest* eyes I have ever seen look my way.

I feel this strange tightening sensation in my chest. *Weird.*

She turns her upper body toward me, places her elbow on the bar, and goes to rest her chin on it but misses. I hide a laugh behind my bottle.

"I *meant*," she enunciates the word, "drink me, as in give me a drink. You know, like *beer me.*"

"Maybe next time, go with *beer me*. It would've sounded way better."

"But I don't want beer. That's why I said *drink me*. Duh."

She rolls her eyes, and I can't stop the laughter that time.

"You're American."

I lower my bottle to the bar. "And you're English."

"Yep. That's me. English and all alone. Like that chick who sings that song in that film. You know who I mean?" She snaps her fingers at me.

"I literally have no fucking clue what you're talking about."

"You do! It's ... crap. What's her name? That film from years ago ..." She keeps on snapping her fingers at me. "She had shit luck with men ... like me ... Bridget Jones!"

"Never heard of her."

"Ugh. You men have no clue." She gives me a disapproving look. "In the film, she's drunk and home alone, and she sings 'All By Myself.' Which is like me. Except I'm not at home. But I'm drunk and alone. Also, she ends up with that hot guy at the end, and that's definitely not me. No hot guy waiting for me."

Okay, so there's no guy, and she is here alone. Which is a bonus for me. She's fucking gorgeous, and I would definitely like to get to know her better. Okay, I want to fuck her. When she's sober, of course.

I decide to ask her. Not to fuck. Not just yet anyway. But for confirmation that there is actually no guy. "So, you're here alone then?"

"Yep. *Alone, alone, alone,*" she sings.

The bartender finishes up making the drinks for the couple and puts them on a tray and down at the other end of the bar for the waitstaff to take it over to them.

He comes over to my new drunk friend. "Sorry about your wait. What can I get you to drink?"

"Do you make cocktails?"

"Yes, ma'am."

"Ohh, goodie." She claps her hands together. "I'll have a Long Island iced tea. That has a lot of alcohol in it, right?"

"Sure does. Gin, vodka, tequila, rum, and triple sec."

"Perfect. And go light on the mixer. Please and thank you," she adds as he turns away to start making her drink. "I hate it when people don't use manners," she says to me.

"Then, we have that in common."

My mom instilled good manners into me.

"The prick never said *please* or *thank you* to anyone."

"The prick?"

"My ex."

"Ah. Gotcha."

She climbs up onto the stool, two down from mine. It takes her a few attempts to actually get up on it. I'd offer my help, but it's fun, watching her try.

"Where's your other half?" she says to me once she's got her sweet ass on the stool.

"My other half of what?"

"You know, your significant other. Wife. Girlfriend. Husband. Boyfriend."

"Not gay. Not married. No girlfriend."

She laughs. "No fucking way you're single. You're hot—like super hot—and super-hot guys are never single."

Good to know she thinks I'm hot. Not that I doubted she would. I mean, I'm a good-looking bastard, and she's not made of wood.

"Well, you know, sometimes, super-hot guys like me are single." I put my bottle to my lips and empty the contents.

"You're really single?"

"Yep."

The bartender puts down her cocktail, and while he's there, I ask him for another beer.

I look at the hot Brit, and she's got her full lips wrapped around the straw, drinking down that cocktail like a champ.

Makes me think of something else I'd like her lips wrapped around and the happy ending I'd like her to swallow down.

Jeez, my thoughts are really straying off into the path of perverted. Which isn't unusual for me. I love women. I love fucking them.

But this one really has me fired up. Maybe it's because it's been a while since I last had sex.

"This drink is really yummy," she says to me.

"You seem like you're enjoying it."

She's drunk down half of it already. She keeps going at that rate, and she's gonna be wasted.

Looks like I'm on drunk-person duty tonight. I mean, she's here alone, and I can't exactly leave her to her own devices. Sure, we're on a small island, and I'm guessing it's safe. But there's a lot of trouble a drunk person can get themselves into, even on an island.

The bartender puts my beer down, and I thank him. I'm only two beers in, this being my third, so I'll cut myself off after this one. I can hold my liquor, but something tells me I'm gonna need to be sober for this, and I wasn't planning on getting drunk tonight anyway. Unlike my new little British friend.

Look at me, thinking of someone else. See, I can be a good guy when I want to be.

She drains her drink and orders another.

"Oh my gosh!" she exclaims out of nowhere, scaring the shit out of me. "I love this song!"

There's music playing quietly in the background, but I've not been paying attention to it. Clearly, she has.

"Can you turn the music up, please?" she asks the bartender, who is more than happy to oblige her request.

She slides off the stool and starts to dance right fucking there. She literally gives zero fucks, and I like it.

"Come dance with me!" She holds a hand out to me.

As hot as she might be, this is when I tap out.

I might move like a motherfucker on the field, but dancing is not my thing. It's not that I can't dance. Dance lessons were forced on me by my mom to get me through the many fucking functions my father would drag us to. Mom always wanted me to dance with her, and I would do anything for her.

But in the middle of a quiet bar, that's where I say no.

"Nope, I'm good. But you carry on."

And I am more than happy to sit here and watch her gyrate and move her body around. I especially like it when she bounces on the balls of her feet and her tits move in her top. It is the best thing I've seen in ages. I haven't seen tits that actually move of their own accord in a really fucking long time.

God bless the British girl's surgically untouched tits.

I could honestly sit here all night, sipping on my beer and just watching her dance.

But it's also a little pervy—okay, a lot pervy now that I think about it. I'm ogling a drunk girl who doesn't know better. And I'm not the only one. The bartender and the guy sitting outside, whose wife just went to the restroom, are also getting a good look at the British girl here.

"Why don't you sit down and finish your drink?" Yes, I'm encouraging more alcohol consumption, but it was the only thing I could think of to say to get her to sit her gorgeous ass down, so the menfolk—me included—would stop watching her tits bounce and her tight ass move around.

"I will when the song ends."

Okay, so that didn't work.

"What song is this anyway?" I ask, having zero clue about the song that has her so hyped up.

"You don't know this song?" She looks at me like I'm an idiot.

She's right too; I am.

"That would be why I asked you what song it was."

"God, you're so sarcastic!" She rolls her eyes at me.

Is it weird that the eye-rolling turns me on even more than seeing her tits move?

She finally stops dancing and sits her ass back down on the stool. Well, after a couple of attempts.

She's sweating, and it's sexy as fuck because all I can think about is another way she could be sweating with me. Yes, I'm that sexually depraved. Sue me.

"God, it's hot." She fans her face with her hand.

"I'll get you a water."

"I've got a drink." She wraps those lips around the straw again.

My imagination sends SOS signals to my dick. *Down, boy. Not tonight.*

" 'Cruel Summer,' " she says to me after swallowing another good amount of Long Island iced tea.

"What?" is my response.

"The song. You asked what it was called, and it's called 'Cruel Summer.' "

"Who sings it?"

"Bananarama."

I laugh. "What?"

"Bananarama," she repeats.

"That's actually a real band name?"

"Yep, '80s British girl band. My aunt Jenny loves them." She grabs the glass of water the bartender just put down and gulps the full glass down.

"Thirsty?" I deadpan.

"No. I just want another cocktail." She smirks at me. "Thank you for the water," she says to the bartender. "Can I have a margarita now, please?"

"Nothing is gonna stop you from drinking tonight, is it?"

"Nope. I want to get drunk."

"You already are."

"Then, I want to get drunker. Until I forget."

"Forget what?"

"That I'm actually unhappy."

What am I supposed to say to that? A better man would ask why she's unhappy, but I'm not a good man.

Thankfully, the bartender places her cocktail on the bar in front of her, distracting her.

She thanks him and immediately takes a sip of it. "God, that's good."

I decide to stop bugging her about drinking too much and let her get as drunk as she wants. I'll watch out for her and make sure she gets back to her room safe and sound.

It's not like I have any other plans for tonight.

"I'm considering changing my name to Eeyore. What do you think?"

"First off, I'll have to ask what your name actually is before I can offer my thoughts."

"What's the second thing?"

"Eh?"

"You said *first off*, which always means there's a *second off*."

There are so many dirty things I could say to that, but I won't. Well, at least tonight, I won't.

"Tell me the answer to my first question, and I'll tell you what the second thing is."

"Fine." She sighs. "My name is Dillon."

"Like Bob Dylan?"

"Exactly like that. Well, minus the Bob. Would have been a bit shit if I'd been called Bob Dylan." She laughs. "My dad was a big Bob Dylan fan."

"Your dad sounds cool."

"I wouldn't know. He died when I was a baby."

Shit.

The normal response for people in this moment is usually to say they're sorry. But having lost my mom when I was fifteen, I know how much I hate it whenever people say that to me.

So, instead, I say, "That sucks. You never getting to know him."

"I thought you were gonna say sorry. People always do."

"Do you want me to say I'm sorry?"

"Nope. I hate it when people say that."

"That's what I figured."

She stares at me for a moment, and I really like her eyes on me. I'd like other parts of her on me, too, but we'll get to that later. But her eyes, they're so fucking blue. A stark contrast to her dark hair. So dark that it's almost black.

"Is your hair naturally that dark?" I hear myself asking her. I blink myself free from her gaze, feeling like a total idiot. I thought I'd upped my game since I was sixteen. Clearly not.

Not that I'm hitting on her right now. But I am laying the groundwork because I definitely want to fuck Dillon when she's sober.

"You know I'm gonna ask why you're asking me that before I answer, right?" She smiles.

"Your eyes are really blue, and you don't see many dark-haired girls with blue eyes. Usually brown."

"Well, to answer you, my hair is all natural. What about yours?"

"Oh, totally natural too." I grin at her, and she laughs.

"I like you," she tells me. "You're funny."

"I know."

She chuckles again, shaking her head. "So, what's your name? You know mine; it's only fair that I know yours."

"West," I tell her.

"Like north, east, and south?" She grins.

"Exactly like that," I echo her prior words. "My parents were big fans of the cardinal directions."

She laughs again, and I really fucking like the sound.

"So, you have siblings called North, East, and South?"

"No. Thank fuck. Only child." I'm relieved that I didn't have a sibling who had to deal with Dad's constant absence or his crappy treatment of Mom or watching her die way too young.

"Only child here too," Dillon tells me, pulling me out of my thoughts. "And you never did tell me the second thing."

"Oh yeah."

"So …" She gestures for me to go on.

"Why Eeyore? There's a fuck of a lot of better names out there. Like the one you currently have."

"Because I'm a sad donkey."

I give her a blank stare.

"You know, Eeyore, the sad donkey."

"Not a clue what you're talking about."

"Please tell me you've heard of Winnie the Pooh."

"Sure I have."

"Eeyore was his buddy. The purple donkey that's always sad and depressed."

I shrug because I don't remember a purple donkey.

"I can't believe you don't know who Eeyore is!" She shakes her head. "So disappointed, and here I was, thinking you were cool."

"I am. Hence why I have zero clue what the fuck you're talking about."

"Eeyore is a sad donkey. I'm sad. Ergo the name change."

"You're really gonna regret this conversation when you wake up sober tomorrow."

"Shut up," she says, but she's laughing.

"And you don't seem sad to me."

She pauses and looks at me. "No, I don't, do I?"

There's a brief moment where we lock eyes again. I feel my skin start to prickle with desire, and my dick is definitely paying close attention.

Not tonight. She's drunk.

"You don't look like a donkey either," I add with a grin to take my mind off all the sex I want to have with her.

Laughter bursts from her, breaking our eye contact. "Thank God for that! Be a bit shit if I did look like a donkey. Not that they're not cute. But I definitely wouldn't make a cute donkey."

I'm grinning at her, and she says, "What?" around the straw she's got in her mouth.

"Nothing. You're just cute, is all. But not donkey cute."

"Thanks, I think." She chuckles.

I watch her as she finishes the rest of her drink, draining the glass. I've got to give her props; she sure can drink her liquor. Although she is kind of cheating, as it's a cocktail.

"So, do you only drink cocktails, or can you handle the hard stuff?" I ask her.

"Asks the man who's drinking beer."

"Touché."

"So, are you only a beer drinker? Or do you fancy joining me in a shot?" There's a wicked gleam in her eyes. A challenge.

And I know I said I wasn't drinking anything else after this beer, but I also know that one shot won't kill me, and I've never been one to back down from a challenge.

"What's your poison?"

A gorgeous smile slides on her lips, and fuck, do I want to kiss her. But I won't.

Not tonight anyway.

Tomorrow though, all bets are off.

"You choose."

I turn to the bartender. "Two shots of Fireball, please."

"Make it four shots," she says.

Okay, two shots won't kill me. I won't get drunk. Well, not before her anyway. She's already halfway to wasted, and I'm a big guy. She's fucking tiny. Couple of shots, and she'll be done.

three

WEST

I WAS WRONG. FOUR shots and another Long Island iced tea later, and she doesn't appear to want to stop drinking even though she's at the point of drunk where terrible decisions usually ensue.

I'm definitely feeling the buzz of the liquor. Fortunately, it's not enough that I can't see her back to her villa safely. Because there is no way she's getting back there alone without getting into trouble along the way.

Honestly, I think she'd have a hard time finding her way out of the bar at this point.

But I have to say, I am impressed at her ability to hold alcohol. For such a small person, she sure can put it away. And I only know what she drank in the bar. I have no clue what she drank before she got here.

"Another drink, barman," she slurs, lifting her hand up. Her other hand is supporting her head, elbow somehow managing to stay put.

Catching his eye, I shake my head.

"No more. I'm cutting you off."

She juts out her lower lip, pouting, and I have the urge to bite it. "I thought you were fun, Westy."

"Westy? Please don't ever call me that again. And I'm tons of fun. But you're wasted, and the only thing you need to be drinking now is water."

"Water's boring."

"It's what will save you from feeling like you're dying in the morning."

The bartender helpfully puts down a bottle of water on the bar in front of us.

I thank him and pop the cap on the bottle. I hold it out to her. "Down this. You'll thank me tomorrow."

"I don't want to thank you tomorrow. I want another cocktail."

"Down this, and we can talk about another drink."

She stares at me again. Granted, her eyes are glazed and off focus, but they're still absolutely fucking stunning.

"Fine," she grumps and takes the open bottle from me. She drinks half of it straight down.

"All of it," I tell her when she pulls the bottle away from her mouth. Putting my hand to the bottom of the bottle, I guide it back up to her lips.

"You're really bossy, you know."

She has no idea.

"Stop complaining and finish the drink."

She sticks her tongue out at me, but she finishes the water. "Happy?" she says, putting the empty bottle down on the bar.

"Yep."

I actually am, and I don't mean from getting her to drink the water. I've had a lot of fun with her tonight. I've laughed a fuck of a lot. She's a funny drunk. It's been a long time since I've enjoyed the company of a woman who I'm not actively fucking or knowing that I will be at the end of the night.

Although I plan on broaching the fucking thing with her tomorrow. When she's sobered up.

"Now, I get to have another drink."

"Bar's closing," I lie.

She looks around. The bar has filled up since she arrived earlier, and everyone is still sitting at tables.

"People are still here."

"They'll be leaving in a minute. We should go now to avoid the rush."

"But you promised me another drink!" she whines.

"And you can have one when you get back to your villa."

"I have none left. I drank everything in the minibar and the fucking free champagne they left."

"You're complaining about free champagne?"

She frowns. "No, the champagne was decent. It was supposed to be a gift for the newlyweds for our fucking honeymoon."

Oh. Shit.

I knew she was here alone and had an ex. But I didn't know she was here on her honeymoon, alone.

No wonder she's hammered.

"You can have a drink at my villa. My minibar is stocked."

"You haven't got fucking honeymoon champagne, have you?"

"Nope. Like I said, no girlfriend or wife."

"I haven't got a husband or a fiancé anymore, but I still got the fucking champagne."

I can see her eyes starting to water, and I don't want her to start bawling in the bar.

"Come on. Let's get you back."

27

I slip off my stool and help guide her off hers. I wrap my arm around her waist. She's so fucking tiny.

She falls into my side, and I walk her out of the bar and into the night air.

"Think I'm a little drunk," she slurs as I start to walk us in the direction of the villas.

"No shit." I laugh. "Where are you staying?" I ask her.

"The nice water villas."

"Number?"

"I can't remember." She laughs.

This should be interesting.

"It's at the end of the jetty. It's one of the nice ones. I'll know it when I see it."

"You know, they all look the same; the only difference is the numbers on them."

"I know, duh," she says drolly. "It's the old ones."

"Eh?"

"Old. Well, not old. Another word for old."

It takes me a good fucking minute to figure out that she means senior.

"You mean, the senior water villas." I chuckle.

"That's it!" She snaps her fingers in recognition. "I'm in the end one."

"I'm in the end one too."

Her head tips back, and she looks up at me. "No way!"

"I'm in seventy-nine. So, if you're at the end, you're staying in seventy-eight."

"That's the one!"

She pats my chest with her hand. I have to force myself to ignore the way I feel at the contact of her hand on me.

"And your chest is really hard. Wowsers."

Fucking hell. She's killing me here.

"Like really hard."

Her fingers are pressing against my pecs, and I'm fighting down the urge to kiss her.

She's drunk. She doesn't know what she's doing.

I pull in a deep breath through my nose and get a lungful of her.

"You're really tall," she says quietly, still staring up at me.

"I'm normal-sized. You're just tiny."

Her brow furrows. She looks fucking adorable. Like a kitten trying to be a tiger. "I'm normal-sized, thank you very much."

"I'm a whole person taller than you."

"You're just freakily big."

I laugh. "I'm six foot three. Ergo normal."

"Maybe for a guy. Woman here, if you haven't noticed."

"Oh, I've noticed." Shit, my voice has gone husky, and she's still staring up at me with those big blue eyes.

I really wish she weren't drunk right now. If she were sober, I'd be kissing the shit out of her and carrying her back to my villa, where I would spend the rest of the night fucking her.

But sadly, the only fucking my dick is doing tonight is in my hand.

"Come on—"

"Ooh, look at that!" Before I have time to blink, she's walking away from me and weaving across the sand toward the water's edge, where a crab is standing. "It's a crab. Fuck me, that's a big crab!" She laughs, stumbling a bit.

"It'll bite your foot off," I tease.

She stops and looks back at me. "Really?"

"No." I chuckle. "But it'll probably try to nip you with its pincers if you get too close."

And she is pretty close now that I'm looking.

She takes a measured step back, and out of nowhere, the crab runs at her.

She screams and runs straight for me. The next thing I know, I've got a drunk Dillon plastered to my body.

"Help me!" she wails. "I don't want to get bitten by that crab!"

I start laughing. I can't help it.

29

The crab stopped the minute she bolted for me. And for a drunk chick, she sure could move, and she jumped on me like a fucking Olympic hurdler.

"It wouldn't bite you." I laugh. "Only nip."

But its pincers are big as fuck, so it would definitely hurt.

"I don't want to get nipped!" she wails. "Why aren't you getting us out of here?! It'll get you now!"

"It's still over there." I point to where it is, watching us. "It stopped the second you screamed. I think you scared the shit out of it."

"I scared it?! Fucking thing ran at me!"

Then, I become very aware of the fact that she's wrapped around me. Her legs hooked around my waist. Arms around my neck. Her face pressed to my chest.

I can feel the heat of her through my clothes. I can smell her.

I know I wanted her legs around my waist, but I was thinking when she was sober and we were both naked and in my villa. And there wasn't an ugly-ass crab staring at us.

I can feel my dick starting to sit up and pay attention, and I need her off me before he salutes her in the ass.

Shit.

"I think you're safe to get down now."

"No fucking way! I'm not getting down there."

"You're fine. It won't bother you."

"Ha! Yeah, right. I bet you the second I put a foot down there, that bastard will come for me. I'll stay up here, where it's safe, thanks."

Fucking hell.

I can't exactly force her to get down, and I can feel my dick getting harder by the second. I'm gonna have to carry her back to the villa—quickly—and think of anything but sex the whole time.

I set off swiftly, and she makes a noise of surprise and holds on to me tighter.

I should secure her, so she doesn't fall off. Hold her or something, but if I put my hands on her … it's game over. She'll know exactly how much my dick likes her up here on my body.

Fuck's sake.

I get us back to the villas in record time. I practically sprinted here. She's lucky I'm an athlete; actually, it's me who's lucky because I don't know how much of carrying her I could have endured without doing something stupid.

She's got her head lying on my shoulder now. I hope she hasn't fallen asleep.

"We're here," I tell her.

"Uh, wha …" She sounds sleepy.

"We're at your villa." I walk up the steps to her villa—well, I'm hoping it's hers. "Number seventy-eight. That's you, right?"

"Yeah."

She makes no move to get down.

"You got your key?"

"My key?"

"Yeah, you know, the thing that unlocks the door."

"Oh, yeah, it'll be in my pocket." She loosens her hold on me and slides down my body.

I'm a strong man. But fucking hell, that was torture.

She lands on her feet and starts patting at her legs. "Oh." She laughs. "I haven't got any pockets."

"So, where's your key then?"

"Um … in my bag."

"You didn't bring a bag into the bar with you."

"Oh. Oops." She laughs again. "Guess I don't have my key. I'm really tired." She leans against the door and starts to slowly slide down to the floor.

"Whoa there." I grab hold of her, keeping her up. "Are you saying you're locked out?"

"Probably."

Probably?

"No worries. I'll just sleep here."

"You are not sleeping in the doorway of your villa."

It's either go to reception and get a key to her place—and that means carrying her back there because I can't leave her here. Or she stays in my place.

For fuck's sake.

Sighing, I make a decision. "You're staying with me tonight."

"Uh … no sex though. You're super hot and all, and I definitely would, but I'm tired. 'Kay?"

Chuckling, I say, "Come on." I pick her up, and I carry her over to my villa.

Reaching the door, I remember my key is in my fucking pocket.

"Get the key from my pocket."

"Mmhmm."

"Dillon. Key. In my pocket."

" 'Kay …"

Sighing, I balance her on my thigh, get the key from my pocket, and then unlock the door.

Walking inside, I kick it shut behind me and walk straight over to the bed, where I lay her down.

"Oh, hey." She opens her eyes, looking up at me. They're glassy but still pretty as fuck.

"I'll grab you some water and Advil."

"Hey … you promised more alcohol. And no tablets. Tablets bad."

"Okay, no tablets."

"And no water."

"Okay, okay, I'll get you some liquor."

"Ah, perfect. You're so lovely … and gorgeous …" She pats my cheek with her hand.

Chuckling, I go over to the mini fridge. Grab a glass. Get out a water and pour some into the glass. I take it over to her.

"Here you go." I hold the glass out to her.

"What is it?" She squints at the glass, attempting to sit up.

"Vodka. Neat." I'm such a liar, but she'll thank me in the morning.

"I love vodka!" She claps her hands together and then grabs for the glass.

She throws the drink back, and I wait for her to realize that it's actually water.

But she doesn't.

"Man, that's good! Can I have some more?"

"Sure." I suppress a grin. "I'll pour you a bigger one this time."

"Perfect."

I go over and empty the bottle into the glass. I am not prepared for what I see when I turn around.

She's standing up on the bed, and she's taking her fucking clothes off.

Jesus fucking Christ. I grip the glass so hard that it almost shatters.

"What are you doing?" The words come out strangled.

Her top is off, and there are inches of soft, pale skin.

"It's too hot!" she whines.

She starts pushing her leggings down her hips, and I'm just standing here, knowing I should stop her, that she's too drunk to know what she's doing, but fuck me ... she's hot.

Nope. Stop. She's drunk.

I avert my eyes when her leggings hit mid-thigh. Putting the glass on the table, I grab the comforter off the end of the bed. I hold it up and wrap it around her body, covering her.

"Hey, what're you doing? I'm hot!"

"Trust me, you'll thank me in the morning. Now, lay yourself down."

"Where's my drink?"

"Lie down, and I'll get it for you."

She does as I asked, thankfully keeping the cover on her.

33

I get the water and carry it over. I sit down beside her on the bed and hold out the glass. "Here."

"Thanks." She takes the drink but only sips it this time.

I take it when she holds it out, and I put it on the floor by the bed, so she can find it if she needs it during the night.

"You're a good guy, West."

"You wouldn't say that if you knew me."

"I know bad. My ex was bad. Really bad … he cheated, you know."

"He sounds like a dick."

"Prick." She laughs. "He's a prick. And a twunt."

"Twunt?" I question.

"*Twunt—because sometimes, twat and cunt just aren't enough.* I have that on a mug. It's one of my favorites. I also have one that says, *Twuntasaurus—like a normal twunt but more awesome.* That one has a picture of a cute dinosaur on it too."

"Well, *twunt* is now officially my favorite word."

She smiles big, lighting up her whole face, and if I wasn't sitting down, it would have knocked me on my ass. She really is beautiful.

"I have this really funny mug that I got as a Secret Santa gift last Christmas. It says, *Finger up the bum, no harm done.*" She snort-laughs, and then her brows draw together. "Actually, I never did find out who bought it."

"I'm getting the impression that you really like mugs."

"I do. I love them. I have a whole collection of Disney ones too." She sighs, and the sound is soft and sweet. "You know, they're all in boxes at the moment, sitting lonely and unused in my aunt Jenny's garage because I'm officially homeless. I'd given up the lease on my place to move into the prick's house. But you know, obviously, that's not happening, so I'm staying with Aunt Jenny, who is awesome—you'd love her—until I can find another place. Ugh." She groans, slapping a hand to her face. "I honestly don't know what I was thinking! I don't even know why I was going to marry him. You know, he was the worst in bed.

34

Total worst! He needed a map just to find my vagina. And I don't even think a satnav would have gotten him to my clit."

Jesus. Fucking. Christ. She really needs to stop talking about her vagina and clit. Because I'm already imagining how her pussy tastes.

"Well, I'd say, you had a lucky escape," I say to move my thoughts away from her pussy because I'm not getting anywhere near it tonight.

"Yeah." She sighs an unhappy sound.

I'm just here, wondering how this bad-in-bed, cheating prick of a guy managed to land a gorgeous girl like Dillon.

"I'm just sad, you know," she continues. "Not so much about him. He was just a small blip in the landscape of my life—my aunt Jenny told me that. Yeah …" Another sigh. "I'm just really sad about my mum."

"Your mom?"

"Uh-huh. It was my mum he was cheating on me with. They were having an affair. I walked in on them kissing a few weeks before he and I were supposed to get married. They were at her house. I'd let myself in. I was there to go finalize the seating plan with her. And they were right there in the kitchen, going at each other.

"Apparently, they'd been sleeping together for three months. Three fucking months! Literally from the moment I'd introduced him to her. Because, you know, that's what girls do—take the fiancé to meet the mother! He drove her home that night, and he was gone a while, told me that he'd had car trouble. Yeah, right. I bet that was the night it started.

"I know my mother. She doesn't waste any time when she's after a man. God! There I was, asking her to help me plan the wedding, asking her to give me away on my wedding day because she's the only parent I've ever had. Desperately trying to bond with her because our relationship has always been difficult. And she said yes to it all. She even helped picked my wedding dress! And all that time, she was screwing

SAMANTHA TOWLE

my fiancé!" She lets out this strangled noise that sounds like a cross between a laugh and a cry.

"I can't even say it without wanting to puke. I was sleeping in his bed with him, and so was she. God, it's just disgusting and incestuous! The day I found out, I literally puked. I threw up everywhere, and then I scrubbed my body raw in the shower. I just needed to get clean. Get their betrayal off me. But even now, I still feel ... gross." A soft cry slips past her lips. "My mum always told me that I was stupid. Guess she was right."

She blinks up at me with wet lashes, those eyes filled with hurt. I have the sudden urge to squeeze the life out of the fucking moron who hurt her, and I'd never lay a hand on a woman, but I might make an exception for her mom.

"You're not stupid, Dillon." I soften my tone even though I feel a confusing amount of anger toward the two people who hurt this woman that I barely know. "They are. To even contemplate doing that to you, let alone actually doing it ... it's cruel." I shake my head. My dad is an asshole, but even he wouldn't stoop that low. "And I'm sorry to say this, but your mom sounds like a total twunt."

She laughs through her tears, and I'm glad that I could at least make her smile when she's feeling so sad.

"She is a twunt."

I reach out, and using my thumb, I wipe a tear from her cheek. She blinks up at me, all wide blue eyes and innocence.

"They're both twunts who aren't worthy of you. And I know it hurts now. But it won't soon."

Her eyes close. "Promise?" she whispers.

And something in my chest splinters. I rub my hand against my chest, trying to erase the weird sensation I'm feeling.

"I promise. Good things will happen for you, Dillon. I know it."

Because good things are owed to people who suffer the awful. Well, that's what my mom always said. But it never happened that way for her. I really hope it does for Dillon.

"West?"

I brush strands of her hair off her forehead, and her eyes open and close slowly.

"Yeah?"

"I ... I ..." Then, she passes out.

I chuckle to myself. Then, I turn her onto her side in case she pukes during the night. Actually ... I grab the trash can and put it beside the bed, so I won't have to clean up vomit off the floor.

I grab some sleep shorts, turn out the light, and head into the bathroom to change out of my clothes and brush my teeth.

When I exit the bathroom, I navigate my way through the room in the dark. Stopping by the bed, I look over at Dillon, fast asleep in my bed, snoring lightly.

A total stranger to me only a few hours ago, and now, I know what brought her to the island and into the bar, drunk and straight into my path.

Sure, she's hurting now, but I'm going to make her time on this island good until she forgets any hurt those two assholes made her feel.

I walk quietly over to the shitty little chaise at the end of the bed. It's either this or the floor. The floor is hard as fuck, and I'm not in college anymore—when it didn't matter where I ended up sleeping. These days, I need comfort. I'm not getting any younger.

I lie down on the chaise, not bothering with a blanket because it's hot as balls in here, even with the AC on.

I stare up at the dark ceiling, listening to the soft, even breaths coming from the bed.

It's the last sound I hear before I fall asleep.

four

DILLON

I ROUSE TO THE sound of the ocean and the squeeze of my bladder.

I make an attempt to open my eyes but decide against it when the morning light nearly blinds me.

Christ's sake. My head is pounding, and my mouth is as dry as sand.

Where the hell am I?

Oh yeah. On my honeymoon. Alone.

And I'm pretty sure I drank the island dry last night.

So, there is that.

I lift a hand to my head.

What happened last night?

I remember starting on that bottle of champagne. On a mostly empty stomach. Except for the banana I ate.

My stomach roils.

Ugh. Fuck. Don't think about food.

I know I left my villa to go to the bar in search of more alcohol. Found the bar. There was definitely more drinking at the bar. Pretty sure I was talking to someone there as well. Then … nothing.

For fuck's sake.

I send up a silent prayer. *Please, God, don't let me have made an arse out of my—*

I hear a low, deep moan. Which definitely didn't come from me. And definitely sounded male.

Oh God, please no. Don't let me have hooked up with a complete stranger.

Peeking open one eye, I wince at the light.

And see that there's a man asleep on the chaise at the end of my bed.

Holy fuuuuck.

My first night here, and there's a guy in my room. At least he's not in bed with me. But that doesn't mean we didn't have sex.

I run a hand over my body.

I'm in my underwear. No clothes.

Shit.

Okay. Don't panic. I have my panties on. That's a good sign, right? I'd be sans panties and the guy would be in bed with me if we'd had sex.

Or at least, that's what I'm hoping.

Drunken sex with a complete stranger is so not what I need right now.

I'm not actually sure what I need, truth be told. Apart from a shower and a coffee. I can figure shit out from there.

First off, I need to find out who the hell this guy is.

Forcing my other eye open, I wipe the sleep from them with my hand and rise up onto my elbows to get a better look at the guy.

Damn, my head is killing me.

He's on his side, facing away from me. All I can see is a mass of dirty-blond hair.

Who the hell is he? And why is he in my villa?

A quick trawl of my memory doesn't bring up anything from last night. But also, my brain is still awash with last night's alcohol, so no surprise there.

Deciding I need to get a better look at him, I crawl down the bed a little.

Jesus, he barely fits on that chaise. His legs are hanging right off it. It can't be comfortable for him on there at all.

He's shirtless. Nice back. There are actual muscles on it. I've never seen muscles on a man's back before. Well, not in real life anyway. Tim definitely didn't have back muscles. He had arm and chest muscles but definitely none on his back.

And I really need to stop thinking about back muscles.

Strange man in my villa also has a large tattoo on his back. It looks like a black bird in flight. It's really cool.

My eyes scan down. He's wearing shorts.

Another plus to the fact that we didn't have sex. No man I've ever known would get dressed after sex. Unless he's weird, which knowing me and the men I attract, that wouldn't be a stretch. Christ, Tim wouldn't even get up to dispose of the condom. He'd tie a knot in it and leave it on the floor, knowing it would gross me out so I'd get up and dispose of it.

My eyes move down those long legs. Also muscular. Tanned with just the right amount of hair on them. Feet are bare. He actually has nice feet for a man.

Why in the hell am I thinking about his feet?

I really do have some fucking weird thoughts at times.

He makes a mumbling sound and turns over onto his back. All of my muscles lock up.

Then, I see his face.

Oh.

OH.

Sweet Lawd.

A flood of memories from last night hits me.

It's the hot guy from the bar. And when I say hot, I mean, *hawt*.

Like Pitt and Hemsworth hawt.

Now, I'm kind of gutted that I didn't have sex with him.

I do a mental tour of my vagina just to be sure, but sadly, everything appears normal down there. Doesn't feel like I've had sex.

Gutted.

I mean, he's a big guy, so I'm figuring I'd be a little sore if we'd had sex. Unless he has a tiny cock.

And that would just be a damn, *damn* shame.

What is his name though? I know he told me last night. It's something to do with a direction … like a compass.

Is it Compass? Of course it's not Compass, you idiot. God, what's he called? What's he called? Come on, brain … think …

West!

His name is West.

That's it. Hot West with the sexy American accent. See, I do remember something from last night!

I might not remember why he's asleep on the chaise in my villa, and I might only be ninety-five percent sure that we didn't have sex due to my investigation into our state of dress. Although I am holding on to that five percent that we did bump uglies—or his gorgeous with my ugly because my eyes just landed on his chest, and holy mother of pearl, it's magnificent.

Muscles everywhere. I've never seen so many muscles in all my life. He has abs. Like actual, real abs. I've never seen abs on a man in real life. Only on TV, in pictures, and in porn movies.

What? Every healthy woman should watch porn. It's educational. And some of the guys are fit as fuck. And they fuck like I've categorically never experienced in real life.

I definitely need to get a better look at these abs.

Stealthily, I crawl down the bed to get a better look.

And … oh, hello there.

He is rocking some serious morning wood. It's showing very visibly through the fabric of his sleep shorts.

Now, I know for sure that we didn't have sex because I would definitely be feeling something this morning if that monster erection had been inside me.

Okay, this is getting creepy, even for me. I'm on the bed on all fours, staring at the abs and morning wood of a complete stranger, and—

"What are you doing?"

five

DILLON

I JUMP BACK AT the sound of his deep voice and fall off the bed.

"Argh!" I cry out, my back and butt hitting the hard floor.

"Um, should I ask if you're okay?" His deep, gravelly voice travels over the bed, to where I'm laid out on the floor.

"No," I grump.

"You need help getting up?"

"Again, no." I push myself up to a sitting position, and using the bed, I pull myself up to standing.

He's still lying there on the chaise, all that glorious bare chest on show.

"You really shouldn't watch people while they're sleeping, you know. It's creepy."

"I wasn't watching you sleep!" My hands go to my hips. Which I realize are bare. As is most of my body, except for the parts covered by my underwear.

A quick glance tells me that, yes, I'm still wearing my comfy, ugly-as-fuck white bra and panties, which I put on to travel here in. I still haven't changed.

It's official. I'm gross.

And I'm standing in front of the hottest man I've ever seen in real life in fugly underwear. And I have no clue what state my hair is in.

Fuck my life.

I quickly fold my arms over my chest, like that's going to fix anything about this situation.

His brow lifts, and it makes him look even sexier if possible. "If you weren't watching me sleep, then what were you doing?"

"Well, I was wondering, why in the bloody fuck are you in my villa?"

"Bloody fuck?" He smirks.

"Don't change the subject. Why are you in my villa?"

"I'm not."

"Yes, you are."

"As much as I'd love to debate the fact with you—because I have a feeling arguing with you would be fun—I can't be bothered because I'm deadass tired. I had a shitty night's sleep on a child-sized sofa. You're welcome, by the way."

He stretches his big arms above his head, and I'm momentarily mesmerized by them. They really are big. I bet he could pick me up and not even break a sweat.

"You're staring again."

"No, I'm not," I bite.

Although I should have no problem with objectifying him. If he doesn't want me to, then he shouldn't go around shirtless. Or have abs like that. Even if he did just wake up. He should put a shirt on.

Says the woman who's still standing in her day-old underwear.

"I thought I saw a mosquito on your arm."

"Sure you did, Double D."

"What did you just call me?" I'm wide-eyed, ready to smack him down. And I'm not even a double-D cup. I'm a D cup. Okay, there's not much difference, but it's so not the point.

"Double D," he repeats.

"And you don't think that's, uh, a tad inappropriate?"

"Your name is Dillon Dawson, right?"

"Yes …"

"So, you're Double D. Dillon Dawson."

Oh, for fuck's sake.

"Hilarious. But Dillon will do just fine."

"Whatever you say, Double D." He gets to his feet and stretches his body out, and I'm too mesmerized to tell him off for the second time.

I mean … fuck me.

With a dildo.

Repeatedly.

He's huge. Like really bloody tall. Six-three, minimum. And he's built. Muscles as far as the eye can see, and trust me, I'm looking. *Really* looking.

He has a jaw that looks like it was carved by the gods themselves. Roman nose that's definitely been broken in his lifetime. Intense gray eyes. Kissable full lips. Basically, he's gorgeous. And his hair … *damn.* It's surfer, sun-kissed dirty-blond hair that grazes those massive shoulders of his. It's hair that you want to reach out and grab hold of during sex or when his head is situated between your legs. Either way, I'm not fussy.

He looks like a movie star. He's that kind of good-looking. Like he should be on TV or in a magazine or up on a billboard somewhere.

I wish I were exaggerating because without even looking in the mirror, I'm guessing that I currently look like a troll that just crawled out from under her bridge.

Trust me to meet the hottest of the fucking hot when I look like this. And also smell like a stale brewery.

As he turns and lowers his arms, I notice that he has another tattoo on the inside of his bicep on his right arm, but I don't get a good look at it.

He walks away from me and over to the coffee machine. "You want a coffee?" he asks.

I can't stop staring at the muscles in his back, and they move underneath his tattoo. It's mesmerizing.

Realizing I haven't answered him, I snap myself out of my stupor. "Pretty sure I can make myself a coffee. And I'm sure you can make one in your *own* villa."

He turns, coffee pod in his hand, that damn smirk back on his handsome face. "Do you remember anything about last night?"

"Um … a little."

Another husky laugh. "I brought you back to your villa, which happens to be right next to mine, and you realized that you'd locked your key inside it, which you thought was funny as fuck. It was too late to go back to reception to get you a replacement key, and honestly, I didn't want to carry you to reception and then back here again. So, I brought you to my villa." He waves a hand around.

I follow his hand around and spot an iPad and laptop on the coffee table, which definitely don't belong to me. I know I left my suitcase in the doorway, where concierge had left it. I decided to get wasted instead of unpacking. I lean back and look at the front door. Empty.

I got wasted, had to be carried back to my villa, which I'd locked myself out of, and ended up sleeping in his.

Which was actually really decent of him.

I wince. "So, when you say, carried me …"

"You just jumped up on me. Didn't have much of a choice."

"Oh." I wince again. "I'm so sorry. I can be … a bit overfriendly when I'm drunk."

He chuckles, and the sound is really nice. "Figured that when you were telling me how hot you thought I was."

No.

Please.

No.

Kill me now.

My whole body is on fire. Pretty sure I'm the color of a tomato.

Why, God, why?! Haven't I suffered enough?!

Not that having a gorgeous man carry me and put me to bed is suffering, but knowing that I was drunk as a skunk and saying the most embarrassing things to him is beyond suffering. And he's staying in the villa across from mine, and we're on a tiny island, meaning I will most definitely have to face him again.

Not that I can get any lower than I am.

Fuuuuck.

I swallow past the rocks of embarrassment in my throat. I'm such an overconfident fucking twat when I'm drunk. "Uh … can I ask … did you and I … well, did we have sex?"

He presses the button on the coffee machine and turns to face me. He leans back against the table and folds his arms across that magnificent chest of his. "Call me old-fashioned, but I like a woman to be sober and conscious when I fuck her."

The way he says *fuck* in that sexy American accent sends shivers all the way down to my toes.

"Okay, well, that's good then." It is because, damn, I would have hated to forget having sex with him. "So, I'll just get my clothes and be out of your way. Thanks for taking care of me."

"No problem at all."

"Um, you don't happen to know where my clothes are?" I ask, looking around for them.

"Should be down near the side of the bed. That's where you threw them when you stripped." He points to the side of the bed I'm not at.

And the hits just keep coming.

I stripped my clothes off? I figured I'd just undressed for bed. But stripped off? For fuck's sake, Dillon.

Cringing, I ask, "Please tell me that I didn't do an actual striptease for you."

He turns back to me, coffee in his hand now, brow raised. "You do that when you're drunk? Damn, if I'd known, I'd have put in a request."

His lips lift at the corner. It's sexy as hell. Well, all of him is.

"Not usually. But I wouldn't put anything past drunk me."

"Noted," he says, a twinkle in his eye before he takes a sip of his coffee.

"Right, well, I'll just grab my clothes then ..." I skirt around the bed, and because I don't want to have to walk past him, I go the long way around, meaning I have to walk around the dividing wall that the head of the bed is pushed up against. Grabbing my clothes and shoes, I all but run into the bathroom.

Locking the door, I drop my forehead against it.

Great.

Just bloody great.

First night here, and I make a total knob of myself.

I embarrassed myself in front of West, told him how hot I thought he was, made him carry me back, stripped my clothes off, and took over his bed.

I suppose it can't get any worse than this.

Unless I made a total arse of myself in front of others in the bar as well. I should ask him, but I don't know if I want to know the answer.

Then, a thought hits me. *Is he here alone?* I mean, everyone on this island is here with a significant other. I should have been.

I mean, from the fact that I spent the night in his villa, in his bed, I'm taking it that he doesn't have a wife or girlfriend here with him.

Maybe he's here with friends.

But that doesn't mean he doesn't have someone back home.

Although, when I asked him if we had sex, he said, "Call me old-fashioned, but I like a woman to be sober and conscious when I fuck her."

If he had a girlfriend or wife, then that would have been the time to say it, right? Unless he's a lying, cheating arsehole, of course.

Although I do have this itch in my brain that I might have already had that conversation with him last night. When I was drunk. And I have no frigging recollection of said conversation or whether it actually happened.

Ugh.

So, I should knock off the lusty thoughts about him until I actually know for sure what his relationship status is. Not that I would ever actually consider doing anything with him.

But he is really frigging nice to look at.

Pushing off the door, I use the toilet and wash my hands. I get a glimpse of myself in the mirror and want to cry.

For fuck's sake. I look awful. My skin is pasty. My lips are dry and cracked. My hair looks like that bird tattooed on West's back made a nest out of it for the night. And my breath is rancid.

Spying some mouthwash, I pick it up and pour some into my mouth, making sure the bottle doesn't touch my lips. I don't want to leave bad morning breath on his bottle of mouthwash as well.

I gargle it for a solid two minutes before I spit.

SAMANTHA TOWLE

A little better, but I need to scrub my teeth clean when I get back to my villa.

Which I have no key for.

Christ almighty.

I'm going to have to go to reception in yesterday's clothes and get a new key. Unless … I left the back door open when I went out. I was drunk enough to forget my key, so more than likely, I'd left it open. I had been drinking out on the deck after all.

I could hop into the water off the jetty and wade around to the steps to my villa, and bingo, I'd be in without having to walk all the way to reception.

Cool. I have a plan. Now, to get dressed and put that plan into action.

I pull on my leggings and top, feeling gross and counting down the seconds until I can get a shower. I push my feet into my Converse. Run my fingers through my tangles, smoothing it down the best I can.

Taking a deep breath, I unlock the door and step out.

Looking right, I see West standing out on his deck, back to me.

For a moment, I consider just sneaking out to save myself more embarrassment that will inevitably come because, you know, it's me. But sneaking out would be a dick move. I just need to thank him for his hospitality and get the heck out of here.

I walk over, stopping where the sliding doors are open—like I'm hoping mine are—and clear my throat. "So, I'm gonna head off … back to my villa. Well, to reception to get a key for it and then to my villa."

Why do I have to ramble? Why can't I just be normal?

West turns around and leans back against the railing. He crosses his legs at the ankles and brings his coffee cup to his mouth, drinking it.

I watch, once again mesmerized by the movement of the muscles in his arms and chest. I'll be shocked if there isn't drool dripping from the corner of my mouth.

When he lowers the cup, there's a smirk on his lips that tells me he's well aware that I'm ogling him. Again.

Shit. I'm not supposed to be lusting over him, remember? Funny how quickly I forget when faced with those abs.

I blink myself free and look past him to the gorgeous Maldivian morning view of ocean and skyline.

"Can I ask, did I do anything—aside from the stuff I already know—to embarrass myself?"

"Such as?"

"I don't know. In the bar or anything? I didn't say stupid shit to anyone other than you?"

He smiles, and it's fucking delightful. "No. Just me."

"Did I puke?" It's been known in the past when I drank too much.

"Nope. You held your liquor like a champ."

"Um, good. So, yeah, thanks again for taking care of me. And I'm sorry I was such a prat."

"Prat?" He lifts a brow.

"Yeah, prat. You know, like idiot."

"Nope." Another drink of coffee. "Never heard of the word before."

"It's a Brit word. And you're American ... so, yeah, of course you wouldn't have heard of it. Unless you've watched British TV shows, that is. But you probably haven't." *Oh my God, stop rambling and get the fuck out of here.* "So, yeah, sorry for being an idiot with the whole me getting wasted, making you carry me back, stripping my clothes off, and telling you I thought you were hot."

"Were hot?"

"Is. Are. Oh, for fuck's sake, whatever."

He chuckles. "It wasn't all a hardship. Especially not the striptease."

Is he flirting with me?

Holy fucking fuck. I think he might be.

Well, hell, he's flirting with me after seeing all of that and seeing hungover me.

Now, this is interesting.

Probably a bad idea, following it up. Because, you know, I'm still heartbroken and also shit at flirting. Case in point, last night. But definitely interesting that a guy who looks like that might have an interest in me.

"Okay, well, next time I decide to do another striptease, I'll let you know."

"Make sure you do."

Yep, definitely flirting, and I've got shivers in places that I haven't had in a long time.

"Okay." I bite down on my bottom lip. I really have nothing else to say. So, I should get the fuck out of here before I mess this flirting business up. "I'll see you later, West."

I turn and walk away, and as I'm nearing the door, I hear him say, "You definitely will."

I let myself out his villa, the door clicking closed behind me.

"You definitely will."

Oh, hot mama.

Part of me dreads seeing him because I'm still embarrassed about last night and this morning's behavior. But I'm also looking forward to seeing him again because, hell, he's the hottest man alive and the flirty comments are absolutely good for my ego.

I'll just have to make sure that I look a lot better than I do right now or last night when I was still dressed in my traveling clothes.

Speaking of, I really need to get them off because it's hot as balls already and it's early and I'm starting to sweat.

I step onto the jetty and immediately see my villa across from me. I'm tempted to try the front door, but I already know it's locked. It has an auto-lock that engages as soon as you close the door. I walk over to the edge of the jetty and peer down. It's not too far. I sit on the edge and take off my Converse. Holding them in one hand, I lower myself into the water.

It's warm, but it still cools me down.

I'm just wading down the side of my villa when I hear that deep, husky voice that I've very quickly become familiar with, and it sends shivers skating up my spine. Along with the embarrassment filling my chest. I seem to feel that particular emotion around him a lot.

"Should I ask why you're in the lagoon, fully clothed?"

Of course he'd catch me doing something weird right after our little flirty moment. Because, you know, life hates me.

I turn to look at him. The sun beating down has me shading my eyes. He's wearing shorts but different ones. These look like running shorts, and he has running shoes on his feet. But the chest is still bare. Yay for me.

"Thought I would check and see if I'd left the door to the deck open. Save me going all the way to reception to get a key."

He nods. "Good idea."

"I thought so." I grin, and he smiles back at me.

"Well, I'm going for a run. You want me to stick around while you check the door?"

"Nope, I'm good. But thanks for the offer."

"Okay. Later then." He waves a hand and takes off jogging down the jetty.

Yes, I stand there in the water and watch until he disappears from my sight. I wasn't going to miss out on the chance to watch him running. All those muscles flexing.

I turn back around and wade my way around my villa until I reach the steps. Grabbing the handrail, I hoist myself up and climb the stairs.

Reaching the top, I see the sliding door is wide open. *Bingo!*

Finally, something has gone right for me. Unless I've been robbed, that is.

Not that I have much to steal. I didn't bring a lot of money, as it's all-inclusive here, and my iPhone isn't the latest one. It's actually a couple of numbers back.

I walk inside, dropping my shoes onto the floor, and see the champagne bottle I emptied last night, discarded on the bed. At least one of us got to sleep on it.

I check my bag and find everything still in there, including my phone, of which the battery is dead and needs charging. Pretty sure I forgot to ring Aunt Jenny—unless that's one of the things I did remember to do.

I'll charge it up later. First, shower.

Six

DILLON

WHILE I WAS HAVING my breakfast, consisting solely of carbs and caffeine, Najam—the really sweet receptionist who checked me in yesterday—came over to my table. She'd forgotten to give me my itinerary of activities yesterday, which I'd already booked and paid for long before arriving here. Most of them are the things that the prick wanted to do. There is only one thing on there that *I* picked out and booked—an island hop, where you get to go and spend the day on a small private island with just the two of you. Not sure I fancy doing that alone. I'd literally shit myself and have visions of being forgotten about and abandoned there, alone for the rest of my life. I have an overactive imagination, okay? That's what having the mind of a writer is like.

And it appears that I'm snorkeling today. For fuck's sake. All I wanted to do was eat my breakfast and then lie on a sun lounger and read a book.

I don't even care about snorkeling. It was the prick who wanted to do it.

"We need to experience everything while we're there, Dill," he said.

He forgot to mention that he was also experiencing my mother.

And honestly, I always hated it when he called me Dill. I'm not a bloody herb, for Christ's sake. Ugh. Total twunting prick. Whom I will not be giving another thought or brain cell to for at least the rest of today.

So, now, I'm on my way to the boat dock—after a quick trip back to my villa to change out of the bikini I had put on under my shorts and tank top, which I'd planned to spend the whole day sunbathing in, and now, I have on a more sensible swimsuit. I figure I'll need to be a bit more covered up to go snorkeling. Alone.

Yay for me.

I wonder what West is up to today.

I haven't seen him since he took off for his run. He wasn't at breakfast, although I did eat late due to showering, washing my hair, and finally unpacking my suitcase.

But I wasn't looking for him, obviously.

Well, I was. But just so I could avoid him.

Suuure.

Okay, I wasn't looking to avoid him. I'm not actually sure why I was looking for him at all.

When it comes to West, I don't know if I want to hide from him or jump into those strong arms of his, which I already did last night when I climbed up that big body and made him carry me back to the villa. So, yeah, it's probably best to refrain from all urges to leap into his arms the next time I do see him. I already made a massive twat out of myself last night. Best not to keep adding more twattish behavior to it.

Thinking about last night though and how kind West was to me, looking after my drunken arse and letting me crash in his bed, maybe I should have offered him the empty place I have on this snorkeling trip, which was meant to be the prick's. I mean, it is already bought and paid for, and he was really nice to me last night.

Although I guess it might be a bit weird, inviting a total stranger on a random snorkeling trip with me.

Only he's not a total stranger. I slept in his bed last night and spent the evening drinking in the bar with him even if I do only remember the tiniest portion of it.

I don't know why I'm even stressing over this. He's probably already got plans today with whomever he's here on the island with. And I'm still not sure whether he's single or seeing someone even though that itch in my brain is telling me I know the answer and that he's single, but I don't know if that's actual truth from something I learned in my inebriated state last night or just wishful thinking on my part.

No, not wishful thinking! Because it doesn't matter to me either way if he's single, married, or has a harem. I'm here on this *honeymoon turned single girl* trip for no other reason than to heal my wounded heart. Not hook up with a gorgeous American dude. Even if he does look like the love child of Brad Pitt as Achilles and Chris Hemsworth as Thor and is the hottest man I have ever seen.

Ever.

Yes, the second *ever* was needed.

Not that any of this matters anyway because I didn't offer him the ticket and I'm stressing out my hungover brain with crap that has zero relevance or point in my life.

Okay, so I'm just going to stop thinking about it now and try to enjoy this solo snorkeling trip of mine.

I walk out of the cover of the palm trees and across the beach. I can feel how hot the sand is, even with my flip-flops on. It's a scorcher of a day. I already applied sunscreen, but I'm glad I put a bottle of it in my beach bag because I'm gonna need another application. I have pretty good skin. I don't burn and tan easily. But I don't want to age my skin prematurely or risk skin cancer, so I always apply a good factor sunscreen in the heat.

Leaving the beach, I step up onto the jetty, where a group of people are already standing under the cover of the open building that sits at the end. To the right is another smaller building, which looks like a hut, and next to that sits a docked boat—or *dhoni*, as they are called here in the Maldives—which I'm guessing is what will be taking us out to the reefs today.

I'm halfway up the jetty when I see West. It's not like he's hard to miss.

He's like a water fountain in the middle of the desert.

My stomach does this little flip-floppy thing at the sight of him standing there, leaning up against the hut, just slightly away from the main group of people. His face is turned down, reading something on his phone. His hair is tied back in one of those man buns, and he has a pair of aviator sunglasses covering his eyes. I've never dated a guy with long hair before.

And you don't plan on dating this one either, Dillon.

He's wearing white flip-flops, red board shorts—the color looks great against his strong, tanned legs—and a white tank with a sports logo over the left pec. Those gloriously muscular pecs and splendiferous arms are on show. Can you tell I went through a phase of reading historical romances? Anyhoo, I can see the flex of muscles in his forearm as he types something on his phone.

And I'm clearly looking at him way too hard if I can see that from here.

I force my eyes away, face forward, and keep walking.

My heart beats faster as I approach everyone. I'm telling myself that it's the nerves of coming here alone, in front of all of these couples, but it's not. It's because West is here.

Should I go up and say hello? Or pretend that I haven't seen him?

As I'm bouncing back and forth in my head over what to do, my eyes unwittingly go in his direction again, and at that precise moment, he lifts his head and looks right at me. I can't see his eyes because of those damn sunglasses, but I can *feel* his eyes on me. Then, his lips lift at one side into a smile. A sexy smile.

And there's that damn flippy-floppy thing going off in my stomach again.

My feet travel in his direction without guidance. Honestly, I don't think I could have stopped myself from going over if I tried. He just has this pull to him. Like the display picture that stands outside of the coffee shop I pass every morning on my way to work—of the caramel latte, topped with a caramel crumb, and a double chocolate muffin, topped with salted caramel—purely left there to lure unsuspecting victims inside. And even though I would give myself a big pep talk the whole way there—that my thighs and butt did not need the fresh calories or fat cells to provide me with new additions to my ever-growing canvas of cellulite—I would still stop at the coffee shop, open the door, go inside, and buy them.

I'm a weak-willed woman. What can I say?

And I'm definitely not the only one who feels the magnetic pull of West. I can see the furtive glances in his direction from the coupled-up women here. Honestly, I don't blame them. If I'd been here with the prick, I'd have been looking at West too. I'm not a cheater—never have been, never will be—even though I have half the DNA of a cheater. But West is a hard man not to look at, and a little window shopping has never harmed anyone. It's when people start making purchases on their maxed-out credit cards that we have a problem.

But oddly, in this moment, with his eyes on me, none of that actually matters, and for the first time since I arrived on this island, I'm really happy that I am alone.

West pushes his sunglasses up onto his forehead, showing me those gorgeous gray eyes of his.

"Hey," I say. *God, I'm so cool and sophisticated.*

His lips quirk into a full smile. "Well, hey there, Double D."

I sigh. "Didn't we already have this conversation?"

"Which conversation?"

"The one where I told you not to call me that and you agreed."

"Did we?"

"Yes."

"Huh. I must have forgotten that. Speaking of forgetting things … I am surprised to see you here."

It's my turn to say, "Huh?"

"Well, I figured you'd be nursing your hangover today after your drinking binge last night. You know, the night you don't remember."

"Oh, well, I would have been, but I'd already booked this trip. Although I didn't remember that until an hour ago, when Najam gave me my itinerary."

"Were you also drunk when you booked it?"

I give him a humored look, and he chuckles. "Surprisingly, no."

"You know though … you didn't actually have to come."

I give him a confused look. "But it was already paid for."

"Yeah, but if you hadn't been given your itinerary in time, you would have missed it anyway."

"But then I would have been pissed off that I'd paid money for something that I didn't use and/or experience."

"And/or?" His lips spread into a grin.

"Oh, I don't know, dude. I'm hungover, remember?"

Our eyes meet and connect. I feel a quick rising of dancing heat in my belly. Unsolicited thoughts about him and me flash through my mind.

What the hell is wrong with me?

I'm fresh off heartbreak of the worst kind, and here I am, mooning—okay, perving—over him. It's just not like me. I'm not like this in normal life.

Sure, I had crushes when I was a teenager. I've fawned over gorgeous celebrities. I thought Tim was attractive when I first met him. But I didn't get an instant hit of lust with Tim like I seem to have with West. With Tim, it was more like … I was taken by how much he seemed taken with me. I got swept up in his feelings. I just didn't know at the time that Tim was well known for getting swept up by women. The workers at his family company had a nickname for him— Fast Love. He'd been engaged three times before me, and I was number four, which I found out after the affair with my mother came to light. Clearly, Tim's "fast love" with me had died out the second his interest transferred to my mother.

To be fair, they're perfect for each other. Both inconsistent, lying, cheating, *will shit on anyone*—even their own children—scumbags.

But I'm not thinking about either of them today.

I'm thinking about West and these sexual feelings between us… well, they're all my own. He's done nothing to ignite them. Except for look so frigging gorgeous, of course. Oh, and the flirt he was giving me this morning … which I'm not actually sure was him flirting with me or just me interpreting it that way. God, I'm so off-balance at the moment; I can't even tell if a guy is flirting with me or not. I didn't used to be this bad with men. I'm hoping it's only a temporary glitch.

And I'm not normally an instant-lust gal.

Maybe it's because I'm on this island, where every fucker is in love, and it's addling my brain. Or it could be his American accent that has bedazzled my hormones. And his face. And his super-hard, insanely fit body. And—

Oh, for fuck's sake. Stop thinking, Dillon. It's bad for your health, and it's all inconsequential bullshit.

You fancy the guy. End of story.

Admitting it doesn't mean I have to do anything about it.

Wow. I feel so much better now.

Okay. Cool.

I have the hots for West, and it's okay because nothing is going to happen.

And I'm spending way too much time in my head and not in the real world. Meaning talk to the guy and stop staring at him like a numpty.

"So—" I start.

"Right, people!" A happy-sounding guy dressed in shorts and a T-shirt with the resort logo claps his hands, getting everyone's attention, cutting off whatever shite I was about to say to West. "Good morning! I'm Aden, and over there is Zaim." He points to the other guy, dressed in the same clothes as him, who is standing by the boat. "Zaim is our boat captain, who will take us to the beautiful reefs. We will both be your guides, here for whatever you need, and I very much hope you are all enjoying your first full day with us. Now, it's time for us to get started. Would you please head over to the hut?" He points to where West and I are standing, and everyone's eyes volley in our direction. "Where Kayden and Mahmoud are waiting to fit you with a snorkel, goggles, and flippers. Once you have them, please board the boat. Once everyone is on, then we can be on our way to see the beauty that the Maldives has to offer."

This guy sounds just like the brochure that got me to book this place.

And bonus: West and I are first in line to get our things, thanks to him standing right by the hut.

"You stood here on purpose to be the first in line," I murmur to him as we head inside and are greeted by the happy, smiling faces of Kayden and Mahmoud.

His eyes flicker down to me, a secretive kind of smile touching those full lips of his. He gives a slight shrug. "I'm not the kind of guy who is ever last in line for anything."

Oh, I bet he's not.

"Hello! You are Mr. and Mrs. …"

"Oh, we're not—" I start to say, but I'm cut off by the deep sound of West's voice.

"Oakley. Mr. and Mrs. Oakley."

I'm sorry, what?

"Welcome, Mr. and Mrs. Oakley!" The guy beams. "You are a very handsome couple."

"Yes, I'm a very lucky man." West slings his big arm around my shoulders, pulling me into his side, giving me a squeeze.

And me? Well, I'm just standing here, mouth open in utter shock. Because apparently, I just got fake married.

Seven

DILLON

WITH MY BRIGHT PINK matching snorkel, goggles, and flippers in hand—Kayden was insistent that I have the bright pink because, apparently, it's my color, although I've always thought red suited me better—I walk back out of the hut, West walking silently beside me, and I have about a hundred and one questions about what the heck just happened in there bursting to come out of my mouth.

The instant we step out of the hut and pass the line of our fellow islanders, we're ushered onto the boat.

I climb aboard with the help of the man already aboard the dhoni. The words I want to say to West burning on my tongue. West climbs aboard behind me.

I quickly walk to the back of the boat and sit down. West strolls toward me like he has all the time in the world. I give him an expectant look, and all I get in return is a grin.

The second he sits in the seat beside me, I jump on him. Figuratively, of course. "Um, what the hell was that?"

He gives me a look of innocence. "What?"

"Um, Mr. and Mrs. Oakley ringing any bloody bells?"

"Bloody bells?" He gives me an amused look.

"Don't change the subject."

"Wouldn't dream of it."

"Why did you tell that guy that we're married?"

He shrugs. "Just seemed easier to go with it than explain that we're not together."

I stare at him, wide-eyed and flabbergasted. "I'm sorry, what?"

"He thought we were married. It seemed like a lot of effort to explain that we're not. Sometimes, it's easier to just go with the flow."

"You mean, lie."

He laughs a deep sound, and it annoys me that my body reacts to it. "If that's what you want to call it."

"Well, it is a lie. So, I'll definitely be calling it that."

"Honestly, I thought I was doing you a favor."

I round on him. "You thought what?"

"You seemed uncomfortable about being here alone, and I just thought I was helping."

Oh. Well, that takes a little wind out of my sails.

"You're alone," I say.

"But it doesn't bother me."

"How do you know it bothers me?"

"I can just tell. You give off a vibe."

"A vibe?"

"Yeah. And also, you made a whole big deal about the fact that you were here alone. You started talking about some movie where a chick sings a song about being alone, and then you said you were gonna change your name to Eeyore or something."

For.

Fuck's.

68

Sake.

I'm never, ever, *ever* drinking again.

"I, uh ... said all that?"

"Yep."

"Wow. That's ... embarrassing."

He laughs.

"And I appreciate the sentiment, West. I do. But in the future, can you please not tell anyone else that we're married or together? I'm sure I'll live through the ensuing conversations that I'm here alone."

"Okay, Double D. I will make sure to correct the next person who assumes we're together and say that we are in fact not."

"Good. Thank you. And for the love of all that is holy, will you stop calling me Double D?"

"Will do, Double D."

Ugh.

We sit in silence as the other guests start to trickle onto the boat. West stretches those long legs of his out. He takes up so much space. His thigh is almost touching mine.

I'm so aware of him. Every breath he takes. Every move he makes.

And now, I sound like that song. Which is about stalking. *Great.*

"So, is your surname really Oakley, or was that made up too?"

"It's really Oakley."

West Oakley.

Dillon Oakley ...

Huh. It actually has a nice ring to it.

Whoa there, Fast Love! You're fresh off one engagement. You definitely don't need another ring on your finger. At least, not for a long while. So, don't be getting ideas about the hot American sitting next to you.

"So, I know you're on this snorkeling trip alone, and you were in the bar alone last night, right?"

"Right."

"So, are you here on the island alone? Like I am. Or with friends?"

"Just me."

"You take trips alone often?"

"Not usually."

"Why this time?" God, I'm so nosy.

His eyes slide to mine. I feel a little jolt inside. "I just needed to get away for a little while."

I can't get a read on what the reason might be. I hope he hasn't been crapped on from a great height by people he cared about, too, and needed to get away from them.

I decide to lighten the mood.

"You commit a crime?" I grin, so he knows I'm teasing.

"Dammit. How did you guess?"

I spread my hands. "It's a gift. What did you do?"

He sighs solemnly. "I stole my neighbor's cookies."

"What flavor were the cookies?" I ask, trying to keep a straight face.

"Triple chocolate. Why?"

"Just wondering if they were worth it."

A sexy grin slides onto his face. "Oh, they totally were. They were *melt on the tongue* kind of cookies."

Sweet. Jesus.

I didn't think I could get any hotter right now, as it's a thousand degrees in the shade, but apparently, I can.

I swallow down and look away.

"Have you snorkeled before?" he asks me.

"Oh. Nope. First time. Total virgin."

Virgin? For crying out loud. Why do I have to say stuff like that?

"Well, I'm experienced in snorkeling. So, if you need any help when losing your snorkeling virginity, just say the word."

Okay. He's definitely flirting with me, right? This isn't me being dense. I mean, I know the whole virgin comment was dense, but him saying what he just said ... that was flirting. I'm almost sure of it. And the cookie thing just then, the whole melt on the tongue *thing. That was flirting, right?*

"Okay then. I will. Thanks." And then I say nothing else because, you know … I'm me.

Everyone is on the boat now, and it starts to move.

Aden is standing up at the front of the boat, and he claps his hands to get everyone's attention. "So, we're now on our way to see some of the most beautiful reefs the Ari Atoll has to offer. Now, you all have your equipment, yes?"

There's a bunch of lowly murmured yeses in response.

"Good. Now, do we have any of you here who have never snorkeled before? Please raise your hand."

I really, really don't want to put my hand up. But I just can't lie, so my hand goes up with a few other people's. Surprisingly, about half the people on this boat haven't snorkeled before.

Makes me feel like less of a loser.

"No problem at all. I will do a quick demonstration of how you are to put your goggles and snorkel on so as not to let in water. Okay, so we have one-half of the gorgeous couple seated at the back, my two Scottish friends—"

"Sorry. Excuse me." That's West, lifting his hand to get Aden's attention.

"Yes?" Aden says in question to West.

"We're not together. You said, one-half of the gorgeous couple, but we're not a couple."

Oh. No.

He fucking didn't.

All eyes on this boat are now on us. I can feel myself wanting to disappear into my seat.

When I said he should correct people, I didn't mean like *this. For fuck's sake.*

"Oh. I apologize. My mistake," Aden says.

"No problem," West says and then lets out a dramatic sigh. "I mean, I'd like to be a couple with her. We'd make a great match. We're both incredibly good-looking, and I'm totally into her. I think she's gorgeous. But she doesn't find me attractive. She's friend-zoned me." He lets out another dramatic sigh.

"What?" That loud exclamation comes from the woman on the seat next to us. She stares directly at me. "Are you nuts?"

"I, er …" I stammer as an imaginary tumbleweed blows across the deck of the boat.

"Shannon," comes from the man I'm assuming is her husband, and he doesn't sound impressed at all.

Her face turns as red as I know mine is.

"Oh, I meant," she sputters, "that she must be nuts if she wants to be alone on this island and not in a couple like everyone else. That's totally what I meant."

Her husband gives her a look that says they'll be having a long chat when they're next alone.

"So …" Aden says, seeming a little startled. He shakes his head, as if to gather his wits. "Let me get this demonstration done for those of you who haven't snorkeled before."

The minute Aden starts talking, I lean in a little closer to West.

God, he smells good.

Focus, Dillon.

"Was that really necessary?" I whisper to him.

"Just doing as you asked." He shrugs.

I can tell he's fighting a smile. The twat.

"You're an ass," I murmur. "That was not doing what I asked. I asked you to correct people when they thought we were together."

A low chuckle. "That's what I did."

"Sure. And what about all the *I'm into her* and *I think she's gorgeous* bullshit?"

"Who said it was bullshit?"

My eyes meet with his, and the look in them makes my mouth dry.

He's definitely not joking now. His gray eyes are dark.

I swallow and turn away, forcing myself to listen to Aden tell us how to put on a frigging pair of goggles and a snorkel.

But how am I supposed to concentrate after that?

I might be shit with men and have zero sense when it comes to them. But I do know one thing, and that was flirting. He was one hundred percent flirting with me.

Holy. Hell.

eight

DILLON

IT'S OFFICIAL. I'M SHIT at snorkeling.

Everyone is off and exploring, West included, and I'm here, choking on seawater. He made that offer to help me lose my snorkeling virginity when we were back on the boat, but he didn't mention it again when we were getting in the water, so I didn't say anything either.

But contrary to what he said before, I don't mind being alone. I mean, it's not my favorite. I like people. I like the company of them. But I can be alone. I came all the way here alone, didn't I?

Now, if I could just figure out this snorkeling business. I honestly don't know where I'm going wrong. I listened to what Aden said about putting it on and ... okay, so I didn't fully listen.

I was too distracted by West. What he'd said, the whole *who said it was bullshit* thing. Yes, I totally said it in a deep

American accent in my head. But it wasn't just that. It was him … his proximity to me. That damn thigh nearly touching mine. Every move he made, down to each inhale and exhale of breath, I was aware of.

It's maddening. Why am I so aware of this guy after such a short period of time? I'm not supposed to be interested in anyone else. Not after what I've just been through.

Unless … this interest I have in West and the attention he's giving me, maybe I'm soaking it up because it makes me feel better. I was so sick of feeling sad all the damn time. It's nice to not feel sad. Around West, I don't feel sad.

Yes, I'm slightly irritated and in a perpetual state of arousal and confusion, but I'm not sad.

And honestly, after what I've been through, I'll take that.

I readjust my goggles, put the mouthpiece back in my mouth, and then lower my head into the water.

All is good for a few seconds, and then I breathe in and take a load of water. I lift my head up, coughing and spluttering, yanking the mouthpiece out.

"Argh!" I shove the bloody goggles up to the top of my head.

I'm tempted to pull them off and launch them into the ocean, but I don't want to get billed for losing them and end up having to pay for a new set for them. I really have no clue how much snorkels and goggles cost.

"Your tube is the wrong way."

"What?" I turn in the water to find West behind me.

Where the heck did he come from? I thought he'd swum off to explore with the rest of the group. Guess I was wrong.

"Your breathing tube. It's the wrong way."

He swims closer, and I find my body tensing in anticipation of his nearness.

"Here." He takes the breathing bit from me and shows me how the tube is the wrong way. "So, when you go under, the tube is in the water too."

76

My cheeks flame red with mortification. "Oh my God. I'm so embarrassed. I'm such an idiot."

"I'd disagree with you, but ..."

I give him a dirty look and splash water at him.

"Hey!" He's laughing. "You said it! Not me! See, this is why you should listen when the guy on the boat—you know, the expert—is talking, telling you what you need to do."

"I was listening." I totally wasn't. I've always had a hard time listening to instructions. Someone starts talking, and I just tune out and go into the stories in my head. My teachers always said I was a dreamer. I wasn't. I was—am a writer. "Kind of. But you weren't listening."

"No, but I've snorkeled hundreds of times. You've snorkeled ..." He gestures his hand for me to finish for him.

"Never," I say begrudgingly.

"Well, seeing as though I like you, you can stick with me, and I'll guide, make sure you don't drown yourself."

He likes me?

That's all I heard in that statement that mattered. I got the rest, and hanging with him for the duration of this trip and not by myself is hardly a hardship.

"You sure you don't mind? I won't be holding you back?"

"I'm sure. I wouldn't offer if I wasn't."

"Then, I accept your offer."

He smiles. "First, let's tighten your goggles a little too. They look like they're letting in a bit of water." He swims behind me and starts tightening the elastic strap.

I'm just here, treading water, with his fingers leaving little trails of fire on my head, wherever they touch.

I've just had the worst experience a person could have. Caught my mother having an affair with my fiancé, my heart shredded to pieces, and I'm literally on my honeymoon alone, lusting over this guy.

My libido clearly hasn't gotten the memo.

Or maybe I just wasn't as into Tim as I thought I was. Maybe I just liked the idea of him more than I actually liked him.

The security he was offering. The way he treated me kindly—until he didn't.

"All done."

West's hands fall to my shoulders. My skin breaks out in goose bumps.

"You ready to snorkel?" His voice is deep and husky in my ear.

I have to suppress a shudder.

I swallow down and say, "Yes." It comes out a little croaky.

"You sound nervous."

I turn in the water to face him. His hands fall from my shoulders. It's definitely easier to think and talk when his hands aren't on me. Those big hands that covered my shoulders ... just imagine what they could do to me ...

Okay, so I was wrong. Removing his hands from me didn't help.

Now, I'm looking into his face because in the water, we're the same height, and all I can think about is him touching me with those hands and my lips sucking the water droplets from his mouth.

An image of me and him having sex flashes through my mind.

My heart speeds up. I can feel my body heating in response to the thought. I'm in warmish water, but I feel like I'm on fire. I know my neck and chest are flushed because West's eyes are now on them.

Stupid body gives my thoughts away every time.

His eyes lift, meeting mine with knowledge.

He knows I want him.

We're already close, but when he tips his head forward, it puts his mouth centimeters from mine.

I gulp down. His breath blows through my parted lips.

I bite down on my lip and try to regain control over my body.

I'm in the middle of the Indian Ocean, and I'm getting aroused over a guy I barely know.

"We'll snorkel now. We'll talk about this later."

This? What's this?

But I don't get a chance to ask because he's swimming away, ducking his head down into the water.

I wait a beat, confused. My mind still reeling over what *this* actually is. Then, I give up thinking, duck my head into the water, and follow after West.

When I catch up to him, he's floating on the surface, staring down at one of the reefs.

The moment I look down at what he's seeing, my insides light with happiness at the utter beauty of the reef.

Then, I feel a hand touch mine. I tilt my head to look and see that West has curled his large hand around mine, engulfing it. My stomach swoops just like the shoal of fish I've been watching.

Hand-holding. Such a small act. But it can be so incredibly intimate when you're hot for a guy.

And I'm hot for West. So fucking hot.

He gestures to something and then starts to swim, taking me with him.

Maybe he just held my hand to get my attention and to lead me over to what he wants to show me. I don't need to be getting carried away.

But on the surface minutes ago, there was definite sexual tension between us, and then there's the *this* that we'll be talking about later.

And I really need to stop overthinking and analyzing about a guy I haven't even known twenty-four hours even if we did share a bedroom last night. What I need to do right now is look at the life and beauty happening right below me.

I follow along with West, moving farther away from the boat and from the group we came here with. It's like we're in our own little bubble.

We could almost be the couple he pretended us to be earlier, and …

Stop being weird, Dillon. And get out of your head.

I toss all thoughts out of my brain.

Something to the right catches my attention. The instant I see it, I freeze. Pretty sure my heart stops, missing a good few beats.

Then, the panic sets in, and I kick into action. Pulling free from West's hand, I push up to the surface, kicking my legs like a maniac. I pull the mouthpiece from my mouth, breathing heavily.

"Oh fuck! Oh fuck! Oh fuck! Shark!" I yell just as West resurfaces. "Th-there's a shark! We have to get out of here! Back to the boat!" I'm literally living every one of those damn shark movies that I've ever seen.

And in each one, the idiot like me almost definitely dies.

I start kicking my legs to get moving. But I'm stopped by West. His hands wrapping around my waist.

"Relax. It's fine. It's not gonna hurt you."

"It's a shark!"

"It's sleeping."

"I don't care if it's having a mani-pedi! It's a fucking shark, and I really don't want to be eaten!"

He chuckles. "You're not going to be eaten. It's only a reef shark. Probably about seven or eight feet long. Not big at all."

"That's almost twice my size!"

He nods. "That's true. You are tiny."

"Oh fuck. It's gonna eat me, for sure. It's gonna see me, the smallest one here, and pick me out as the easy snack!"

"It's not going to eat you or me or anyone else."

"What is wrong with you? I'm concerned by how unconcerned you are! Are you missing the fear gene?"

"Shark attacks in the Maldives are almost nonexistent."

"Almost! You said, *almost*. What percentage are we talking here? Actually, why are we still in the water, talking?"

"I don't know the exact percentage—"

"You know nothing."

"Did you just quote *Game of Thrones* to me?"

"Not intentionally."

"Sounds like you did."

I sigh. "I'm from Yorkshire. Ygritte's accent is Yorkshire. Everything I say sounds like I'm quoting either her or Jon Snow."

West chuckles. "Look, Dillon, I promise you, it's more scared of you than you are of it. You go near that shark, and it'll swim away—I guarantee it. If it was dangerous, don't you think I'd have gotten you out of the water already?"

"I don't know. You could be one of those weird adrenaline junkies who likes to stare death in the face."

He laughs low. It actually sounds really sexy.

Why am I thinking sexy thoughts in the middle of a shark-and-death situation? I need serious help.

"Nope. I quite like living. And I prefer to get my rushes of adrenaline in other ways," he says.

"How?"

"Having sex."

With me?

The thought just popped in, unbidden and uninvited. Thank God it stayed in my head and didn't come out of my mouth.

What does come out of my mouth though is a croaky-sounding, "Oh."

I feel one of his hands slide up my waist a touch. Teetering on the bottom of my rib cage.

He's staring at me in that way again. The one where he looks like he's hungry as fuck and I'm his next meal.

And it's weird how much I like it.

Maybe it's because of the hurt I've been feeling and still continue to feel that I'm soaking up the attention he's giving to me. It makes me feel a little less shitty about myself for that brief period of time.

Then, I remember about the shark. "That shark is still down there, sleeping, right? It hasn't moved?"

West pulls down his goggles over his eyes and dips his head into the water. He resurfaces a moment later, pulling up his goggles, wiping the water from his face. "It's still in the reef."

"Good. Now, I'm going back to the boat and getting out of this water before that seven- or eight-foot shark wakes up and decides to be brave."

West laughs. "I'll come with you."

I give him a look. "I'd expect you to. I mean, who the fuck would want to stay out here to be shark food? Maybe we should warn the others?" I give a quick glance. They're quite far away. "Nah, they'll be fine."

West chuckles and holds out his hand to me. "Come on. Let's get you back to the boat."

nine

DILLON

OFFERING HIS HAND, WHICH I take, West helps me down from the boat and onto the jetty. I notice how callous and rough his skin is. I didn't notice it when I held his hand in the water earlier. I wonder if that's from his job. Whatever that might be.

I should ask, get to know him. It'd be nice to have a friend here on the island for the next two weeks.

But we want to be more than just his friend, Dillon.

That's just my vagina talking. I'm choosing to ignore her.

"Wanna grab a drink?" West asks as we start walking down the jetty.

"Yeah, sure. That'd be great."

"Bar we were in last night or the bar by the pool?"

"Bar by the pool." It has nothing to do with the fact that I got shitfaced in the bar I went to last night and that I'm planning to avoid it for a good few days, so the bar workers forget who the drunken girl from last night was.

"Cool. They serve food as well if you're hungry."

"I can always eat."

"Good. I like a girl with an appetite."

"Well, I definitely have an appetite. A big one."

"You still talking about food here?" he says.

I look across at him. He's already staring down at me, and I feel myself starting to heat under his gaze.

"Of course," I manage out.

"Shame."

I look away, a smile on my face. Because he's definitely flirting with me.

We reach the bar a few minutes later and take a seat at one of the tables closest to the water. I put my bag down on the floor beside me.

"It's bar service here," West tells me. "Let me know what you want, and I'll go to the bar and order for us."

I grab the small menu off the table and give it a quick look. "I'll have a burger and fries."

"Drink?"

"Beer." Maybe I shouldn't be drinking after how much I drank last night, but I'm on holiday, and it's an unwritten law that you have to day drink. Especially when you're at an all-inclusive.

"No cocktails today?"

"Was that what I was drinking last night at the bar?" I ask. A lot of last night is still blurry.

"Long Island iced tea. Margarita. Then, you moved on to Fireball shots."

"Ugh." I groan. "I really have no control once I start drinking."

"You were going for it last night. It was pretty impressive. I've never seen someone as small as you drink that much liquor."

"Thanks. I think."

He chuckles. "It was a compliment."

"Yeah. I was … letting off some steam, I guess. Coming here and it was supposed to be my … and seeing the card and champagne in the room … yeah, anyway, I just needed to get drunk."

"Well, you definitely did that." He smiles. "Did it help?"

"Kinda. Not really. I don't know." I look away to the water.

"So, beer," he says, stepping over the awkwardness in the air that I put there. "Bottle or tap?"

"Bottle."

"What brand?"

"I'm not fussy."

"Okay." He stands. "I'll be back in a few."

"Thank you," I say as he walks over to the bar.

While he's gone, I pull the tie out of my hair and give it a spray with my detangling-and-conditioning spray. I love having long, thick, wavy hair, but it's a bitch to take care of at times. After being in the seawater today, it'll need another wash when I get back to my villa. I brush through my hair, getting out the tangles, and then I tie it back up into a bun. Then, I get out my sunscreen and apply some to my arms, face, and neck. A little protection if I'm going to be sitting out here in the sun while I eat.

I'm just putting my sunscreen away when West puts down a beer bottle in front of me on the table and sits down in his chair.

"Food will be about fifteen minutes," he tells me.

"Cool. Thank you."

"So, Double D, I'd ask if you enjoyed losing your snorkeling virginity, but I think I know the answer."

"Ugh. Are you going to call me that the whole time I'm here?"

"Probably." He grins.

"Fine. Then, I'll call you … Compass. No, Westy!" I have a flash of memory of calling him that last night and him hating it.

He stares at me a moment, weighing this up. Then, he shrugs and sips his beer. "Fine."

Ugh. Whatever.

"So, snorkeling …" I go back to his question. "Well, before Sharkgate, it was actually okay. I had no clue just how pretty the ocean was."

"There are some stunning reefs here."

"Where else have you snorkeled?" I ask him.

"Hawaii, Fiji, Thailand … but it was mostly scuba diving then."

"So, just a few places then."

"I'm fairly well traveled." He leans back in his chair and rests his right foot on his left knee.

He looks so relaxed and at ease with who he is. Although, if I looked like him, I probably would as well.

Picking up my beer, I take a sip of the ice-cold liquid, enjoying the feel of it going down, cooling my overheated body.

It's so bloody hot here.

I press the base of the bottle to my chest to try and cool me down. When I look up, West is watching me … well, the bottle really and where it is, and his pupils are super dilated.

I freeze for a moment, unsure of what to do. I don't want him to stop looking at me. I know it's vain, but I don't care.

But I also can't sit here with this bottle on my chest for much longer without looking weird.

And I really don't want to look weird.

Decision made, I lift the bottle back up to my lips and take another drink. When I look back at West, he's still watching me, but his eyes are on my face now.

"Look … Dillon, I'm a straightforward guy, so I'm just gonna say what I wanted to say to you last night but couldn't because you were trashed."

"Okay …" My heart starts to thrum in my chest. I lift my bottle to my lips and take another sip of beer.

"I think you're hot," he continues. "And I want to fuck you."

I choke on my beer. Actually coughing, spluttering choke on my beer.

For Christ's sake.

"Are you okay?" he asks.

"Fine." I bang my fist on my chest. Cough. "I'm fine." Another cough.

"You want some water?"

"I'm fine." Cough. "Really fine." I clear my throat and take a small sip of beer.

It doesn't help, obviously.

But I keep hold of the bottle for the need to do something with my hands. "So …" I say.

"So"—his lips lift at the corner—"I figure I shocked you."

"Shocked me? No! Not at all!" I glance down at the table before looking back up at him. "Actually, yeah, you really did. I've never had a man say that to me before."

"Then, you haven't been around the right type of men."

"Yeah, no shit, Sherlock."

He laughs, and I really like the sound. It makes my chest light up in the best kind of way.

"I like you, Dillon. You're funny and quirky, almost as honest as me, and you are seriously sexy as fuck."

He thinks I'm sexy. Holy crapping hell!

"And I would really like to have sex with you, but I also know that you recently went through some shit with your ex …"

And my moment of happiness over hot West calling me sexy plummets to the sand at my feet. "Did I, um … tell you last night? When I was drunk?"

"Yeah."

"What exactly did I tell you?"

"That your asshole fiancé was sleeping with your mom."

"Oh my God," I groan, covering my face with my hands. "I can't believe I told you. I am so embarrassed."

He reaches over the table and tugs my hands from my face. "You've no reason to be embarrassed. About the snorkeling? Definitely. That was pretty bad. And Sharkgate? Totally embarrassing." He laughs softly. "But what they did to you … betraying you like that? Especially your mom. Dillon, you have nothing to feel embarrassed about. It's them who should be feeling shame."

His words should make me feel better, but they don't. Knowing my mum, she's probably convinced herself that her cheating with Tim was somehow my fault. That's how a true narcissist works.

And me, well, I really shouldn't be allowed to drink or be around people ever because I can't keep my stupid, big mouth shut.

"Look, I know this would be classed as bad timing," West continues, "with what you recently went through, but we're only here for two weeks, and then we'll both go home to our sides of the world and never see each other again. I'm attracted to you, and you're attracted to me. The sexual chemistry is there between us already, so imagine what it'd be like if we actually hooked up."

I'm pretty sure my jaw is on the floor. No man has ever spoken so openly and directly to me about sex before.

It's actually kind of a huge turn-on. Who knew?

He's suggesting that we hook up. Don't people just do that naturally, without a whole conversation about it? Not that the conversation isn't hot, but …

"When you say *hook up* … do you mean like a one-night stand?" I say because honestly, I don't know what else to say. I'm new to this *talking about sex before doing it* business.

He smiles, and it's just so frigging sexy. "Well, I was kind of thinking more along the lines of you and me hooking up for the duration that we're here on the island."

Oh.

Wow.

"You mean, like … a two-week stand?"

He chuckles low, and I feel it like a hand between my legs. "If that's what you want to call it."

"I'm really not sure what to call it," I whisper.

His look is searing. "Sex, Dillon. You call it really fucking hot sex for two weeks straight. If you let me, I'll make you come so hard and I'll fuck you in so many ways that you'll still be feeling me for weeks after."

Oh, that sound you hear? Well, that's the sound of the elastic in the crotch of my swimsuit snapping open in anticipation.

ten

WEST

DILLON IS STARING AT me like she's seeing me for the first time. Lips agape. Those gorgeous blue eyes of hers wide and totally scandalized.

I have an image of her lying beneath me, looking up at me in the exact same way, and my dick twitches in my trunks.

I like that she has this kind of sexual innocence about her. She's not inexperienced, but she's not sexually confident either. She's not used to someone talking so openly about sex with her.

Well, when I'm done with her, she'll be experienced in both by the end of this vacation.

I know she's recently gone through a really shitty breakup. But I'm not the kind of man who is indecisive. I can't be that way on the field. When I have a pass to make, there's no room for hesitation. And I'm not that way in life.

I always know what I want, and I always go for what I want. I'm clear from the get-go if I want a woman. I tell her what I'm willing to offer her—which is sex. If she's happy with that, then let the fucking commence. If she isn't, then I won't lose any sleep over it.

Well, maybe I'll lose a little if Dillon says no.

Knowing that she will be sleeping in the villa just across from mine and I don't get to know what it's like to sink my cock into her pussy … yeah, that might cause me to lose some sleep.

I'm not sure what it is about her. She's just so different from any woman I've ever met. And I've met a lot of women.

I honestly can't remember the last time I was so hot for a chick as I am with Dillon. Probably when I was back in high school and discovered what it was like to get my dick wet for the first time.

Maybe it's the English thing, or the way she has absolutely no clue how fucking gorgeous she is, or those eyes that seem to see everything, or her funny and smart mouth, but I wanted her the moment she wobbled into the bar. And I would have absolutely gone for her that night if she hadn't been drunk. But she's not drunk now. She's sober, and I'm not holding back on saying what I want.

And what I want for the next couple of weeks is her.

I want to fuck her real bad. Actually, I need to do a lot of things to her that would require us spending a hell of a lot of time in bed together. Things that I bet her dipshit of an ex never did to her. I'm gonna make her come so fucking hard and so often that she won't be able to wipe the smile from her face for a fucking month.

For the time we're together, I'll be good to her. I'll make her feel good about herself. All the while making us both come hard and often.

I might not be cut out for a relationship. But I will never make a woman feel shitty about herself.

I'll make her feel beautiful and sexy. I'll make her feel everything that attracts me to her.

You don't need to be a prick to be a player.

I'm just a guy who likes sex but who knows that a relationship isn't for him. But I don't want to be the asshole who hurts people who really don't deserve to be hurt. And Dillon is definitely one of those people.

Wordlessly, she picks up her beer bottle and presses the mouth of it to her lips. Tips it up, pouring the liquid into her mouth.

I watch the way her delicate throat works on a swallow as she takes the beer into her body. *Lucky fucking beer.*

Her tongue sneaks out and licks her lips.

And my mind goes straight to the gutter. Thoughts of that tongue of hers licking the length of my dick. Parting those lips as I slowly feed my cock into her mouth, hitting the back of her throat.

Fuck.

I'm getting hard, just thinking about it. And getting a boner while wearing these fucking swim shorts isn't the best idea. I have a big dick. That's not bragging. Just a fact. And these shorts ain't concealing any boner. I've already shocked and scandalized Dillon. I don't want to tip her over the edge.

Not yet anyway.

She places the bottle back on the table, keeping hold of the neck of it with her delicate fingers.

"I have to ask, for obvious reasons … are you single? Or do you have someone back home? Wife, girlfriend, husband, boyfriend? And I want you to be honest with me."

"Like I told you last night when you asked me, no. I don't have anyone in my life."

"Bloody alcohol fog," she mutters, and I chuckle. "So, this … what you're suggesting …"

"Us fucking."

"Yeah, um, well, isn't this … a bit … I don't know … strange? Sitting here, talking about it. What I mean is, people usually, you know, meet, and then it just happens … naturally. There's an instant attraction, a spark or whatever. They catch each other's eyes a few times. One strikes up a conversation. They spend time talking. Eventually, it leads on to a kiss, and then maybe, you know …"

"They fuck."

"You say that word a lot."

"It's a good word. Great in fact. And, yes, what you said is how most of the population hooks up. I'm not most people."

"I'm starting to see that."

I chuckle before taking a drink of my own beer. "Look, Dillon, if I'm upfront with you, then there's no chance of mixed signals. Sure, I could do all the romancing stuff. Long gazes, accidental touches. Find a reason to move closer to you. Pull you in for a kiss and then take you back to your villa and fuck you senseless. But then, a few hours later, when we were done fucking—"

"A few hours?" she interrupts, her eyes widening again.

I hold back a smug grin.

There are two things in life I excel at. Football and fucking.

I put the bottle down on the table and hold her stare. "Minimum. And after the hours of fucking and we both came down from the high, I'd then have to broach the subject of how I wasn't interested in ever having a relationship and that sex was all I could offer you. So, yeah, I could be that guy, who isn't upfront and ensures I get to fuck you even if just once and lays it all out afterward. But I'm not that guy. I will always be upfront with the women I want to fuck. And currently, *you* are who I want to fuck."

"I don't think anyone who comes on holiday is looking for a relationship. Especially a woman who is on her honeymoon, sans groom." She points a finger at herself.

"Fair enough. But I still won't lead you into something without you knowing the rules."

"Rules? You make it sound like a game."

I smile. "Games can be fun. Especially when both people are playing the same game and are fully clear on how to play."

Her delicate neck moves on a swallow, and she looks away, finally breaking our gaze. "You said you never want a relationship." She looks back to me. "As in ever?"

I could question why she's asking me this. Maybe it's curiosity. Maybe it's because she's the type of woman who needs to be in a relationship. She was getting married after all.

"No," I answer honestly.

"Have you ever had a relationship?"

"When I was in high school, for about a month."

"I'm sorry." She starts to blink rapidly. "You're telling me you haven't had a relationship since high school. Which doesn't count as a relationship because it was a month long and you were in high school."

"That's exactly what I'm telling you."

"How old are you?"

A little thrown by the change of direction, I give a mock frown, slapping my hand to my chest. "Don't you know that you should never ask a man his age?"

Her brow lifts. "Pretty sure it's okay to ask when said man is asking to get inside my panties."

"I don't want inside your panties, sweetheart. I want them off. It's my dick I want inside you."

Her full lips part, creating a perfect O. A flush creeps across her chest, rising up to her neck. Her breathing has increased its tempo, her chest rising and falling.

I love how responsive she is to just my words. I can't wait until I can get my hands and mouth on her.

"And to answer your question, I'm twenty-seven. How old are you?" I'm guessing, considering she was supposed to be getting married, she's not eighteen or under. I like women, not jailbait.

"Twenty-three."

Thank fuck.

If she'd said eighteen or under, I might have actually cried.

Not really. I'm not a crier. But I definitely would have been disappointed. Massively disappointed.

"Perfect. So, we're both consenting adults. We're both single. And we're incredibly attracted to each other."

"You are so confident."

"Attractive, isn't it?" I give her a smile that's been getting me laid since the ninth grade.

Her teeth sink into her plump bottom lip. "Oddly, yes."

I like that answer. I like it a hell of a lot.

Leaning forward, I lay my forearms on the table. "I get this is different for you. I'm a direct guy. I see something I want, and I go for it. And I really want you, hence this conversation. But I also understand this isn't straightforward for you. You want me—I'm clear on that, and I'm not being arrogant," I interject when I see her mouth open to speak. "I'm only stating what you've already told me. But I know you're fresh out of a shitty situation with your mom and your ex. Obviously, you are in no way ready for a relationship. But you know that's not what I'm offering. You just have to think over and decide whether you want to do something about this sexual chemistry between us."

"So, if we were to have sex, how would it work?"

"If you don't know that, then I'm not sure that I want to do it with you," I joke.

She rolls her eyes, and I chuckle.

"What I meant is, how would this fling work?"

I like that she's asking. It means she's fairly close to saying yes.

"However we both want it to work."

"So, say we had sex at your villa. I then what, leave and go back to my place?"

"If you wanted to. But I'm not opposed to sleepovers. Sometimes, I wake up thirsty in the night, and when that happens, I usually like to get my tongue wet. *Repeatedly*."

She swallows. "What about during the day?"

"We can fuck in the daytime."

"When we're not fucking and it's daytime and we're both, say, I don't know … on the beach at the same time?"

I shrug and lean back in my chair. "Then, whatever. We can hang out when we're not actively fucking, if you want. I'm not opposed to that."

She lets out a nervous-sounding laugh and looks away, over at the ocean view. "God, this is so …"

"What?"

Her eyes come back to mine. "Strange."

"What would you have preferred? Me to come on to you while you're vulnerable? We fuck because ignoring the chemistry between us is damn near impossible, and then afterward, you feel like shit because maybe you weren't ready to fuck another guy? Or me laying it all out to you, giving you time to think it over and know for sure what you want either way?"

She picks at the label on the bottle. "When you put it that way … maybe it's not so strange."

"I like to call it smart." I give her a little grin. "More guys should be like me. Then, less hearts would get broken and—"

"Okay, Romeo. Do you want a medal?"

"I could take a medal. But Romeo was a douche, who fell in love at the drop of a hat. So, yeah, I'm nothing like him."

She laughs a sound that makes my dick twitch.

I lean forward, bringing me closer to her, and lower my voice. "There's no pressure. I'm seriously hot for you, and I know you're hot for me. Give me a chance, and I'll make you feel things you never knew existed."

"How do you know I haven't experienced those things already?"

"Because you haven't been fucked by me." God, I'm a confident bastard. But I also have the goods to back it up.

She sighs, and I'm not sure I like the sound. "I didn't come here, looking for anything with anyone …"

"Believe it or not, neither did I."

She looks at me, and I can see the mistrust in her eyes.

"I came to get away from my life. Same as you."

"Your fiancée sleep with your mum?" She lets out a small, self-deprecating laugh.

"No relationships, remember?"

"Duh. Of course." She slaps a hand to her forehead.

I see the waiter walking over with our food, so I make sure to get this last part out quickly.

"I just came here to get away from real life for a while, like you. But then I saw you, and when a situation as gorgeous as you presents itself, with the sexual chemistry I know is already between us, then I'm not going to ignore it. I'm going to pursue it. Pursue *you*. I'm simply offering no-strings sex for the time that we're here, and when the vacation is over, we both go back home to our lives. We don't stay in contact, no phone numbers or social media exchanges. Think on it. And when you've made a decision, let me know. If it's a no, then we'll go back to just being vacation neighbors. But if it's a yes, then … get ready for the fucking of your life."

Leaving my words there, I lean back in my seat and watch her gorgeous, flushed face until the waiter reaches our table.

eleven

DILLON

I CAN HEAR THE wash of the waves and the low hum of the air-conditioning that's keeping me cool on this hot Maldivian night.

I should be sleeping.

Obviously, I'm not.

I can't stop thinking about what West said to me earlier. I've thought of nothing else since. I thought of it all the way through dinner. Which I saw him at. But he was coming in as I was leaving to come back to my villa.

But seriously, I mean, who could sleep after hearing that?

Sex for two weeks, no strings.

I mean, firstly, a guy who looks like that wants to have sex with me. Um … best thing ever. My confidence is at an all-time high right now.

But …

And it's a big *but*.

SAMANTHA TOWLE

I'm fresh off heartbreak. And not the run-of-the-mill heartbreak. Ultimate betrayal. *The Jerry Springer Show* kind of betrayal.

If I'm being totally honest with myself, yes, I was hurt by what Tim did and the demise of our relationship. I thought I'd loved him. I wouldn't have agreed to marry him if I didn't think that. But now, looking back, I know that I was more in love with the idea of him and what he could give me—a family, security, love, happiness. All the things I'd never had, growing up.

I've never felt loved by my mum. We've never felt like a family. The only family I had growing up was my grandparents and my aunt Jenny. They're my dad's family. So, of course, Mum used me as a tool to get whatever she wanted from them. Which was almost always money.

She is a shitty parent.

But all of that aside, I am most hurt by her betrayal. I shouldn't have been surprised. She'd spent my whole life finding ways to screw me over.

But even still, all the things she's done over the years … the hurtful words she spat at me, the blows to my confidence she gave me, the friendships of mine she ruined … I never thought she would go as low as to sleep with my fiancé.

It hurts like hell when the one person who is supposed to love you and have your back stabs you in it.

So, yeah, getting involved with West might not be the best idea.

Sure, I've had one-night stands before. I did go to university.

But when I hooked up with those guys, I wasn't putting the pieces of my broken heart back together. And I wasn't currently on my honeymoon, alone.

My head is a mess. I mean, it's only been a few weeks since I found out about their affair.

West is only offering a couple of weeks.

And it is only sex. I mean, we don't even live on the same continent, for God's sake. It's not like I'll see him again after this, and knowing that, there's no way I'll get attached to him.

And really, how attached could I get to someone in such a short period of time? I know West won't get attached to me. He made that abundantly clear. Attachments are not his thing.

Why the hell am I making this into such a big deal? Why am I even thinking this through?

It would just be sex with a really, *really* good-looking guy. A holiday fling. People have them all the time. We're only here for two weeks, and truthfully, it would be nice to not feel so shitty about myself.

Having sex makes you feel good. Great in fact. Especially when done with the right person who knows what they're doing, and if West does sex as well as he talks about it, then I would be in for one hell of a fan-fucking-tastic time.

I'll get to have a couple of weeks of great sex and then leave the island, high off all the sex we'll have had, and I'll be happy as a pig in shit. And I'll take that feeling back home with me. I'll be able to wear the good sex feelings that West will have given to me like an armor to protect myself from the reality that's waiting at home for me.

And they do say the best way to get over someone is to get under someone else. I'm not exactly sure who *they* are, but if it is the right way to get over heartbreak, then who better to get under than West?

So, I can lie here, lamenting over my crappy life, or I can go have sex with the hot American.

Hmm. Tough choice.

I sit up and slide my legs over the side of the bed.

But …

What if I do start to like him? What if I get attached and when it's time to say good-bye, I'm sad, and I have no good feelings to take back home with me? Just more sadness.

I could get hurt again.

But could I possibly get any more hurt than I already have been? I highly doubt it. Some guy I just met isn't going to hurt my heart as much as my own mother did.

God, why am I such an overthinker? Why can't I just take a chance and have some fun with a gorgeous guy who is offering me orgasms? Well, I hope that's what he's offering.

Shit.

What if he's really bad at sex? I mean, I've seen the morning wood that was straining against his shorts, but just because he's got a big dick doesn't mean he knows how to use it. Or how to give a woman an orgasm.

Tim couldn't find my clit with a torch and a map. Seriously. I had to give him directions every time.

West could be just as clueless. A totally selfish lover.

But I won't know this unless I have sex with him.

I could just have sex with him once. I don't have to commit to anything.

Argh! For fuck's sake.

I'm doing my own head in.

Why did he have to proposition me like that anyway? I mean, who does that?

Maybe it's an American thing. Back home, a guy usually just hits on you in a bar, flirts a bit. Maybe you end up kissing, and then he asks you back to his place.

West laid it out like a transaction. I was half-expecting him to give me a contract to sign to say that I understood his terms of service.

It wasn't the sexiest thing.

But the way he talks so openly about what he wants … *me.* Jesus, so fucking hot.

But no, it's not a good idea.

No matter how hot he is, it's just not a good idea for me to get tangled up with another guy so soon. I came here to get some space and give me time to clear my head. Not to get serviced by Captain America over there.

No. I'm gonna have to decline his offer.

In a year's time, I'll probably want to punch myself in the face for my stupidity at turning down sex with West, but I know it's the right thing. I'm just not in the right place in my life right now.

Now, I just have to tell him.

I bite my lip, thinking.

I should wait until morning. It is just past midnight. But I know me. I'll only lie here all night, chewing over it, and I won't get a wink of sleep.

And he might still be awake. Or asleep.

But I won't know that unless I go over there.

Okay.

I stand up.

I'll go over there now. Knock on his door. If he doesn't answer, then I know he's sleeping, and I'll just wait until morning to tell him. And if he answers, then I'll tell him that I've thought it over and I have to say no.

See, easy.

I stride over to the door and open it.

Then, I stop, run back, and grab my key off the table. Don't want to lock myself out again. The sliding doors are closed and locked, so there'd be no getting back in that way. And honestly, I wouldn't fancy wading through the lagoon in the pitch-dark. Knowing my luck, a shark would come along and bite my fucking leg off. No way would I want to walk to reception in the dark in my pajamas either. And sleeping in West's villa again would be a no-no after telling him that I don't want to be in a fling with him for the next couple of weeks.

Actually, should I change out of my pajamas? Is it a bit weird, going over there, wearing them?

Honestly, I don't know why I'm worrying about this. The guy saw me in my ugly bra and panties yesterday. My Primark pajamas aren't going to faze him.

And I'm not trying to impress him anyway.

Okay. Maybe I am a teeny-tiny bit.

Fluffing my hair, I walk out into the night and close the door behind me, locking it.

I walk down from my villa onto the jetty and pause to look at the night sky. It's so clear, no smog here. I can see every star in the sky. It's beautiful. All those other worlds out there.

I wonder if there's some female alien on some other planet, going through the same thing I am right now.

Trying to fix her broken heart after the worst betrayal. And currently going to turn down sex with the hottest man alive. Or hottest alien alive in her case.

You know, I'm so glad that no one can hear my thoughts because I'm really fucking weird at times.

Sighing, I look over at West's villa and walk over to it.

When I reach the door, I lift my hand and knock. Not too loudly. But loud enough that if he's awake, he'll hear me.

I hear movement inside, and my stomach takes a dive south.

Even though I want this over with, I'm really nervous now.

The door swings open, and West is standing there.

In boxer shorts.

That's it.

There's inch upon inch of his golden-tanned skin on show. And I know I've already seen him in a similar state of undress before, but it seems to do nothing to dull my reaction to the way he looks now. To that body of his. His hair is down, kissing his shoulders. He looks gorgeous.

My mouth dries, and all words fail me.

Those abs are gonna be the death of me.

"Hey," he says. "You okay?"

I try to speak, but nothing comes out. I'm just staring at him.

"Dillon?"

"Uh, yeah?"

"What can I do for you?"

"Oh." I blink. It doesn't help. I just go straight back to staring at him like a sex-starved nympho. "I was, uh, thinking about what you said."

He leans a shoulder against the doorframe. "Oh yeah?"

"Yes."

"And?"

And … what was I supposed to be coming over here to tell him? I forgot.

No. I'm supposed to tell him no to all the sex.

But just look at him. He's a once-in-a-lifetime kind of sexual experience. Something to tell the grandkids about. Or not because that'd be gross. But when I'm home and alone in bed, I'd have those memories to keep me warm at night.

But it's not a good idea, Dillon. Remember, you could get hurt again.

Hurt is bad.

But sex is soooo good.

No. Stop it. Stop thinking about the sex and how big his cock might be and how good it would feel inside you. Or how that sexy mouth of his might taste or if his muscles would feel as hard as they look.

Just say no to all of the sex with the hot American man. Say no and turn and walk back to your villa. And then get a cold shower.

Right. I'm gonna do it.

"And … well, I thought it over, and it's a … yes."

Twelve

DILLON

YES? WHAT THE HELL, Dillon?! You were supposed to say no.

Oh, who am I kidding? I was always gonna say yes. Look at him, for fuck's sake. I'd have to be crazy to say no to sex with him.

Those full lips of his pull up into a smile, and I almost come on the spot. His hand reaches out and grabs hold of mine. I'm tugged inside his villa. The door is closed, and I'm pushed up against it.

My breath whooshes out of me.

I've never been manhandled like this before. I really like it.

West presses his body up against mine. And it's fucking heaven. He feels so good. Hard against my soft. Except for my nipples. They're very much hard.

West stares down at me. His lips so very close to mine. "Are you sure you're okay with everything we discussed? Just sex and no contact after we leave here?"

I feel his warm breath against my skin.

I swallow and lick my lips. "I wouldn't be here if I wasn't."

"Good."

Then, he kisses me.

And holy hell.

We both dive straight into the kiss. There's no sweeping brushes of lips or gentle pecks.

This is an *I'm kissing you like I really wanna fuck you* kiss.

The feel of his mouth against mine is amazing. His lips are soft yet firm.

He tastes of toothpaste and utter sin. He smells like sex and the ocean. He's in all of my senses. It's overwhelming but in the best kind of way.

Total aphrodisiac.

But to be fair, he could just stand in front of me, fully clothed, and I'd get turned on. Because hello, hotness.

When his tongue touches mine, I feel sparks shoot through me.

Kind of like when the battery dies on your car, so you put jumper cables on it and use another car to get it going. That's what West is doing to me. Charging me with his jumper cables.

And that sounds really lame. So, yeah, never say that out loud to him.

But whatever it is that I'm feeling right now, it's exhilarating, and all he's doing is kissing me.

I never felt like this when Tim kissed me.

West kisses like he knows exactly what he wants … me.

Why the hell am I thinking about my ex right now? I'm wrapped around the most physically beautiful man I have ever seen in my real life. And on television.

My hands slide up that hard chest of his, and my arms loop around his neck. His skin is so much softer than I expected. But his muscles are as hard as I thought they would be.

I wiggle closer to him. Our bodies are already pressed together, but I need to get closer to him. Impossibly close.

West's arm goes around my waist, pinning me to his body. His other hand grabs a handful of my hair, tilting my head back slightly, taking control of the kiss.

I hear a whimper and realize that it came from me.

God, I love the way he kisses. Lush and deep. He kisses with meaning. Telling me that this kiss is leading to somewhere really fucking good.

The hand around my waist slides down to my butt, gripping it, and he urges me up onto my tiptoes.

I feel so tiny compared to him.

He's so fucking built. I've never been with a man as big as him. It's probably stupid to think, but he makes me feel girlie. Feminine. And I really like it.

His other hand leaves my hair and grips my other butt cheek. He lifts me, and my legs go around his waist.

We don't even break the kiss.

He presses me back against the door. His lips move from mine, kissing down my neck. He starts thrusting his hard dick against me, sucking on a sensitive spot on my neck. The sounds coming from me are unintelligible.

"You feel so fucking good," he murmurs, trailing his tongue over the swell of my breasts.

My hands slide into his hair, and I tug his mouth back to mine, and then we're kissing again.

His hand moves up my side and under my top.

His fingers trail just below my breast. My braless breasts. I came over here, forgetting that I had no bra on. Because I was in bed, and really, who wears a bra to bed? Not me—that's for sure.

When his fingers touch the bottom of my boob, he freezes. "You're not wearing a bra," he says against my lips.

"I was in bed."

He groans. "I need to see them. You. Now." He pushes off the door, taking me with him.

He strides into the main area of the villa, and I'm lowered to my feet next to the bed. I tilt my head, staring up at him. His lips are swollen from my kisses, his hair messed up from having my hands in it.

He looks fucking beautiful.

And right now—and for the next two weeks—he's mine.

Rough, strong fingers curl into the hem of my pajama top, and it's lifted. I raise my arms above my head, and West tugs it off.

My hair falls around my shoulders.

Dropping my top to the floor, West takes a few steps back and stares at me.

My skin prickles under his perusal.

Normally, I feel self-conscious when I'm naked in front of a man. Even one I know well. But with the way West is looking at me right now, I feel nothing but desired.

I can't ever remember anyone looking at me the way that he is right now. With such open hunger. Like he's going to devour me whole. And I'm going to let him.

A shiver moves through me.

"I was right." His voice is rough.

A gulp. "About?"

"Your tits. They're real."

Huh?

"You thought I had fake tits?"

"No, I thought you had real tits, and I was right."

"Okay … question … is this what men think about when they see a woman naked for the first time—if she has real or surgically enhanced tits?"

"I don't know what other men think about. But I'm just a tit man. It's been a long while since I last saw a pair that hadn't been under the knife."

"I honestly don't even know what to say to that."

His lips quirk up into a dirty grin. "You don't have to say anything." He takes a step forward, back to me, and cups my boobs in those large hands of his.

My breath stutters. Nothing has ever felt so good as his rough hands against the soft skin of my breasts.

"They're perfect." He rubs his thumbs over my nipples. "You're perfect."

Then, he lowers his mouth to mine and kisses me again. His lips trace a path down my throat and to my chest. When he lowers to his knees and slides his tongue down the valley of my breasts before wrapping his mouth around my nipple, my legs almost buckle.

Holy sensations.

His hands grip my hips, like he knows I'm having trouble keeping upright, while his mouth and tongue work their magic on my boobs.

When his tongue slides lower, down my stomach, and dips into my belly button and his fingers start to tug my pajama shorts down, I know I'm not gonna be able to stand up, even with his help, if he's heading where I'm really hoping he's heading.

He slides my shorts and panties down my legs tortuously slow. When they reach the floor, I step out of them and kick them aside.

West's hands slide around my calves and up my legs to my thighs, fingers curling around them.

I'm standing here, completely naked, in front of this man that I barely know, and I feel nothing but sexy and wanted.

It's strange, yet it feels amazing.

He sits back on his heels. "Fucking gorgeous," he says, eyes roaming my body. His voice is as rough and dirty as the look in his eyes.

He stares up at me. "Sit on the bed and spread your legs, so I can fuck you with my tongue. I wanna taste you, Dillon."

Holy. Fuck.

He's so demanding. His mouth is so dirty.

And I bloody love it.

I sit down on the bed. Heart pounding, I part my legs.

"Wider," is his command.

I'm embarrassingly wet. But it doesn't stop me from doing as he said.

I spread my legs open as far as they can go, and I let my eyes slide down his bare chest and lower. I can see his erection straining against his sleep shorts. My mouth waters.

I've never had such a visceral reaction to the sight of an erection before. Sure, I like cocks, but I've always been more concerned with just having sex with them more than how they'll look and feel and taste.

But I really want to know what West's cock looks like. Tastes like. How it'll feel in my mouth.

"Like what you see?" West's hand curls around his erection, giving it a squeeze.

My pulse races as my eyes lift to his. Inside, I'm jittery with nerves, but I give my cockiest smile. "I haven't seen anything yet."

His lips turn into a grin that's all fox. "You will."

Then, he dips his head down and puts his mouth on my pussy.

"Jesus." My hands go to his head, gripping.

Gray eyes stare up at me. "Not him. Me."

He slides a finger inside me, and my muscles clench around it.

"Fuck. You're tight. Can you take more?" he asks, and I nod.

He puts another finger inside and starts fucking me with them both. The palm of his hand is pressing up against my clit with every thrust of his fingers, and it feels divine.

"Touch your tits. I wanna see you play with them."

I cup my breasts with my hands and roll my nipples between my fingers.

"Fuck yeah, just like that," he rasps and then pulls his fingers out of me. He replaces them with his tongue and starts fucking me with it.

I cry out at the sensation of his hot tongue inside of me.

My hands leave my breasts and fall back onto the bed, supporting me.

When I feel his tongue slide out of me and over my clit, I nearly come off the bed. And I almost come too.

Hey, don't judge me. It's been a while.

I somehow manage to stave off the orgasm because I'm not ready for this to be over just yet.

His fingers slip back inside me, and his mouth works my clit over while he fingers me.

My hands fist the duvet.

"You taste so fucking good," he murmurs against me.

The rumble of his deep voice against my clit is too much for me to take, and I go off without warning.

"West!" I scream out his name, plus a few curse words, as my hips shamelessly pump against his mouth while I ride out my orgasm against his tongue.

The most intense orgasm I have ever had.

I collapse back against the bed, out of breath, heart pounding, like I just ran a marathon. When in fact I did nothing, except come harder than I ever have in my life. It was West who did all the work, and he was really bloody good at it.

Amazing. Incredible. Mind-blowing.

And I get two weeks of this. With him.

Sex and orgasms.

Shutting my eyes, I send up a silent, *Thank you.*

I hear movement. A drawer opens and then closes.

Opening my eyes, I push up to sit, just as West comes to stand before me.

He has a condom wrapper in his hand, and he's still wearing his boxer shorts.

I look up at him. "You're still dressed." My voice comes out raspy. Dare I say … sexy. I sound nothing like I usually do.

Must be all that screaming I just did.

He tosses the condom on the bed beside me. Then, he shoves his boxers down his hips and …

Holy fucking cock.

There's length. And girth. Lots of both.

I swallow down.

I'm a small woman. I have a small vagina. I don't honestly know if it's gonna fit in me.

But one thing I do know is that I'm gonna have fun trying.

I drag my eyes from his cock, which is right there in front of my face—I could literally stick my tongue out and lick the tip—and tilt my head back to look up at him. His jaw is clenched tight, and the look in his eyes … he looks like he's holding back from tearing me in two right now.

And with a cock that size, he just might.

"Impressive," I say. "Did your parents give you growth hormones as a child?"

A dark chuckle. "All natural."

"Lucky me," I whisper.

Then, I lean forward and lick a path up his cock with my tongue. When I reach the tip, I suck the pre-cum from it.

"You taste good," I murmur.

His breathing stutters, and then he growls a sound so sexy that I could come again just from hearing it.

Parting my lips, I take him in my mouth, sliding down excruciatingly slow.

I want to tease him. I want to make him crazy with want for me.

I don't know who this sexually confident woman is who's crawled inside of me tonight. But I'm liking her a lot.

"Jesus," he rasps.

I let his cock pop from my mouth, and I stare up at him. "Not him. Me." I grin after giving him his words back from earlier.

That earns me a sexy smile.

I curl my hand around the base of his cock and take him back in my mouth, sliding down as far as I can go, taking as much of his cock as I can take.

I've never had a dick this big in my mouth before, so my gag reflex has never truly been put to the test …

It hits the back of my throat, and … nope. I can't take it all.

I ease back a bit, knowing my limit, and then I start working him over with my mouth. Bobbing my head up and down, letting his dick slide between my lips, gripping and squeezing the base.

"Fuck …" he growls through gritted teeth. "Keep doing that … and I'm gonna come."

Well, we don't want that, do we?

I give him one last suck and then let his dick slide from my mouth.

I reach for the condom and hand it to West. He tears open the wrapper and slides it down his dick with impressive speed.

Then, he lowers down to his knees on the floor, putting us face-to-face.

He lifts a hand, reaches out, and cups my chin. Then, he leans forward and kisses me. He slides his tongue into my mouth, and I taste myself on him from earlier. It's such a turn-on.

His hands come to my hips, and he guides me forward, off the bed and onto his lap, so I'm straddling him.

Lips kiss along my jaw and nip my earlobe. "Ride me," he whispers.

I rise up onto my knees and take his cock in my hand.

I press down, and the wide crown of his dick spreads me open.

I slowly lower myself onto him. He's so damn big. Stretching and widening me. It's a pleasure pain.

"You're so fucking tight," he grunts.

His jaw is clenched tight, eyes shut. He looks like he's in actual pain.

"Do you want me to stop?" I ask him.

Please say no.

Gray eyes flick open and stare back at me. "Definitely fucking not."

His hands grip my ass, and he guides me down the rest of him until I'm fully seated in his lap.

I take a moment to adjust to him. The way he's filling me is delicious. But he's all the way up in there, and my muscles are clenched around him.

"You okay?" he asks.

I smile at him. "I'm good. You?"

"I've wanted to be inside you since I laid eyes on you last night, so yeah, I'm fucking great."

His admission sends my confidence soaring.

I bring my mouth to his and kiss him hard. Then, I place my hands on those broad, muscular shoulders of his and lift up. Then, I slam back down.

"Fuck yeah," he grunts. "Keep going, babe. Fuck me hard."

So, I do. I ride him hard and fast.

He has one hand on my ass and the other on my boob. Squeezing and tugging on my nipple, sending little jolts of pleasure straight to my clit.

Then, his hand wraps around my hair, and he tugs my head back. His mouth replaces where his hand just was, and he sucks and licks my nipple. My hands land back on his big thighs, putting me at a new angle, which feels incredible, as I continue to ride him.

The hand that was on my ass comes between us, and deft fingers rub over my wet clit.

I don't think I've ever been as wet as I am right now.

He turns me on so fucking much.

With his fingers on me, it doesn't take long before I feel that telltale tug in my lower belly, telling me that an orgasm is approaching.

"Keep … doing … that …" I pant. "And … I'll … come."

His head lifts, eyes meeting mine. "I don't plan on stopping. Come for me, Dillon."

He covers my mouth with his. His tongue licking my mouth, fucking me like his dick is, while his talented fingers coax my orgasm out of me.

"Fuck!" I cry, my head falling back as I start coming hard.

I thought the first orgasm was off the charts. This one beats the hell out of it.

My arms are trembling, and I can barely hold myself up. Sensing that, West wraps his hand around my back, holding me up as my body contracts around his.

Just as the orgasm is starting to recede, I'm moving. West stands, taking me with him. Then, we're on the bed. His hard body over mine, he pins my arms over my head to the mattress and then starts to fuck me with abandon.

Jaw clenched, eyes bright with lust, hips slapping against me, he screws me into that mattress and looks like a fucking god while he does it.

"Dillon! Fuck!" he yells. "I'm coming!"

His hips start to jerk against mine, and then I feel his cock pulse inside me as he starts coming.

When he's finished, he falls on top of me. His breathing is heavy. I slide my hands from his and press them to his back, holding him.

Lips press a soft kiss against my shoulder. My skin tingles at the contact.

"That was …" I breathe.

"Fucking amazing." West lifts his head and rests up on an elbow, removing his weight from me. He stares down at me.

"Yeah," I sigh happily. And it really was amazing.

Literally the best sex I've ever had. I mean, I came twice. Twice!

That's never happened to me during sex—ever.

No man has ever bothered to try to make me come twice. Tim definitely didn't bother. But then he was too busy—nope, not going there right now. I'm feeling great. Nothing is going to steal my glow.

Because … orgasms.

West definitely knows what he's doing in bed. I'm guessing he's had a lot of practice. More than me.

I mean, I've dated my fair share of men, but I'm reckoning that West's number is a hell of a lot higher than mine.

Not that it matters.

Because I'm currently reaping the benefits of that experience.

I can't believe I was even considering saying no to doing this with him. Right now, I could be lying in the bed in my villa all alone.

Thank fuck I didn't say no. Finally, I did something smart. And now, I've got two more weeks of this.

I'm in paradise with the hottest man I have ever seen, and I get to have sex with him and have multiple daily orgasms.

Guess I'm not so stupid after all.

Thirteen

WEST

FUCK ME. THAT WAS incredible.

She's incredible. Even better than I thought she would be.

She's got more sexual confidence than I initially gave her credit for. She rode my dick like a champ. And she definitely likes being told what to do during sex, which is a bonus for me because I'm a bossy fuck in bed.

I know what I want, and I say it.

I did go easy with her this first time. Let her take the lead to start with. I wasn't sure how much she could take. But she took all of me and more. Although I was a little rough with her toward the end.

"I didn't hurt you, did I? Kind of lost my mind a bit toward the end there."

She gives me a shy smile. "No. I mean, you got a little rough, but I liked it."

"Yeah?"

A blush creeps up her face. "Yeah."

I love that she gets shy after what we just did. And that she likes it rough.

"I'm just gonna go clean up," I tell her before easing out of her. I climb out of bed and head into the bathroom to dispose of the condom and wash up.

When I come back to bed, she's not in it. She's standing by the glass doors, looking out into the night, a blanket wrapped around her, covering that gorgeous body of hers.

"You okay?" I ask, sitting down on the bed.

She turns, smiling. "Yeah. Just looking at the stars. I love that you can see them so clearly here."

"It's pretty cool."

"So, you finished in the bathroom? I'm gonna go clean up."

I watch her walk past, and then I lie down on the bed, arms behind my head.

She seems uncomfortable. I hope she's not regretting what we just did. Because I'm sure as fuck not. But I know her headspace is a little messy at the moment.

I hear the toilet flush, and the bathroom door opens a minute later.

I push myself up to a sitting position and cover my junk with a sheet.

Dillon appears back in the room. She stops a distance away from the bed. Her hand is holding that blanket to her body like her life depends on it.

"You okay?" I ask her.

"Yeah"—she smiles—"I'm fine."

There's a beat of silence.

Then, she says, "So … I should probably go back to my villa."

It bothers me that she's suggesting going. I'm not actually sure why. It's never bothered me before when a woman has wanted to leave straight after sex.

Maybe it's because I don't feel anywhere near done with her tonight.

And we did have that whole conversation about it before, and I don't want her going because she thinks she has to.

I slide my legs off the edge of the bed, so I'm sitting, facing her. "Are you going because you want to or because you think I want you to? Because we had that whole conversation earlier today."

She lifts those delicate shoulders. "I don't know."

"Do you regret us fucking?"

Her eyes snap up to mine.

"Because I know you're coming off a shitty time."

"No. I don't regret it at all. Do you?"

"Fuck no. But I'm not the one being weird."

"I'm not being weird."

"You are."

"Fine. I am." She huffs out a breath. "I've just never done this before."

"Had sex? Because I'd never have guessed. You were really fucking good."

She gives me a look, but she likes the compliment—I see it in the way her cheeks redden. "I've just never slept with a guy I don't know much about. It just feels a bit"—she shifts on her feet, looking down, and lets out a breath—"strange." Her eyes come straight back to mine. "I don't mean the sex was strange. The sex was incredible. Best ever. When you went in the bathroom, I was just thinking and realized I only know your name, age, and that you're from America. I guess I freaked a little bit."

I've had sex with women and not even known their name before, and it's never bothered me. But then I've never been in a relationship before. I don't want her to feel weird. I want her to feel good.

She wants to know some stuff about me? Fine, I can tell her stuff. Just not everything.

"What do you want to know?"

Those small shoulders of hers lift again. "I don't know … just like … where in America are you from? Not that I know tons of places in America, but I might know where you're from."

"I grew up in DC."

She moves to lean back against the wall, taking her farther away from me, which I don't like. "Washington, DC?"

"Yeah. But I live in Baltimore now."

"Not heard of it."

"It's in Maryland."

"Like the cookies?"

"What?"

"Cookies. Back home, we have cookies called Maryland cookies."

I shake my head. "Never heard of them."

"Guess they're not named after there then." She laughs softly. "What's your job?"

"Sports."

"Sports, as in …"

"Football. I play football."

"My football or yours?"

"There're two kinds?"

She gives me a look. "Don't be facetious; you know there are."

I lean back on my hands and raise my brow. "Oh, you mean, soccer."

"Football. Yours is American football. My country and the rest of the world—"

"Except for America."

"Call it football," she carries on without acknowledging what I said. "So, I'm taking it, you play American football?"

"Yes, I play *football*." I grin, knowing I'm annoying her and really enjoying it. It's a turn-on, watching her getting flustered and pissed off with me. And I'm also enjoying the fact that she's more concerned with being annoyed over the football/soccer terminology than she is with the fact that I play football. Back home, when a woman finds out I play for the NFL or she realizes who my father is, she's more interested in that than who I am as a person. Which generally works for me because I'm not interested in any woman knowing the real me or me knowing her.

Yet here I am, telling Dillon things about myself because she asked and I'm finding myself curious to know stuff about her.

"Are you a quarterback?"

I chuckle and shake my head. "Fucking TV and movies have everyone outside of the sport thinking it's the only player that exists on the team. Nope, I'm not a quarterback."

"Hey, it's not my fault that your American movies and shows only talk about quarterbacks. So, what position do you play?"

"I'm a wide receiver."

"I have no clue what that means."

"It means, I can catch like a beast, evade like a ninja, run like a motherfucker, and pass like the star I am."

"Beast, ninja, motherfucker, and star. Sounds … modest."

She grins, and I chuckle.

"Just telling you like it is."

"Uh-huh. So, I'd ask what team you play for, but it would mean zero to me."

Good. I'm not sure I want her to know. But then she'd only have to Google my name, and everything would come up. Who I am. Even outside of football.

"What about you?" I ask, deflecting the conversation from me to her.

"What about me?"

"Where are you from? I know you said your accent is Yorkshire."

"I'm from Hull."

"Never heard of it."

"Not many people have." She laughs. "It's in East Yorkshire. At the end of the motorway. You only come there if you live there."

"What do you do for work?"

She sighs and looks down at her feet. Her toes are painted a pale pink. I have the sudden urge to get down on my knees and lick a path from her pretty pink toes all the way up her leg to her pretty pink pussy.

"I was, uh, working as a receptionist for my ex's family's company. That's how I met him."

Ah.

"How long were you with him?"

I see a slight wince to her expression that makes me curious. "Um … six months."

"And you were getting married?" I can't stop the surprise that comes out of me.

I couldn't imagine getting married, period. But marrying someone after six months of knowing them?

Fuck. That.

"I know it was quick. It was a bit of a whirlwind. He proposed after six weeks of dating. I guess … I, um … got swept up in it all. In all honesty, I'd probably been feeling low when I met him. My grandparents died within two years of each other. My grandmother's passing was only eight months before I met him."

"You were close?"

"Very." She releases a sad-sounding breath. "I suppose I just wanted to feel happy. So, when he proposed, I took the good feeling that came with it and ran with it. It was stupid and naive; I see that now."

"We're all capable of doing stupid things when we're in pain."

"I know," she says, and then her eyes widen, like she's just thought of something worrisome. "West, I hope you know I'm not doing this with you because I'm in pain.

Because I'm not in pain. I mean, I am hurting, but it's not why I had sex with you."

"I know," I reassure her because she sounds so concerned.

"Good." She smiles, relaxing. "And I know now that getting engaged and married so quickly was a dumb idea. Don't get me wrong; being engaged was exciting, and I would have waited to actually get married, but he didn't want to wait. Then, an opening came up at the hotel he wanted to get married in, so he booked it."

"I'm hearing a lot of what he wanted in there."

She sighs again. "Yeah. It wasn't like me to do something so rash. He kinda took charge. I thought it was romantic."

She looks embarrassed, and I feel bad for her.

"I guess I can understand how that could happen."

I can't. But I'm not going to judge her for her decisions. We all make mistakes. I'm the fucking king of them.

"Yeah, so we were engaged and getting married." She looks up, and I hate the sadness in her eyes. "So, I figured I should introduce him to my mum …" She trails off.

I sit forward and rest my forearms on my thighs. I remember what she told me last night when she was drunk, about how she'd caught them together. I can't even imagine what that was like.

My dad is a monumental prick, who had a hard time keeping it in his pants when he was married to my mom, but I don't think even he would stoop so low as to fuck my girlfriend, if I ever had one.

"So, you don't work there now?" I ask.

She shakes her head. "I quit as soon as I found out what was going on. Probably stupid to quit a job when you don't have another to go to, but I just couldn't work there anymore."

"I get it. I'd have done the same. Anyone would."

"Yeah." She lets out a breath. "I have some money in savings, and I earn a little from my books, but when I get back, I need to get another job to keep me afloat. I don't want to waste all of my savings."

"Books?"

"Oh." She lifts her head, and I see that lightness that she lost back in her eyes. "I write them. Books. Self-published. I don't make a lot, but yeah, that's what I do."

"You're an author."

"A badly paid one, but yeah, I guess I am," she says shyly.

"What kind of books do you write?"

"Romance. Contemporary mostly. But I've written some romcoms, and I even wrote a romantic suspense once. That was fun."

I smile. "You'd like to write full-time?"

"Yeah." She sighs. "That's the pipe dream. But it's a hard dream to make happen. I know so many amazing writers who still have to work day jobs to make the ends meet."

"But still, you're getting to do what you love even if it doesn't pay all the bills," I say to her.

"Yeah." She smiles that smile that knocked me on my ass the moment I saw her, and it makes me want to stick my dick in her and do many, many dirty things to her. "When I write … I create these whole worlds where anything can happen. There doesn't have to be sadness or shitty people or cheating fiancés and crappy mothers …" Her smile weakens, and that I don't like. "In the worlds I create, anything can happen. And I get to write HEAs. What could be better than that?"

"HEAs?"

"Happily ever afters."

"Is that what you were looking for with your ex?" I ask, and then I want to smack myself in the face because her smile disappears altogether.

"Probably. Maybe I just wanted to live one of the stories I wrote for once."

"So, in these stories of yours, with these happily ever afters, do the characters have sex?" I lean back and part my legs a touch, causing the sheet to slide from my lap. I want that smile back on her face.

Actually, I want her beneath me and screaming my name again.

Her eyes zero in on my cock straightaway, and a flush covers her chest.

I fucking love how responsive she is to me.

"Yeah," she croaks and clears her throat. "Yeah, they do."

"And you write these sex scenes?"

"Yes." She hasn't taken her eyes off my cock yet, and he's preening under her attention.

"Any particular sex scene that you've ever wanted to act out?" I cup my balls with my hand and then slide my hand up and palm my dick, giving it a firm squeeze.

A hot breath leaves her, but she doesn't look away from my hand. She's standing there, watching me jack myself off.

It's seriously fucking hot.

"There, uh … was this one scene I wrote, where, uh …"

She licks her lips, and the action makes me even harder. I want her mouth on me so bad.

"The girl, she, uh … had sex with the guy before she even knew his name."

"Sex with a stranger?"

"Yeah." Her breaths are coming in fast. Lips parted. Her gorgeous chest rising up and down. The grip that she's had on that blanket is starting to loosen.

Funny that that's her fantasy when after having sex with me and knowing my name but not knowing other stuff freaked her out.

I guess the fantasy is always different from the reality.

Taking my hand off my dick, I crook my finger at her. "Come here."

She walks over to me. Coming to a stop between my parted legs.

I tug at her blanket, letting it fall to the floor.

My eyes roam her naked body. She's fucking gorgeous.

"You are stunning," I tell her.

She stares down at me. Those insane eyes of hers are glassy with lust. Her chest flush with want. Reaching out, I hold her hip with my hand, brushing my thumb over the soft skin of her stomach. She shudders.

My other hand cups her cheek. Her face is flawless, except for a tiny mole above her lip. I press my thumb over her lips, dragging it down. She captures it between her teeth, surprising me.

I feel the touch of her tongue against the tip of it, and the feeling shoots straight to my dick, making him even harder.

She releases my thumb from her mouth. I slide my hand into her hair and tug her mouth down to mine, stopping just before our lips meet.

"You ready to forget my name?" I whisper to her right before I slam my lips to hers and waste no time in kissing her like I'm gonna fuck her. Hard.

Her tongue seeks entry into my mouth. When it slides against mine, it's like a cattle prod to the spine.

My arm curls around her ass, and I lift her and turn, putting her on the bed and me on top of her.

No foreplay this time. I just want to fuck her. Fast and hard.

I leave her for a moment to grab a condom. I have that fucker on in record time.

Then, I'm back on top of her, my mouth ravaging hers as I slide inside her.

Fuck. Yes.

I've never been inside such a tight pussy. I don't know if it's because she's so physically small—the women I usually fuck are taller than Dillon—or if it's because she has the magical unicorn of pussies.

Well, whatever it is, I don't care.

I just care that I'm inside her.

128

I could literally fucking live in here. She feels that good.

When I'm buried to the hilt, she moans into my mouth.

The sound of her moan vibrates in my chest, and it's like pouring gasoline on an already-raging fire.

I don't know what it is about her, but she has my dopamine levels going fucking crazy.

I grab her hands and pin them to the bed. "What's my name?"

Her eyes blink open, and she stares up at me. A dirty, sexy fucking grin comes on her lips.

"I don't know." She plays along.

"You wanna know?"

She shakes her head.

It's my turn to smile. "Good. Now, hold on tight 'cause I'm gonna fuck you hard."

Her legs lift and wrap around my back, and her fingers slide between mine, gripping my hands.

"Kiss me," she whispers, so I do.

And then I start to fuck her.

Hard.

"Oh my God!" she cries as I pound into her. Her nails dig into the skin of my hands, but it only spurs me on. "Feels so good. Don't stop."

Like I would ever. I'll fuck Dillon for as long as she wants me to.

I mean, for the two weeks we're here. I'll fuck her as many times as she wants in that time.

"Are you gonna come for me?" I pant, staring down at her tits bouncing with every hard thrust I give her.

"Yes. Just keep doing that."

But I don't. I angle my hips so that my dick hits deeper inside her and the base drags over her clit.

"Oh my God!" she cries. "No, keep doing that … please …"

I increase my tempo but keep the angle.

I can feel my balls drawing up tight, and the telltale feeling of heat spreads at the base of my spine. I'm gonna come real fucking soon if I don't do something to slow myself down. A woman has never come after me, and I don't intend to let that happen now.

She just gets me going so fucking bad.

I grit my teeth and clench my ass cheeks as I focus on getting her there first.

Knowing that her tits are super sensitive, I lower my head to them and take a nipple in my mouth. One good suck, and she goes off. She cries out my name, forgetting we're supposed to be strangers in this little scenario. Her muscles tighten around my dick, squeezing the shit out of it, and I couldn't stop my orgasm if I tried. And I ain't trying.

My dick jerks inside her, and I start coming. And I keep coming. I've no fucking clue where all this spunk is coming from, considering I came like a motherfucker not that long ago.

When I'm done, I collapse on her. A huff of air comes out of her.

I forget how small she is compared to me.

Rolling over, I take her with me, putting her on top, keeping my dick inside of her. He's not ready to leave the warmth of her quite yet.

"Better?" I ask her, smoothing her hair back from her face, which is plastered to my sweaty chest.

"Yeah," she whispers. "That was … epic. Even better than the first time. And that had been amazing."

"Yeah," I murmur.

She's right. It was better than the first time, and the first fuck had been incredible.

But that …

It was fire.

Again, something I've never encountered in all my years of fucking. Nothing has ever beaten the first time with a woman before. You know the excitement of knowing what it's like to fuck someone for the first time? It's usually downhill for me after that.

But apparently, not this time.

"West?" she whispers.

"Yeah?"

"Thank you."

"You're thanking me for sex?"

She laughs softly, and the sound tickles my chest. "No. Well, yeah. But no. I'm thanking you for telling me that you wanted to have sex with me. If you hadn't, I wouldn't be here right now, feeling the best I have in a long time."

I'm happy she feels that way. If anyone deserves to feel good, it's her.

"Well, I'm really fucking glad you said yes to us fucking."

She tilts her head to look at me. "You have such a way with words." Her eyes are smiling at me.

"It's a gift." I shrug.

Then, I thread my fingers into her hair, bringing her face to mine, and I kiss her. Gently. Slowly.

Complete contrast to the way I just fucked her.

We kiss for a while. It's the first time in a long time that I can remember kissing a woman without it ending in sex.

Because I never kiss a woman like this after sex. I usually leave or fall asleep.

Our kisses slow until they stop, and she lays her head back on my chest, snuggling into me.

I stroke my hand over her long hair and down her back. After a few minutes, I feel her breaths start to even out.

"You tired?" I ask her.

"Mmhmm," she murmurs. "You want me to move?" She sounds reluctant, and to be honest, I'm kind of liking having her lying up here on me.

"No. You're good. Just let me get rid of this condom."

I shift my hips, so my dick slips out of her. She makes a noise of displeasure, and I wonder if it's because my dick is no longer inside her or if it's because I moved her a little.

I reach down and tug the condom off my dick, and then I blindly reach for the tissues on the nightstand, wrap it in one, and toss it on the nightstand to dispose of in the morning. I reach behind me and flick the light switch off, plunging us into darkness, and then I grab the sheet and pull it over us both, covering us.

"Night," I murmur to her, pressing a kiss to her forehead.

"Night," she whispers, her lips pressing a soft kiss to my chest.

She's asleep a minute later.

While I'm still lying here wide awake five fucking minutes later. Which is another weird thing. Because I can go to sleep in a nanosecond. Especially after sex.

I stare down at her dark head and wonder just what it is about her that has me doing things I don't normally do.

It takes me a hell of a long time before I fall asleep.

fourteen

DILLON

MY SECOND DAY ON the island, and I woke up in West's bed again.

Not that I'm complaining. Because this time, we'd had sex. Multiple times. And I didn't wake up with a hangover.

Bonus.

I did wake up with West's morning wood poking me in the ass.

Not literally *in* my ass. It was prodding my butt cheek. Although anal with him would be … quite possibly painful. His dick is huge. I have had butt sex once before, but the guy was nowhere near as big as West, and we used a ton of lube. I don't have lube here with me, and I'm not sure that it's something they stock at the shop.

And why am I thinking about anal?

Oh yeah, because of how I woke up this morning. To his hard dick, which led to us having sex. Again.

Out of this world. Hot as sin. Sex.

We'd had sex twice last night. Then, we'd woken in the middle of the night and fucked again. Doggy style. Then, we did it again this morning. Total lazy morning sex. It was awesome.

So, in total, we'd had sex four times. FOUR!

Sorry, but that had to be shouted. Because … FOUR!

And each time was better than the last.

Like, how is that even possible? But it is. Seriously.

And don't even get me started on the orgasms.

Okay, get me started. Because I have lost count of how many I've had with West so far.

I'm totally lying. I haven't forgotten. I had two orgasms the first time we did it. One the second time. One when we sexed in the middle of the night. And two this morning. That's six orgasms.

SIX!

Can you believe it? I don't think I had that many orgasms in the first month with Tim.

And there's more to come. I have twelve more days' worth of orgasms.

Hallelujah. And praise the Lord.

After our morning round of sex, I went back to my villa to shower and get ready for breakfast. We'd arranged to go together. And it was him who had asked me to go to breakfast with him. There was no way I was going to ask him. I was totally playing it cool.

After breakfast, West went to the gym, and I decided to go for a wander around the resort. Check some of the shops out.

There wasn't much going on at the shops, so I hit up the beach. Got myself set up on a lounger with a mocktail and a book and just lounged and read. Took a nap. Grabbed some lunch from the bar and just chilled. It was perfect.

I felt all light and happy. Literally nothing could burst my happy glow.

Well, except for maybe finding out that my mum had also had sex with West.

Which would be impossible. So, yeah, not ever gonna think about that.

And I also didn't think about West or what he might have been up to all day.

Nope, not me. I was chill.

Okay, maybe I did think about him a little bit. You know, just wondered what he was up to.

I didn't see him for the rest of the day, and he wasn't at dinner.

I might have knocked on his door on my way there to see if he wanted to come with me. But there was no answer. And he wasn't in the restaurant.

I might have glanced around, looking for him.

But I didn't knock on his door when I came back from dinner.

I resisted.

Go me.

So, now, I'm out on the deck, relaxing on a sun lounger. Sigala and James Arthur's "Lasting Lover" playing out of the speakers on my phone. I'm enjoying the peace and gorgeous night sky while basking in my afterglow from all the sex and orgasms I had last night and this morning while not thinking about what West might be up to right now.

I stare up at the stars. I just can't get over how clear the sky is here. No smog and clouds blocking up the view. It's gorgeous.

Shooting star! Oh my God! I've never seen one before.

And I have no one to tell because I'm here alone.

West is off, doing whatever he's doing. Which is perfectly fine because we're not together. We're just fucking.

I could text Aunt Jenny and tell her that I just saw—

"Hey."

"What? Fuck!" I scream, jerking up to sit, seeing the dark outline of a very wet West emerging out of the water like fucking Aquaman and coming up the steps and onto the deck to my villa.

"Christ on a bloody cracker," I huff, pressing my hand to my chest. My heart is beating like crazy.

I actually shit myself then. Well, I didn't *actually* shit myself. But it was close.

I hit pause on the music on my phone. "You scared the actual crap out of me."

"Sorry."

He doesn't look it. He's standing there, smiling, looking all hot.

Bastard.

"So, should I ask why you just emerged from the water in the dead of night like Aquaman and not used the front door like a normal person?"

He laughs low. The sound runs over my bare skin like invisible fingers, leaving goose bumps in their wake.

"I knocked, but you didn't hear me. Thought I'd try your way of entry. And it's hardly the dead of night."

He's referring to how I got in my villa yesterday after drunkenly locking myself out.

Smart arse.

"Well, it's not fucking daytime. And how'd you know I was out here anyway?"

"Heard the music. Thought I'd surprise you."

"You definitely did that." I curl my legs under me, tucking my hair behind my ear. I'm suddenly very self-conscious of how I look right now. Which is stupid because the guy has seen me wasted, wearing day-old clothing.

He's also seen me naked.

Shiver.

"So, um"—I clear my throat—"how was your day?"

"Good. Went scuba diving, which actually turned into a night dive. I didn't mention it to you because I didn't think it'd be your thing."

"You don't have to let me know your every move."

That's the right thing to say, right? Play it cool. He doesn't need to know that I've been thinking about him today, worrying a little that he was avoiding me, which was totally silly because we'd had breakfast together. Which he'd invited me too. Even though we probably would have both ended up there at the same time.

Fuck's sake, I really need to get out of my own head. It's not a healthy place at times.

I have to stop acting like I'm cool and actually be cool.

"And you would be right about the dive. Scuba diving sounds … fucking awful, and doing it at night is just like a death waiting to happen."

He chuckles, stepping forward, coming more into the light. Droplets of water slide down his chest and in between those gorgeous abs, heading for the prize encased in those swim shorts.

I suddenly feel very, *very* thirsty.

"How was your day?" he asks me.

"Good. Yeah. I chilled on the beach. Read my book. It was nice." *Wow. For a writer, I'm truly shite with words.*

"Cool. So, I come bearing gifts." He walks toward me and pulls a bottle out from behind his back.

"Um, where was that? Strapped to your back?"

He grins down at me. "Tucked in my trunks."

"You swam over here with a bottle tucked in the back of your swim shorts?"

"Yep."

He really is Aquaman. Just less tattoos and blond. And no beard. But he does have a five o'clock shadow right now, so there is that.

I could be his mermaid tonight.

I feel giddy all of a sudden.

Okay. Enough of that.

"Where did the bottle come from? Aside from your pants," I ask him.

137

The villas have a minibar, but that's stocked with wine, beer, and soft drinks. And from here, that looks like either vodka or gin. That's only stocked in the bar, and you can't take bottles from the bar back to your room.

Unless he's getting special privileges that I don't know about. But if he is, then I definitely need to know.

"I might have slipped the guy who cleans my room some money this morning in exchange for a bottle of liquor. This is what he left for me. It was there, waiting for me, when I got back to my villa. I thought we could have some fun tonight."

I take the bottle from his hand and read the label, "*Death's Door*." My brow lifts as I look up at him. "It's called Death's Door."

He grins. "I didn't exactly get a choice in what I got. Just asked for something strong."

I turn the bottle, reading the back, "*Forty-seven percent ABV*. That'll do it." I chuckle.

He sits down on my lounger across from me, straddling it. Those thick thighs spread wide and his junk very much outlined in his trunks. He's definitely rocking a semi in there. Which I like. Because he's rocking that semi from just being here with me.

I get him hard on sight.

There's a certain kind of power in that.

"I thought we could have a drink together," he says to me.

I purse my lips in thought. "I did say I was gonna stay off alcohol after my drunken night."

"You had a beer at lunch yesterday and a mimosa at breakfast."

I also had a few cocktails on the beach when I got bored with mocktails and a glass of wine with dinner, but I don't need to point this out to him.

"I know, alcohol police. I meant, hard liquor. And I'm on holiday. Most people drink mimosas at breakfast when they're on holiday."

"Sure they do, Double D."

"Ugh. We still going with that nickname?"

"I like it. Suits you." His eyes drop down to my breasts.

"I thought it was Double D because of my name, not because of my boob size."

His eyes drag back up to my face. A cheeky grin in them. "Are they a double D?"

"Nope."

"Well, there you go then. The nickname can't apply to your tits."

Is it weird that I get all shivery when he says stuff like that? Tits. Just so openly, but it sounds so dirty.

"What size are they?" he asks. "Just for educational purposes, of course."

"Of course. They're a D." I place my hands on either side of my boobs and pretend to cup them.

His pupils flare as well as his nostrils.

"Definitely not a double?" he asks, eyes on them again. He is definitely a boob man, like he said.

"Nope. Just a solo D."

"Well, I like them." Gray eyes, almost blacked out by his dilated pupils, come back to mine. "A lot."

My mouth suddenly dries. I lick my lips. "So"—I clear my throat—"are we drinking this then? See if it tastes better than it's called? Although I don't have any shot glasses."

He pulls two from a back pocket in his shorts. "He left me these as well."

"You got anything else in there?" I scan my eyes over his shorts. "Bottle of champagne? Cigarettes?"

"Just my big dick and some condoms, obviously. And you smoke?"

"No. But it's been known to happen when I'm drunk and cigarettes are lying around. You never smoked?"

"Cigarettes, no. Weed, yes."

I give a pretend shocked gasp. "But you're a sportsman! You're not supposed to do drugs."

"It's just a little weed. You never smoked it?"

"Course I have." I grin, and he laughs.

"On the outside, you're all sweetness and light. But on the inside, there is a bad girl just waiting to get out."

"I have no clue what you're talking about." I flutter my lashes innocently. "I'm pure all the way through. Although it's a shame we haven't got any weed. Then, we'd have ourselves a hell of a party."

"I said, have a little fun. Not a rager. I don't want you wasted. I have plans for you tonight."

My brow goes up. "Sex plans?"

"Are there any other kind between you and me?"

I press my lips together and shake my head. Droplets of excitement trickle into my belly.

"But before sex, I was thinking we could have a little fun. Play a drinking game."

"Ooh, I like games." I give a little shimmy of excitement. "Which game are you thinking?"

"Never Have I Ever."

"I've never played that before."

"Seriously?"

"Seriously."

"What drinking games did you play when you were a teenager and wanted to get drunk?"

"None. I just drank and got drunk. Didn't need a game to excuse my underage drinking habits." I shrug.

"Badass." He gives me a smile of approval.

"I know. So, what are the rules of the game?"

"Well, for example, I say something I've never done, like … *Never have I ever eaten shit.* And if you've done it, then you have to do a shot."

"Well, I've definitely never eaten shit. But hypothetically, if I have done something you say you've never done, then I just drink my shot?"

"And remove a piece of clothing."

Staring at him, I tilt my head to the side in question. "Is this an actual rule or your own rule?"

"Aren't they both one in the same thing?"

"Hmm." I glance down at him wearing only his trunks, and I'm only wearing a summer dress, panties, and a bra. "But I'm not wearing much. You're wearing even less."

"Then, it should be a nice, quick game." He lifts a brow with the suggestion that when the game ends, meaning we're both naked, then the sexing begins.

And I am down for that, but it kind of seems a little pointless to play if it's over in a flash.

"No, we need a few more items of clothing. Well, you do."

"Babe, I'm not going back to my place to get clothes just so that I can take them off. And I doubt you have anything I can wear."

Babe. He called me babe. Why has that got my insides melting like chocolate?

"Bathrobe," I say, getting up.

I go get one of the complimentary ones. Oh, and the complimentary slippers. I grab those too. I take them back outside and hand them to him.

"There, that makes us even. We're each wearing three things."

His eyes graze over my dress and down to my bare feet.

"Dress, panties, and bra," I explain.

I watch as West pulls on the robe, leaving it open so I still get to look at his chest. The robe does look a little tight on him. I got the large one too.

"Slippers, too, I prompt."

He gives me a look. "Just pretend I'm wearing them."

"Spoilsport." I stick my tongue out at him. "Okay, so who's going first?" I clap my hands with excitement. I've never played a drinking game before. And not one that leads to sex.

I mean, what's not to like? Drinking shots to get West naked?

Hell. To. The. Yes.

fifteen

DILLON

"I'LL GO FIRST," HE says.

"Such a gentleman."

"Double D, I go first because it means a higher chance of me getting you naked faster."

"But what if I want you naked before me?"

He raises a brow. "You literally just put more clothes on me."

Ah. Good point.

"But that was for the game. And it's a robe. Not a bloody snowsuit."

He chuckles, and I watch as he pours out two shots and hands one to me. "I know the game better than you. It was my idea. Ergo I'm first."

"Ugh, fine. Whatever." I lift the shot to my nose and sniff it. "Jesus. This stuff smells potent."

He lifts his glass up and inhales. "Fuck, you're right." He chuckles.

"Good job we'll only be doing three shots each."

"Babe, I literally watched you down four shots of Fireball along with two Long Island iced teas and a margarita. And that was after you drank a bottle of champagne, plus whatever else you'd swallowed before you came into the bar. Three shots of this won't even touch you."

I smirk proudly at him. I might be a loser in many aspects of my life, but I've always been able to hold my liquor. "It was two mini bottles of red and white wine, plus the bottle of beer that was in the minibar, along with the champagne, of course, before I came to the bar."

"I honestly don't know if I should be concerned or impressed at your tolerance for alcohol."

"Definitely impressed." I grin at him. "Right, come on. Let's do this. Hit me with your first question."

"Okay. Never have I ever … been to Hull."

"Really?" I raise a brow at him.

He grins. "I never said I played fair."

Narrowing my eyes at him, I put the glass to my lips and tip my head back.

The gin scorches my throat on the way down. "Fuck, that's strong." I wince, putting down the glass and blowing out a breath, which feels like it's actually fire and not air.

"Now, off with the dress."

Getting up on my knees, I take the hem of my dress, pull it over my head, and set it down on the lounger behind me. Thank the Lord I'm wearing decent underwear. It's my nicest set. Lacy and black. Which was obviously put on in anticipation of possibly seeing him tonight.

And from the look in his eyes, he definitely likes my lacy black underwear.

Without taking his eyes from me, he picks up the bottle and refills my glass. "Your turn," he says.

"Hmm." I tap my fingers on my chin, thinking for a moment. "Okay. I've got one." I'm confident that I've got him here because all men do this. "Never have I ever ghosted someone."

West doesn't move or attempt to drink.

My confidence deflates like a popped balloon. "You've never ghosted anyone?"

"Told you, Double D. I'm a straightforward guy. I don't wanna fuck someone anymore, I tell them."

Ugh.

"My turn," he says. "Never have I ever … sent someone a naked pic."

"You've never sent someone a naked selfie?" I'm honestly shocked.

If I looked like him, I'd be sending them out to whoever wanted one. Maybe even people who didn't.

Kidding.

"Nope. Can't have pics of my dick floating around the internet. The NFL wouldn't like that."

Is it weird that I didn't actually register until this point that he's probably something of a celebrity back home? I mean, the NFL is like our Premier League, and footballers back home are famous. Granted, I don't know many of them. But if there was one who looked like him, I'd definitely know about him.

Sighing, I toss back the shot and hand him back the glass to refill.

While he's topping my glass up, I reach back, unhook my bra, and pull it off. Thank God no one can see onto my deck. Unless there's the actual Aquaman out there and he's gonna pop up out of the water any moment now. Which, in all fairness, I wouldn't be opposed to Jason Momoa seeing my bare breasts.

I toss my bra at him. He catches it and hangs it over his shoulder, like a bloody trophy.

145

Okay. So, I'm two shots in, two items down, and he's still had no shots and got all of his clothes. I need something good here.

Think, Dillon. Think ...

There has to be something I haven't done that he definitely has.

Ooh. I've got it! A guy who is as sexually experienced as he is, is sure to have done this.

"Okay." I clear my dry throat, which I'm pretty sure no longer has any flesh left covering it because the alcohol has burned it all off. "Never have I ever had a threesome."

He grins. "Well played." He puts the shot glass to his lips and tosses back the gin. "Fuck!" he growls. "That's some strong-ass gin!"

"Told ya," I say as he puts his glass down. "Clothes now. I'll refill for you."

He removes the bloody slippers he's not wearing and not the robe or trunks. Of course, this is my fault for putting more clothes on him.

And it's also his turn now. I just know I'm gonna lose my panties.

"Okay. Never have I ever faked it."

Oh! I'm safe! I've never faked an orgasm before.

I grin and shake my head.

His brow lifts. "You've never faked an orgasm before?"

"Nope." I give a winning smile.

"Not even with the ex who ... *needed a map just to find your vagina and a satnav to your clit?*"

I wince. "When did I ... oh, for fuck's sake. Was there anything I didn't say or tell you that night?"

A playful expression slides onto his face. "Maybe. But not much. You did tell me *a lot* of stuff that night."

I stare down at the small glass of gin in my hand. "Might not be a good idea for me to keep drinking these. I might just get wasted again and tell you all the things I didn't get around to telling you the other night."

"Sounds like a fun time to me." His tone is dry, so I can't tell if he's being for real or sarcastic. But I'll go with the latter because I can't imagine listening to drunk me drone on about boring shit is much fun.

"So, okay, it's my turn. I need to think about this because you're still fully clothed and I'm not so … oh, got one!"

Every guy has said this without a doubt. West might be a good guy, but he was also a teenager once, and teenage boys will do anything to get laid.

Biting back a grin, I say, "Never have I ever told someone I loved them just to get laid."

His gorgeous gray eyes narrow on me, and I know I've got him.

Shaking his head, he tosses back the drink and thrusts the empty shot glass out at me.

Laughing, I take the glass and refill it from the bottle while he takes off that robe.

"In my defense," he says, taking the now-full shot glass that I'm holding out to him, "it was one time, and I was sixteen. She was the hottest girl in school, and getting my dick wet was the only thing I thought about back then."

"Isn't getting your dick wet the only thing you think about now?" I tease.

He gives me a serious look. "No. I also think a lot about getting your pussy wet."

Oh. My.

My mouth dries again, and I'm almost tempted to throw this shot back to moisten it.

"Okay." Another clearing of my throat. "It's your turn."

I've just got to get through this round and catch him on my next turn, and I'll win. And I love to win.

I'm a little competitive, if you haven't guessed.

West stares at me and says, "Never have I ever watched *Keeping Up with the Kardashians.*"

I smile winningly. "Never watched it."

He frowns. "I thought every woman on the planet had watched at least one episode of that crap."

"Not this girl." I grin.

He totally thought he was gonna win with that basic one. That's what he gets for underestimating me.

"Oh no. You lost that turn, and now, it's my turn to ask a question. What could I ask? Hmm … let me just think." I tap my finger on my chin.

West stares back at me, amused. "Don't drag it out, Double D."

I'm not even gonna bite at the nickname because I'm too busy trying to think of a good one to get those shorts off of him and crown me the winner.

Think, Dillon. Go for something to do with sex because I can't imagine there isn't anything he hasn't done or tried, whereas I've experienced only the basics.

"Oh, I've got one. Never have I ever eaten food off someone's naked body."

He frowns, nostrils flaring, and I know I've won.

I have to stop myself from jumping up and doing the Carlton dance.

West throws back the shot, dropping the empty glass on the lounger. Then, he stands and drops his shorts.

Oh, hello there, lover.

His dick is fully hard. My mouth waters at the sight.

But still, I won, and I have to gloat a little.

Okay. A lot.

"Oh dear. You're naked. Guessing that means I won."

West sits back down, and I'm having a hard time not staring at his cock, which is currently kissing those abs of his that I like so much.

"Nope. You have to be naked too."

I lift a questioning brow. "Now, that just sounds like you're making the rules as you go."

He gives me a look of innocence. "As if I would."

"Fine. You take your turn. I'm happy to get naked now that I've officially won. Not that I think you'll get me on this round."

West looks at me and says, "Never have I ever slept with a coworker."

Fuck. Fuckity fuck.

Okay, maybe I shouldn't have been so confident. But he does know that the prick was my coworker and technically my boss.

"Hey! That's not fair," I grumble. "You already knew that I had."

"Did I?" He feigns innocence. "Can't say that I recall knowing that."

"Yeah, right. You remember everything else I told you, except for that."

He lifts those broad shoulders. "Weird, right?"

Fighting a smile, I decide to do this a little differently, inspired by my winning question. Putting my shot down, I stand up and hook my fingers into the waistband of my panties, and very slowly, I drag them down my legs, bending at the waist, until they reach my ankles.

West watches the show with laser focus.

I step out of my panties and then sit back down, closer to him this time. I pick up the shot glass, but before drinking it, I lean in and press my lips to his, giving him a swift, hard kiss.

Then, I put my lips to his ear and whisper, "Never have I ever sucked gin off a cock."

Then, I pour the gin over his dick and quickly dip my head. I take him in my mouth and start to suck the liquor off his cock.

"Fuck," he groans, his strong fingers threading into my hair, gripping the strands tight.

I like the feel of him pulling my hair. It's turning me on. I can feel myself getting slicker between my thighs.

It's true. I've never sucked any liquid of any variety off a cock before. But this seemed like a good idea. And he seems to like it. And the gin actually tastes better, coming off him.

I'm surprised by how confident and daring I am with him. I don't know where it's coming from. Actually, I do. It's because his confidence is infectious. He makes me feel like I can say or do anything, and he won't judge me. He might tease me a little. But he wouldn't think any less of me. That I'm sure of.

I can be more myself around him than I've ever been around anyone my whole life. Maybe it's because I know this thing with him is only temporary. But whatever it is, I like it.

For the first time in my life, I actually like the person I am right now. The one who's been trapped inside, desperate to get out.

More confident. Happy. Sexy. Maybe even a little bit naughty.

I suck his dick harder, bringing out my A game. If his whispered words of praise and labored breaths are anything to go by, I'm doing it just how he likes it.

"Jesus. Fuck. Dillon. You're too fucking good at this. Babe, I'm gonna come. You need to move if …"

I look up at him, letting his dick slide out of my mouth. "Never have I ever swallowed before," I whisper. Holding his stare, I take him back in my mouth.

It's true. I've never swallowed before. But for some reason, with him, I want to. I want to taste him. I want to know what it's like to have West come in my mouth.

His hand cups my cheek. "You're fucking amazing. Have I told you that?"

I shake my head.

"Well, I should have, and I will do so every day from now on. But right now, suck me like the bad girl that I know you are."

I love it when he talks dirty. Also, he thinks I'm amazing. So, there is that.

I start working him over with my mouth again. Hollowing out my cheeks, I suck him harder, which he seems to really like.

"Fuck yeah, that's it. Suck me dry, babe. Fuck … harder … shit … Jesus … I'm fucking … coming!"

He grunts. I feel his thighs tense under my hands. Then, his cock starts to jerk in my mouth.

I feel the first hot spurt hit my tongue as he starts to come in my mouth. And come. And come some more.

My eyes water, and I have to breathe through my nose, but I take all he has. I swallow everything down.

When he's done, I release his dick from my mouth and sit back on my heels, wiping my mouth with the back of my hand.

West just stares at me, chest heaving up and down.

Then, the next thing I know, he's on me, pushing me down onto my back and kissing me hard, leaving me totally breathless.

His lips leave mine and brush over my ear. "My turn."

He picks up the bottle of gin and pours it all over my breasts. The feel of the cool liquid hitting my heated skin is exhilarating. "Never have I ever licked gin off a woman's tits before."

His tongue laps the liquid sitting in the valley of my breasts before moving over and licking and sucking every drop off my boobs.

He pours some onto my stomach. "Never have I ever drank gin from a girl's belly button before." He leans his head down and sucks the liquid off my stomach.

He moves down my body and parts my legs with his hand. Dark, heated eyes meet with mine. The look in them has my lower stomach coiling tight with excitement.

"Never have I ever fucked a woman with a bottle of gin before."

Holy fuck. Does he mean …
Jesus. He does.

He waits there, watching me, waiting for me to let him know if I'm okay with this happening or not. My body starts to tremble at the thrill, at the thought of what he wants to do to me. What I'm considering letting him do to me.

I feel crazy and so unlike myself in this moment. And I'm starting to think that's maybe a good thing.

I can't believe I'm actually considering it. Maybe the gin has loosened my inhibitions. Maybe it's being with him, such a sexually confident guy. A guy who I don't know well and will also never see or hear from again in a few weeks.

Holy shit. I'm actually going to say yes.

I'm going to let him do this. Fuck me with that bottle.

I bite my lip and give a small nod of my head. His jaw tightens.

He slides his hand up my inner thigh, opening me up to him. I feel the first touch of the bottle pressing at my entrance, and I suck in a breath.

Why am I so turned on right now? I'm starting to wonder if I've actually lost my mind.

Before I can think any further, he pushes the small neck of the bottle a little farther inside of me.

I hear a hot gasp and realize it came from me.

West's eyes are focused on where the bottle is right now. His teeth digging in his lower lip. His still-damp hair hanging around his face.

He looks so fucking hot.

He slowly starts to fuck me with the bottle. Intense eyes lift to mine. "You are so fucking hot," he growls.

Tension is building inside of me. My clit throbbing. I feel like I'm about to burst; I'm so turned on. "West, please," I moan, needing him to touch me there. Make me come.

Sensing what I need, he slides the bottle out of me and then tips the gin on over my pussy. His head dips down between my legs, and he starts to lap at my clit.

And I start to come in naught-point-three seconds after the first touch of his tongue on me.

"West!" I cry. My back arches as I come hard against his mouth. The most explosive orgasm I've had with him so far.

I fall back against the lounger, panting. West kisses his way up my body. Lips grazing over my sensitive nipple, making my body twitch.

He presses his mouth to mine, slipping his tongue inside, kissing me. "So fucking hot," he murmurs again.

"I can't believe I just let you do that to me," I whisper, reality washing over me.

I just got fucked by a gin bottle labeled Death's Door. I'm not sure if that's a bad omen or not. But considering I just came like a motherfucker, I'm gonna say, not. And I know I should probably feel shame or embarrassment, but I just don't.

West ducks his head, looking into my eyes. "It was seriously fucking hot, babe. Easily the hottest sexual experience I've ever had."

That lights me up inside because I figure West has had a lot of awesome sexual experiences in his life.

"Mine too," I whisper.

His eyes smile at me, and his lips kiss me again. "Come on. Let's shower this gin off us." He pushes up to stand and holds his hand out to me to help me up, which I happily accept.

He reaches down and grabs his swim trunks.

"You need those in the shower?" I question him as we start to walk through my villa, in the direction of the bathroom.

"No. I need the condoms that are in the pocket because I plan on fucking you in the shower."

Okay then.

As he tugs me along to the bathroom, I'm reminded of the day I arrived. How was that only a few days ago? I said to myself that this villa was a romance-free zone, and yet here I am with West.

But then, this thing I have going on with him definitely isn't romance. It's fucking. Raw, animalistic, *I've never experienced anything like this in my life* fucking.

And it's bloody awesome.

Sixteen

DILLON

"HAS EVERYONE PLACED THEIR bets?" the host calls through his microphone.

A chorus of yeses rings out from the crowd around us.

"I can't believe I'm betting on a crab. Or that I'm actually excited about it."

West's deep chuckle brushes over my ear. He's standing behind me, his hands resting casually against my hips, the bottle of beer he's holding in one of his hands pleasurably cool against me in this hot air, as we stand around a circle that's been worked into the sand, near the beach bar. A black-and-white racing stripe encircles the outside of the racetrack, and in the middle waits our competition, covered by a big, clear bowl.

"Our sources of entertainment are limited here," he says into my ear. "Aside from us fucking, of course."

I glance back at him. It's early evening. The sun has set, and the light is provided from the bar just behind us and the fire lanterns situated all around in the sand. I lightly brush my lips over his. And I really like the shiver I feel in his chest when I do it.

"We do have good sex," I whisper.

"Correction: you and I have fucking amazing sex. Wanna ditch the crab race and go back to my place and fuck instead?"

My teeth dig into my lower lip. "You have no clue how tempting that offer is. But ... I really wanna see if my crab wins."

He arches a brow. "You're choosing a crab over my cock?"

A laugh escapes me. "Well, there's a sentence I never thought I'd hear. And, no, my competitive need is demanding that I stay here and find out if that little crab—the one I cannot currently see, but he's over there somewhere with the number fourteen painted on his shell—is gonna win for me. We can go have all the amazing sex right after I'm done winning."

"You know, it's cute that you picked number fourteen because you thought it's how big my dick is."

I quirk a brow. "I picked it because it's the number of orgasms you've given me."

"That'll work too."

I stare at him a moment, and then I put my lips to his ear and whisper, "Actually, how big is your dick?"

Him implying fourteen inches has got me thinking now. Of course I know it's not fourteen inches like he just said because I'm pretty sure I'd be dead from impalement if it were. But his cock is the biggest I've ever seen in real life.

I've seen big cocks in porn, but it's hard—pun intended—to compare the screen to real life, and measurements are not my thing. All I know is that a standard ruler is about twelve inches, and I don't think it's quite ruler-length long.

Not that I've seen a ruler in a long while. So, it could be, but I don't know. And I wouldn't even have a clue on the girth.

He turns his face to mine, dipping his chin down so his nose touches mine. "I don't know. I've not measured it in a while. It might have grown since then. How about we have a little fun later, finding out?"

Oh, yes, please.

"Okay, ladies and gentlemen!" the host's voice rings out loud and clear, snapping me from my little fantasy of getting West hard with my mouth and then whipping out a tape measure. "The rules of the race are: No going inside the circle or touching the finish line. You can encourage your little racer with your voice only. Anyone who crosses even a finger over the finish line will be squirted with my water!" He waves around a squirt bottle filled with water.

Honestly, with how hot and humid it is tonight, I could see people breaking the rules just to get squirted with the cold water. I'm actually considering it myself.

"The winner is whichever crab reaches the finish line first, and the person who picked that number will receive the grand prize of an island hop! Yes, that's right, ladies and gentlemen. The winner will get to spend one full day on our neighboring uninhabited island, alone. You will be taken by boat and dropped off with a luxurious picnic to spend the day however you choose and then picked up later. Now, that is a prize, yes?"

Everyone cheers and claps.

I turn my head and speak into West's ear, "I feel kind of bad about entering now."

His brows pull together. "Why?"

"Because I didn't realize what the prize was. I figured it'd just be a bottle of booze or something. I already have one of those island hops booked."

It was booked and paid for ages ago. I thought it would be a romantic, honeymoonish thing to do. But I'm not on my honeymoon. I'm currently having a two-week fling with the hot guy pressed up against me.

"Are you gonna go on it?" West asks me.

I screw my face up. "Spend the day on an island, alone? Nah, thanks. I would legit shit myself. I'd have thoughts of being eaten by a shark or being forgotten about and left there alone forever. And I'd have to build a house and learn to fish and stuff to stay alive."

West laughs. "Your imagination is … vast."

"Why, thank you." I smirk. "To be honest, I need to cancel the trip." I know I won't get my money back, but there's no way I'm going and spending the day out there, alone. Not when I can be here and hang out with West.

Unless …

"I mean, I could not cancel it if you, um … want to come with me?" I ask him, lowering my voice.

We've been hanging out a lot these last few days. And I mean, a lot. Most of it spent having sex. So much sex that I honestly don't know how I'm still walking. We have eaten dinners and breakfasts together. Okay, all of them. And lunches too. Also, snack times and drinks at the bar. But we'd be eating there separately anyway, so it just makes sense to eat together. We've also spent each night in bed together, but that's purely for the sex.

But asking him to come on an island trip with me feels almost like I'm asking him on a date. And that's not what this is between him and me. It's sex. Nothing more.

West's eyes stay unchanged on me, and my heart starts to beat faster in my chest as I think I've made a big error in asking him. That I've given him the wrong impression. And I need to rectify this immediately.

Before I can muster up any words to take it back, he says, "You and me, alone on an island. Definitely sounds like fun."

A sigh of relief runs through me. Then, I catch the look in his eyes, and a shiver quickly follows that sigh of relief.

He's thinking about sex.

Well, he's almost always thinking about sex. To be honest, so am I recently. But this time, he's thinking about sex with me when we're completely and utterly alone on an island.

Holy … sex fairies everywhere.

Are sex fairies even a thing? Well, they are now because there's a ton of them fluttering with excitement in my lower extremities. I have to press my thighs together to stem the throb that's now there.

"When is it?" West asks, his voice sounding rougher than it did a moment ago.

I lick my lips. "Uh, I booked it for the middle of my second week here, so it's in five days' time."

"Can't wait."

A Klaxon sounds, making me jump and snatching my attention from West. I turn back to see the host now standing in the middle of the ring, his hand on the handle of the bowl.

"Attention, ladies and gentlemen! It's now time to race! I will count down, and when the Klaxon sounds again, I will free our racers! Make sure to cheer on your crab! So, on the count of three. Three … two … one!"

The Klaxon goes off again. The bowl is lifted, releasing all forty-five of the numbered hermit crabs, and the host makes haste out of the race ring.

People start yelling numbers. Excitement rings through the crowd, everyone wanting to win that prize. I can't spot my bloody crab among them all even though I'm really looking. Yes, of course I want my crab to win because I'm a competitive bugger, but I don't want the prize. Although, if I won, I could just give it to someone else. It'd be greedy to do two island hops. Although two days on a private island with West and all the sex we could have with not a soul around to hear us, not that I'm particularly quiet now, but goodness, I could scream my head off without even the worry of someone hearing me.

Sweet Jesus, just thinking of it …

That's it. I want to win.

"Come on, number fourteen!" I holler, cupping my hands around my mouth, still trying to locate the little crab.

I mean, he can't understand me, but he can hear me, right? Crabs have ears, don't they?

"Oh! There he is!" I say excitedly, pointing at him. Then, I quickly realize that I've only spotted him because all the other crabs have scattered and are on the move, and my crab is still sitting in the middle, not fucking moving.

I backed a dud.

A frigging dud.

"Come on! Move!" I shout at my crab. "Run, you lazy little sod!"

I feel West's chest press even closer to my back as he leans forward. "Is yours the one in the middle? That one that looks like it's dead?"

"He's not dead! He's just … taking his time. Weighing up his options. He's gonna move any second now."

A second ticks by, and he still doesn't move.

"He's definitely dead," West imparts.

"Shut up. He's not dead," I bite. "Run! You little … crab! Run!"

Still nothing. I can feel myself starting to get wound up.

I might be a tad competitive from time to time.

"Move! You lazy frigging crab! I've got an island trip riding on your lazy arse!" The words just burst from me.

Okay, so I'm *a lot* competitive.

A deep laugh rumbles through West. "Thought you didn't want to win anymore? You know, because you already have the same trip booked."

I glance back at him, my gaze narrowed, meeting his grinning one. "I never said I didn't want to win. I said I felt bad because I technically already have the prize."

"So, you do want to win then?"

"No. I mean, yes. Oh, what-the-fuck-ever!" I look back at my crab, eyes zeroing in on it. "I'm not gonna win at this rate anyway because my bloody crab is still in the same spot." I frown at it. "You know, I think he might be dead. Or asleep. Actually, is there even a crab in that shell?"

I feel another rumble of West's laughter against my back and then the soft brush of his lips against my temple, and I can't stop the smile that spreads across my face and the happiness that trills through my body. Because even if I am currently losing this stupid crab race and also totally losing at all aspects of my life, standing here with West right now, his hard body pressed up against mine … it kind of feels like I'm finally winning at something.

Even if it is only a temporary win.

seventeen

WEST

SHE DIDN'T WIN, AND she's not happy about it. It's cute how competitive she is.

Seriously, I thought I was competitive, but I'm starting to wonder if she might have the edge on me. Because I can take a loss. I don't like it. Losing is hard as fuck. Especially when it's a loss with my team. But I can handle it because I take that loss and use it as my focus to make sure I win the next time.

Dillon, however, really cannot take a loss.

She's been complaining the whole way back to my villa about it.

Turns out, there was a crab in the shell, and no, it wasn't dead because she made the host check.

And, no, I'm not kidding.

Then, she said that the crab was faulty somehow.

A faulty crab. I know, right?

It took everything in me not to laugh at that. But I figured if I laughed, there would be zero chance I'd be getting laid tonight. And I really want to get laid tonight because she's looking hot as fuck in the white dress she's wearing. It has total virginal vibes going on. It's begging to be dirtied up.

Also, it was my fault she lost because she picked the number fourteen because of me.

You know, because of the orgasms I've given her. Somehow, the making of the number became not as important at that point.

It's honestly funny though because her complaining isn't irritating me or bugging me. It's actually cute as fuck.

I walk up the steps to my villa with Dillon trailing behind me.

"I mean, they all moved, except for mine. That's fucked up, right?"

"Uh-huh," I answer as I unlock the door to my villa, planning to shut her up with my tongue in her mouth the moment we're inside. I push the door open and stand aside to let her in first.

"I bet they put a few lazy bastard crabs in there, you know, so people couldn't win," she grumbles as she walks past me into the villa.

I follow her in and shut the door. "But someone did win."

Why, West? You had her inside and could have shut her up with your tongue and then been inside of her a few minutes later. But no. Instead, you decide to open your mouth and tip her over the edge.

Nice going, jackass.

She stops, turns, and glares at me. Her hands go to her hips. Her eyes are like lasers on mine.

My balls literally shrivel up and start to climb up inside my body.

But weirdly, my dick gets hard.

I guess he likes a pissed off Dillon.

"Yes," she retorts. "An old couple. Like, the only old couple here. Whose fortieth wedding anniversary it is, might I add. I mean, that's a total noncoincidence. They might as well have given the prize to the only kid there. Which would have been weird because what would a kid do with a prize like that anyway? Suppose his parents could have used it. But whatever! I mean, really, what the fuck are two old people going to do on a private island anyway? Knit? Play Scrabble?"

Hide from your complaining probably.

Of course, I don't say that.

"Well, I'm guessing they'll fuck in between the knitting and Scrabble playing."

"Ew, dude!" She screws up her nose. "Don't say that!"

"You do know that old people have sex too, Double D?" I say in a jokey, conspiratorial whisper.

Her eyes narrow. She crosses her arms over her chest, and the action pushes those gorgeous tits up. Of course, my eyes instantly go straight to them, and now, her tits are the only thought in my mind.

"Yes, I know that. I just don't need to know that right now."

Well, that makes no sense. But who am I to question her?

Actually, I just don't want to question anything because my dick is painfully hard, and all I want is her mouth on mine and my dick in her pussy and my hands on those tits of hers.

I slide my arms around her waist and pull her hips to meet mine. Her eyes flare at the contact as she realizes what's waiting for her once she stops moaning about that fucking crab race and starts moaning my name instead.

"You do remember that you have an island trip in five days and that we're going on it together, right? And we're gonna spend the whole time there fucking, and I'm going to spend an inordinate amount of that time finding outrageous ways to make you come."

Her tense body goes lax. A flush creeps over the swell of her breasts. Her arms unfold, and her dainty hands press against my chest. "Outrageous?" she whispers.

I lean in and press my nose to her temple, inhaling the berry scent of her shampoo and the floral scent of her perfume. I slide it down her cheek and press a soft kiss to the corner of her mouth. "Outrageous." My hand moves up her waist, and my finger traces a path along the base of her tit. "Scandalous." I drag my finger up her cleavage. "And dirty as fuck." I pinch one of her nipples and then swallow her breathy gasp with my mouth.

She opens instantly for me, and I take full advantage and shove my tongue inside.

Fuck. I love the way she tastes and responds to me. It's addictive as fuck. So is the feel of that tight pussy of hers. I can't get enough of her at the moment.

But it'll pass. It always does.

Okay, so I've never actually felt this sort of addiction to a woman's pussy, mouth, body, face, and mind before now. So, basically, all of her.

But it doesn't mean anything.

It's just because we're here on this island, spending a shit-ton of time together, fucking and talking and fucking some more because there's not a lot else to do.

My hand slides into that thick, dark hair of hers, and I grip a fistful of it and pull her head back, exposing her throat to me. I kiss my way down her neck and chest. I yank down the front of her dress and the cup of her bra and put my mouth around one of those sweet nipples.

"West," she moans, her hips pressing harder against mine, seeking my cock.

I feel this sudden, desperate urge to be inside of her. Which isn't exactly abnormal. I feel like that all the time I'm around her. But this time, the urge is more insistent. It feels primal.

I want to dominate her.

Releasing her tit from my mouth, I spin her. Grabbing her hands, I lift them up and pin them to the wall above her head. I press my hips against her ass and bite her earlobe. "Keep your hands there. Don't move them unless I tell you to."

Her breaths are coming in fast. She's excited, and her excitement is only fueling me on further.

Pulling the hairband off my wrist, I tie my hair into a bun, keeping it out of the way. I kick off my flip-flops and lower to my knees. I shove her dress up over her ass. She's wearing a pretty pink thong. So pretty, and I'm gonna dirty it all up.

Grabbing the scrap of fabric, I yank it aside and shove two fingers inside her.

She whimpers, and the sound goes straight to my dick.

"You're soaked, Dillon. Do you like my fingers inside of you?"

"Yes."

I start moving my fingers in and out, fingering her pussy, loosening her up, getting her ready to take me inside her. I'm not planning on spending a lot of time on foreplay. Tonight, I just want to fuck.

Pulling my fingers out of her, I spread her ass cheeks with my hands and run my tongue from that puckered little hole that I'm dying to get inside of to the hole my fingers were just inside. I slip my tongue up there and move my mouth and face, knowing that my stubble will rub over her clit.

"West ... shit, that feels ..." Her hips start to move against my face, grinding down.

I fucking love that about her. Even when I'm dominating her, she still can't help but move that hot little pussy of hers against my mouth. She's unabashed, and she doesn't give a single fuck when she's seeking her own pleasure.

But she's not coming yet. Not until I'm inside her anyway.

Standing up, I enjoy the sound of her cry of displeasure at losing my mouth against her. She looks back at me over her shoulder, resting her chin on it. But she doesn't make a move to turn around or take her hands off the wall.

Good girl.

Holding Dillon's stare, I unbuckle the belt on the cargo shorts I'm wearing and unfasten the button and zipper. I shove my shorts and boxers down just far enough to free my cock.

Getting my wallet from the pocket of my shorts, I get out a condom. I toss my wallet to the floor. Rip open the foil packet and roll the condom on.

I step up close to her, my cock pressing against her lower back. My hands slide around her chest and cup her tits. I start to roll her nipples between my fingers and pinch them just how she likes.

"You want me."

Her head falls back against my chest. "I thought that was obvious," she pants.

"It wasn't a question."

"Cocky twat."

"You like my cockiness."

Her head tilts, and those blue eyes meet with mine. "No. I like your cock."

Fuck. I like you.

"Spread your legs."

She does as I asked, widening her stance. Bending at the knees—because she's small as fuck and heels aren't conducive to walking around on the island and in the sand so she's always in flip-flops—I lower myself to her height. I take my cock in my hand and rub him over her pussy.

I slide my hands up her arms, and covering her hands with mine, I link our fingers.

Then, I thrust up inside her. I don't even give her a chance to adjust to my size. I just start fucking her.

I seem to lose my mind in this moment. I lose it in her body. The feel of the tight walls of her pussy squeezing my dick. Her breathy moans. The smell of sex around us.

I'm reduced to nothing but the need to make her come and for me to come.

I'm pounding into her, fucking her into the wall, like the world is about to end.

I bite her neck. Her shoulder. Suck on that spot behind her ear that makes her hips buck against my dick.

Pleasure shoots down my spine, like I've just been hit with a taser.

Fuck, I'm gonna come.

"Tell me you're close," I pant. "Because I'm gonna fucking come."

"Almost ... there ... just keep doing that ..."

The first minuscule tightening of her pussy around my dick, and I start coming. My dick jerks, and hot spurts of cum start to fill up the rubber. And my coming seems to only intensify her orgasm further, and her muscles almost vise-grip my cock, making me come even harder.

Jesus fucking Christ.

I'm almost sure that I black out at one point. Because the next thing I know, I come to with my forehead pressed against the back of her head, my mouth breathing in her hair.

"Fuck," I croak.

"Right?" she whispers.

"That was intense."

"So intense. I've never ..." She trails off.

"What?"

"Sex has just never been like that for me. That vigorous."

I tilt my head back from hers. "Dillon, we've been fucking five days. If you think that was the first time we've had vigorous sex, then I'm clearly doing something wrong."

"No." She laughs softly. "That's not what I meant at all." She turns her head, and soft blue eyes look at me in the dim light of the hallway. "You're doing everything right. Better than right. I just meant … I don't know what I meant."

She takes her gaze away from me, but I catch her chin, bringing her eyes back to mine. "Yeah, you do. Say what you mean."

She blinks. "I've never had sex before where I felt so lost in it. I mean, I get lost in sex with you—of course I do. But that was … something else. Like we were the only two people who existed in that moment. Does that make sense?"

Touching my thumb to her lip, I nod. "Yeah, it does."

I know exactly what she means. Because I felt it too.

I'm just not really sure what it means.

If it means anything at all.

A yawn escapes her.

I chuckle. "Tired?"

"Yeah. You wore me out."

I slide my dick out of her and take her by the hand, bringing her into the bathroom with me. I undress her and then myself. I tie her hair up into a bun, so it doesn't get wet because I know she doesn't like to sleep with wet hair. I turn the shower on and lead her into the running water. We both brush our teeth in the shower to save time. Then, we're out of the shower and drying off. Mainly me drying myself and her because she's tired and I can't seem to stop touching her.

I lead her out of the bathroom, turning the lights off as I go. I pull back the cover, climb into bed, shift over, and tug her down in bed beside me.

She snuggles into my body, tangling her legs with mine.

Honestly, it's kind of nice. I've never done any of this with anyone before.

I guess I get to play house with Dillon, knowing that there's an expiration date on it when we leave the island. No worry or risk of her getting attached to me, which could happen if I did this kind of thing with anyone back home.

"West."

"Hmm?"

"Do you have a side of the bed?" she asks on another yawn.

"No." Then, I yawn because that shit's contagious.

"No?" Her voice perks up a little. "How can you not have a side?"

"Because I live alone."

"So? People who live alone still have a side of the bed. I lived alone and had a side of the bed. How can you not have a side of the bed?" She suddenly sounds a fuck of a lot more alert than she did a few moments ago.

And there I was, thinking we were going straight to sleep.

"I don't know. I usually just sleep in the middle of my bed."

"But …" She sounds really confused by this, and it's pretty fucking cute, to be honest. "Which nightstand do you put your stuff on?"

"What stuff?"

She lifts her head and stares at me in the dark. "I dunno. Your lamp. Phone. Drink. General shit."

"General shit." I chuckle. "Well, I have a lamp on both nightstands. And the rest, well, I guess it just goes on whichever nightstand I happen to drop it on that night."

"I can't even. You're really freaking me out."

"I'm getting that."

"I just … it's not normal."

I laugh again because she's funny as fuck. "It's perfectly normal. I'm a big guy. I take up a lot of space. So, I just sleep in the middle."

"What size bed do you have?"

"A really big one."

"Bigger than this?"

"Yep."

"But you fit on one side of this bed, and it's a king."

"My ass is hanging off the edge of the bed."

"Really?"

"No. But it's close to it."

"Do you need me to move over?"

"No, you're good."

She goes silent, but I can hear her mind ticking over.

"This really bothers you, doesn't it?" I laugh softly.

"I can't help it!" Her hands go up in the air. "I've just never met anyone who doesn't have a side of the bed."

"Well, you have now."

Silence again.

"So, I'm guessing you have a side of the bed?" I say to her because this conversation is amusing the shit out of me.

"Duh. Of course."

"Which side?"

Silence.

"Dillon … which side?"

She lets out a soft sigh. "The right."

"Where I'm lying."

"Uh-huh."

"You want to sleep on this side?"

"Yes, please."

I chuckle as she scrambles up to climb over my body, but I catch her as she's moving over me, holding her there. One hand on her back, the other tangled in her hair. "Why didn't you tell me this the other nights we slept together?"

"Because the first night we shared a bed, I slept on top of you."

"Good times."

"And the second night, we passed out at the bottom of the bed, and sides of the bed don't count there."

"Why not?"

"They just don't. And the other nights, you slept on the left. So, all was good."

"Seems legit."

"It's totally legit."

"Well, considering it's my bed you're in tonight, I think there should be some form of incentive for me giving up my side of the bed."

She arches her brow. "Oh, so now, you have a side of the bed? And FYI, it's not your bed; it's the resort's bed."

"I'm paying to rent it."

"Don't you think that's weird when you really think about it? Paying a shitload of money to rent a bed that hundreds, possibly thousands, of different people have slept in? Done God knows what in? Christ, just think of all the sex that's been had on this bed."

I love the way she gets sidetracked so easily. "Let's just think about the sex we're gonna have on this bed—right now."

"We're having sex? But we only just did it a few minutes ago."

"Dillon"—I tug her head down and bite on her plump lower lip with my teeth—"we're always having sex." I lick the spot that I just bit. "And it was fifteen minutes ago, not a few minutes. And I was ready to go to sleep, but I'm not now because you got my dick all hard again when you climbed up on here and rubbed your sweet ass all over him."

"I did?"

I grab her hand and shove it down between us, putting it on my cock.

"Oh." She lets out a breathy sigh as her fingers curl around my fully hard shaft. "I guess I did. My bad."

"We can totally do bad. Hot, hard, and dirty all over this bed. Unless you're still tired, that is?" I know full well she's not tired anymore from the way her hand is now slowly jacking me off.

"I'm not tired anymore."

"That's what I thought." Then, I roll her over and spend the next hour fucking us both into exhaustion.

And finally, we pass out, our bodies tangled up together, lying right in the middle of the bed.

eighteen

DILLON

AS BEAUTIFUL AND RELAXING as the island is, there's not bucketloads to do. It really is a place for relaxation. I spend most of my time on the beach. Bonus is that my tan is killer. There is a spa, which I do want to go to, to have a facial and massage, which I need to book. Of course, there's snorkeling and scuba diving—the former I'm not sure I ever want to do again and the latter I know I never, ever want to do.

West is all about the water and exercise. He spends a lot of time in the gym, toning those muscles of his. Running on the beach. Shirtless.

Honestly, when he goes running along the beach, which is usually mid-morning when most of the women on the island are sunbathing out on the beach, it's like a cacophony of ovaries exploding as he passes them by.

These women might be married or coupled up and happy, but they ain't dead.

And me … well, I just sit there and watch him with a massive smile on my face and usually a cocktail in my hand, knowing that I get to spend the rest of my days here on this island kissing and licking that body and taking his big dick inside of me.

Currently though, there's no beach because it's raining. But honestly, it's welcome.

I've been ridiculously hot since I arrived here, and this is the first time I'm actually feeling a sense of coolness without having to have the air con blasting in the villa.

West is here at my place, and we're sitting outside on the deck, close to the doors, under the cover of the awning. The rain is pelting down, and we're playing rummy.

West had a deck at his place. He also brought over his stock of alcohol and snacks from his mini fridge, and along with mine, we have a little beer, wine, and snack fest going on.

So far, we've played two games of rummy. I won the first. He won the second. This third game is the decider. And I have to win.

Have to.

I grab a handful of Haribo gummy bears and toss them in my mouth.

I notice West staring at me as I chew.

"What?" I ask, curling my tongue around a bit of a gummy bear that's gotten stuck in my back tooth.

"Nothing."

"So, why are you staring at me like that?"

"Like what?"

"With that furrow in your brow. Total concentration. Hey … you're not trying to read my mind, are you? Find out what cards are in my hand?" I raise a brow.

"Yes, Double D," he deadpans, "that's exactly what I'm doing."

"Knew it!" I pop the gummy bear piece out of my tooth and then grab another handful from the bag. "Cheater,

cheater, compulsive eater," I sing, and then I toss the handful of gummy bears into my mouth.

I chew on them and stare down at my cards.

When I look back up, he's staring at me again.

"You're staring again."

His lips quirk at one side into a sexy smirk. "Fine. I like watching you. You're nice to look at. And I especially like watching you put something in your mouth. Preferably my cock. But the gummy bear will do. For now."

For now. I'd say I love his confidence. But it's warranted. Because he's right. There's a hundred percent chance that his dick will be inside of my mouth at some point tonight.

But I definitely won't be chewing on that.

"That's weird. But kinda hot."

"I know. And it's your turn."

Sighing, I pick up a card.

For crying out loud. Not one I need. I dump it back on the pile.

"So, have you used the bath in your villa?" I ask him.

I've been here a week and still not used it yet. I can't believe it's been a week. It's flown by. You can bet your sweet arse if I'd been here alone and miserable, that time would have dragged. But because I'm with West, having lots of sex and fun, it's flying by.

One week gone. One week left.

"Nope, not used it. You used yours?"

"Nope." I pick my wineglass up and take a sip.

West picks up the card I just put down and then lays one of his cards down.

Not one I need. Ugh.

"I want to though before I leave. I mean, when else will I get the chance to have a bath outside, where no one can see me and I get to see the view of the ocean from the tub?"

I pick up another card from the deck. *Ooh, I can use this one.* I ditch one of my useless cards onto the stack.

"We should take a bath. Together," West says to me.

"When?"

"Now."

"Now?" I frown. "But it's still raining. And we're in the middle of a deciding game here, in case you forgot."

"I didn't forget." He picks up a card from the pack. "We're taking a bath, Dillon." He glances out at the rain. "I reckon it's gonna stop soon anyway."

I kid you not; it's like the clouds themselves are listening to him and are willing to give him what he wants because it stops raining not even a minute later.

I stare at him and then at the outside, where the sun has come out to play. Then back at him. "If I didn't know better, I'd think you could actually control the weather."

He grins. "Maybe I can." He drops a card on the stack. "Now, go run that bath because rummy," he says, laying his cards down.

Motherfucker.

He won.

He bloody fucking won.

Ugh!

I stand up, tossing my cards on the table between us. "I can't believe you won," I huff. "Stupid fucking game anyway."

I stomp away from him in the direction of the bathtub to the sound of his low chuckle.

I can't believe he won again. I always win when I play cards.

Well, we're definitely having a rematch because I'm not leaving it there.

I turn on the bath taps and pop the plug in. Testing the hot water, I go in and grab the complimentary bubble bath. I pour some under the running water. It smells divine. So, I pour a little more in.

I love lots of bubbles in the bath.

I'm standing, watching the bath fill, when the sound of West's voice turns me around.

"Have you stopped sulking yet?" He steps out of the bathroom to join me on the concealed deck, where the bathtub sits, and hands me my refilled glass of wine.

I take it from him and toss some wine back. "I wasn't sulking," I mutter.

"Uh-huh."

"Losing doesn't bother me. At all."

"Okay."

"I just know I can play that game well and—"

"Dillon."

"What?"

He plants his lips on mine, kissing me, stealing all words and thoughts from me.

"Hmm," he murmurs against my lips. "You taste sweet from those gummy bears."

"I taste sweet because I am sweet."

West takes the glass of wine from my hand and sets it down on the ledge beside the bath along with his bottle of beer.

Then, he reaches a hand back and pulls his T-shirt over his head in one swift move. His shorts are next to go.

Of course, I'm standing and watching the show.

Because wowsers.

Honestly, I think I could be with this guy a lifetime and still never get used to how he looks naked.

Not that I have a lifetime with him. Just one more week.

"You're naked," I stupidly say as he's tying his hair back.

A chuckle. "Not totally naked." He gestures to his boxer shorts. "But I am about to get in the bath, and usually, nakedness accompanies that."

"True."

"You, however, are still fully clothed."

"How many hours in the gym did it take to get those abs?" I haven't taken my eyes off his abs. They're like the sun. You just have to look, even knowing you'll get retinal burns.

"A lot."

"I have honestly never seen abs like yours in real life. They're amazing."

A deep laugh rumbles in his chest. "Your honesty is good for my ego."

I lift my eyes to his. "Seriously. I have never seen a body like yours outside of television."

"I've never seen a body like yours."

"Uh, yeah, sure." I laugh. "Unless you're calling me fat?" I tease.

"Definitely not calling you fat. And I'm serious, Dillon. You're fucking beautiful. You know that, right?"

I don't say anything because I don't know. When I look in the mirror, I see how much I look like my mother. My eyes, nose, chin, hair … all her. We get told all the time that we could be sisters. My mum, of course, loves that.

I know she's beautiful.

But when I look at myself in the mirror, it's not beauty I see. I just see a really sad girl who wants more than anything for her mother, who she looks so much like, to love her.

West takes my silence and reads it well. "Well, you should know. Because you are fucking stunning."

I lick my dry lips. "Yeah, well, I'm sure you've known a lot of beautiful women."

"I have. But like I said, none quite like you."

Sometimes, his honesty is hard to hear, and it's this exact moment that it bugs me most. I feel irrational jealousy at the other women he's been with. It's stupid, I know. It's not like I don't know he's been with other women. That he'll be with other women after me. But it's there all the same.

I shove it down. Deep down inside of me to deal with later.

"And … is that a good thing?" I ask him. "That I'm different?"

He stares at me. His expression impossible to read. Then, he says, "Very."

That one single word lights a spark inside of my chest that I'm not sure I know how to put out.

But I have to. Because I can't get attached to him.

"Bath's getting full." I busy myself with turning the taps off and testing the water with my hand. "Temperature is perfect," I tell him. "You can get in if you want."

West shoves his boxers down over his hips and climbs into the tub. Sitting back, he rests his arms on the edges of the bath.

I pull my tank top off and remove my shorts. I'm wearing a bikini underneath.

Usually, I have zero problems with getting naked in front of West. But after that conversation, I'm fully exposed. A bit vulnerable.

"I need to tie my hair up. Just gonna grab a hairband." I nip into the bathroom, thankful for the moment alone to gather myself. I grab a scrunchie and tie my hair into a messy bun, so it doesn't get wet in the bath.

Then, I suck it up and go back outside.

West's eyes come to me the moment I step through the doorway.

This moment feels etched in tension, and I know it's because of me. Because I'm feeling weird. I'm being weird. I need to quit with this shit.

I know how this thing with us ends—with him flying back to America and me to England—and that's in a week.

Reaching back, I pull the string tie on my bikini and the one around my neck. Catching it in my hand, I push my bikini bottoms down my legs and leave both items on the floor.

I walk over to the bath. West bends and parts his legs, so I can get in. I step into the bath and turn, putting my back to him, and sit down in the space between his legs. West tugs me back, bringing me to rest against his chest.

"You okay?" he asks me.

"Yeah." I tip my head back and look at him. "I'm okay."

He smiles and kisses me. "Good." He reaches over and gets my wine, passing it to me before getting his own beer.

The hand not holding his beer rests against my stomach. His fingers start drawing circles over my skin. He's always touching me, and I really like it. It makes me wonder if he's naturally a tactile person or if he's just like this with me.

And I really shouldn't be thinking things like that. *God, what is going on with me today?*

"This is nice," he murmurs. "I never get baths back home."

"You not have a tub?" I ask.

"I do. But I never use it. Always just get a shower. Quicker. But this, sitting here with you, it's nice. Obviously, the best part is that you're naked and wet and your sweet ass is pressed up against my dick."

"Obviously."

"I have a question," he says a moment later.

"That I might or might not answer."

"You'll answer."

"How do you know?"

"Because I do."

"Okay. Go ahead with your question."

"So, I've been sitting here for a good few minutes, tickling your stomach, and you haven't so much as twitched."

"I'm not ticklish."

"Told you you'd answer—and before I even asked the question."

Fucker. "Ugh. Whatever."

"Seriously though, how are you not ticklish? Everyone is."

"Not me." I shrug and take a sip of my wine.

"Maybe I should try tickling you harder."

"You could try. But you'll get nothing."

"Really?"

"Yep."

"So weird."

"Also awesome."

"No. Just weird. You're a freak of nature, Double D. You know that?"

"Yep. And I wear my freak badge proudly."

"As you should. Lucky for you, I happen to quite like freaks."

I tilt my head back and look at him, my blues tangling up with his grays, and I feel this tug in my chest that I force myself to ignore.

I push a smile onto my lips. "Well, luckily for you, I like freaks too."

His lips tip up into a sexy grin. "Then, it's a good thing we met each other."

And it is. For sure.

If only I could get my pesky heart to stop getting ideas around him … then everything would be perfect.

For the next seven days, of course.

nineteen

DILLON

THE SKY IS BRIGHT blue and clear, and the sun is shining down. I'm snuggled up on a hammock with West, who is currently asleep.

We did some morning yoga and then went for breakfast. After, we took a walk around the island, and we ended up here at the hammock, which is set out on a stretch of sand that runs through a lagoon. It's really peaceful and private.

West nodded off about twenty minutes ago, and I've just been lying here, listening to the waves of the ocean. The steady beat of his heart beneath my ear. Wishing I could stay here forever. With him.

Yeah, I know. I'm dumb.

I have feelings for him. But it's just a crush though. Nothing major.

But it's still stupid of me to even have a crush on him because I knew from the start what this was with us. A fling.

A two-week stand. Nothing more. I won't see him after we leave here. And I was on board with that. Totally. Because I'm not in the right headspace to even be thinking of another relationship. I'm still working through the debris from the explosion of my last relationship.

And it's not even what he wants. West has given me no signals that he sees me as anything more than his fuck buddy that he'll say good-bye to at the end of his holiday.

Therefore, I have to keep this little crush of mine to myself. I want to keep having sex with him. I want to spend the rest of my time here with him.

I just need to push down any little happy, wandering thoughts that I might have of West and me sitting in a tree, K-I-S-S-I-N-G. First comes love. Then comes marriage. Then comes the baby in a baby carriage.

Yeah. None of that.

Act like I don't have a crush on him. Keep on enjoying the sex and the time I have with him.

Then mourn my crush once I get back home.

God. Home.

I really do not want to go home. I know my city is fairly big. Maybe more medium-sized. So, it's not like I have to ever see Tim or my mum again.

But it can also be a really small place. And I just know that Sod's Law will guarantee that I bump into either one or both of them.

I'm so far from ready for that.

Maybe I'll just stay here on the island. I could move here permanently.

And do what?

I could write. And earn not enough to even pay for a tent on the beach.

Yeah, that's not gonna happen.

A crab skitters past, catching my attention, and I see it has the number ten written on its shell. I chuckle quietly to myself. Must be one of the crabs from the race the other day.

Still walking around in its little numbered shell. Wonder where my number fourteen losing crab is. Probably off napping somewhere.

I tip my head back and look at West. He looks totally peaceful. Man, he's just so damn pretty. And why am I just only now noticing how long his lashes are? I have to pay for extensions if I want to look like that.

But seriously, how did I get so lucky to land a guy like him to have a fling with?

I mean, I know I'm not hideous. But he's out of my league. He's out of most people's leagues, to be honest, except for maybe Bella Hadid. She is beautiful.

And here's little old me, getting to do lots of dirty things to him and with him.

I'm taking this as my cosmic payment for having such a shitty mother. Two weeks in paradise, being screwed into oblivion by West.

Well, I've definitely earned it.

This is getting a little boring though. Not the staring at him. No, I could do that all day. I just mean, lying here while he sleeps and I've nothing to do. I don't even have my phone with me. I left it back at the villa. No pockets on my bikini to put it in.

Someone needs to invent that. A phone pocket on a bikini.

Maybe I will, and it'll sell millions. Then, I can stop working crap jobs to support myself while I try to make it as a writer.

And I'm still staring at him like a little stalker because there's nothing else to do. Can I be classed as a stalker if I'm here by invitation? Not that he invited me here, but you know what I mean.

I don't think this classifies me as a stalker. Still, I think watching him sleep would definitely stick me in the creeper category.

"Are you watching me sleep?"

"What? No!" I nearly crap myself, jumping out of my skin. My voice is all high-pitched, clearly giving away that I was in fact watching him sleep. Also, is he a frigging psychic or something?

He blinks open his eyes and smiles lazily at me. "You're a terrible liar, Double D."

"Am not."

"So, you admit that you're lying?"

"Nope."

He stretches, yawning at the same time, and then his hand rubs at his abs. "What were you doing then?"

"Just lying here ... contemplating life."

"You were contemplating life?"

"Yep."

"How'd that go?"

"Okay."

"You figure anything out?"

"About what?"

"Life."

"Oh. Yeah."

"Was it to lie about watching the incredibly good-looking guy sleeping next to you?"

"Ugh! You're such a jerk."

I give him a shove in the chest, and he laughs.

"A hot jerk who's right."

"A jerk who's wrong."

"If you say so."

"I do."

"Just letting you know though ... if roles were reversed, I'd have definitely been watching you sleep."

I stare at his gorgeous face, untrusting of that innocent look he's giving me. "You're only saying that so I'll say I was watching you sleep."

"No, I'm not. I'm being serious."

He moves his arm up over his head, and my eyes are drawn to his tattoo. It's a small cross that's entwined with rosary beads and surrounded by what I think is holly. Perfect subject change. I've never asked him about that or the one on his back before, and now seems like a good time. So we can get off the *me watching him sleep* subject.

I reach my finger out and touch it. "I like this tattoo. Is that holly around the cross?"

"Yeah."

"When did you have it done?"

"When I was eighteen."

"What about the one on your back?"

"Twenty-one."

"Do either of them have any meanings? I know not all tattoos do, but I know some people get them for specific reasons."

"I got the one on my back after I was drafted into the NFL."

"It's a raven, right?"

"Yeah. That's my team. The Baltimore Ravens. They drafted me straight out of college."

"And you still play for them now?"

"Yeah."

"What about this one?" I'm still tracing it with my fingertip.

"My mom's name was Holly."

Was.

"When did she die?" I ask softly. I stop tracing the tattoo and instead curl my fingers around his bicep.

"When I was fifteen. She started getting these headaches. Finally, she went to the doctor. There was a tumor … she was gone six weeks later."

"West …"

He stares up at the sky. "It was a long time ago, Dillon."

"I know. But … it's still shit though. Still unfair." I take a breath. "My dad died when I was a baby."

His eyes come back to mine. "I know. You told me that first night."

"Figures. Did I tell you when and how he died?"

"No. Just that you were a baby."

"I was eleven months old. He was eighteen. He was on his motorbike on his way to work. A car pulled out, didn't see him. He died from his injuries while he was in the hospital. He and my mum weren't together. They'd broken up before she even knew she was pregnant. They were just kids when they had me. But from what I've been told from my aunt Jenny, he really stepped up as a dad. I spent more time with him those first eleven months of my life than I did my mum. I don't think she ever really wanted me."

"Your mom is a fucking idiot."

Can't argue with that.

"Were you close to your mom?"

"Yeah." A smile touches his eyes. "She was awesome."

"What about your dad?"

I feel his body tense up.

"I still see him. But we're not close."

I can tell there's a story there, but I don't push the subject.

"What about brothers and sisters? You got any?"

His lips curve into a grin.

"We've had this conversation already, haven't we?"

"Yep."

"For fuck's sake." I sigh. "And what was your answer to that question?"

"Only child."

"Same."

"I know."

"Of course you do. I wish I had a video recording of that night, so I'd know everything that I told you."

"I wish I had one too. For a totally different reason."

"So you could watch it and laugh at me?"

"Yep."

"Twat."

He chuckles, and I'm glad I made him laugh since I'd bummed him out when talking about his mum and dad.

"Any clue what time it is?" he asks me.

"No clue. I left my phone back at the villa." I kind of like that about here. Not needing to constantly have my phone with me. Spending time away from the real world and the pressures of social media.

"Probably well after lunch now."

"Yeah, probably."

"You hungry?"

"Not really."

I've eaten and drunk my body weight and probably West's since I got here. If I haven't gained weight, it'll be a damn miracle. I'm just holding on to hope that any weight I might have gained, I've sweated out from the insane heat.

"You did eat enough at breakfast to feed a small family, so not surprising."

"Hey." I poke him in the side, and he jumps a little. "You're ticklish." I grin.

"Of course I am because I'm normal. Unlike you."

I run my fingernails over his abs and down to the trail of hair that leads to my happy place. I get nothing from that. So, I do the same to his side, where I just poked him, and he jumps again. The hammock rocks a little.

"You wanna tickle me? Fine. But just remember that we're lying in a hammock together. Any big movements, and we're both going out of this thing. And when I'm being tickled, I make some pretty big movements."

I don't fancy landing on my arse. But tickling him is so tempting.

"Good thing I wasn't planning on tickling you then," I lie.

Instead, I decide to do something else. Because he makes some pretty big movements when we do this, too, and I'm wondering if this is also out of the question.

SAMANTHA TOWLE

I slip the tips of my fingers into the waistband of his shorts.

I hear his sharp inhalation of breath.

Smiling to myself, I slide my hand right inside his shorts and wrap my fingers around his hot, hard cock. "No big sudden movements, you say?" I move my hand up and down his thickening shaft. "So, I guess sex is out of the question."

Eyelids half-mast, he hisses out a moan. He rolls to his side. His hand cups my breast over my bikini, and his mouth descends on mine. "Sex is never out of the question," he rumbles right before he takes my mouth in a deep, sultry kiss.

Lust bolts straight to my center.

"But we could fall," I murmur against his lips.

"So we fall. Nothing could stop me from fucking you right now."

"What if I die from the fall?"

"You'd fall onto sand. I think you're good."

"It's a biggish drop though. I could sprain something."

"It's a couple of feet. You'd be fine. And you can still fuck through a sprain."

"Your concern for me is overwhelming."

"I know. Now, take my dick out of my shorts, so I can fuck you."

I do as he told me, and I free his cock from his shorts.

"Do you have a condom?"

His brow rises, answering my question. Of course he has one. He doesn't go anywhere on this island with me without a condom in his pocket.

We have a hell of a lot of sex.

He slides his hand in the pocket of his trunks and pulls out the familiar foil wrapper. Just seeing it has my insides tightening with anticipation.

A quick tear, and he's rolling it on. Then, he unties the string on the side of my bikini bottoms and pushes it out of the way. Taking hold of my thigh, he hooks it over his hip, and he slides inside me.

He fucks me with slow, shallow thrusts. The base of his cock drags over my clit while he makes love to my mouth with his tongue.

Just when I think sex with him can't get any better, that we've finally reached our peak, he goes and proves me wrong with hammock sex.

There is literally nowhere that he won't screw me.

I'm fairly sure he'd do me on the table at breakfast if I gave him the green light to go ahead.

I don't know if he just has an insatiable sexual appetite or if he has this appetite for me, but whatever it is, I'm grateful for it. And for all the orgasms that he gives me.

I know that in just this past week, I've had so many more orgasms than I had in my entire relationship with Tim.

I've never wanted sex as much as I want it with West either.

I just can't seem to get enough of him.

I'm in the middle of paradise, and it's hard to care about any of it when I'm with West. All I can see is him, and it's scary as hell.

I need to keep reminding myself that this is a holiday fling and nothing more.

And when it's time for us to both go home, we'll part on good terms, and I'll go back to England with a smile on my face and an entire suitcase full of memories of my time with him and all the sex we had.

But in the meantime, I'm still here, and he's inside me, making me feel amazing.

His hand slides over my butt, gripping it.

Our breathing grows heavier. My breasts brush against his chest. The material of my bikini top feels harsh against my nipples.

I reach up and untie the string around my neck, allowing my breasts to be free. I know how much of a boob man he is.

West immediately ducks his head and wraps his mouth around a nipple, sending a bolt of desire straight through me and to my clit.

"Jesus," I gasp.

He's all over me. Inside me. His smell. His taste. Him. It's too much. It's not enough.

When my orgasm hits, I have to bite my lip to stop from screaming. My inner muscles clamp tight around his dick.

"Fuck, Dillon. You're making me come." He presses his forehead to mine, and I feel his cock start to jerk inside of me.

His eyes are on mine, and we're just staring at each other. I worry he can see my feelings in my eyes, so I close them.

He makes no move to pull out of me, and I don't want him to. I like having him inside of me.

His rough fingertips trace a path over my cheek, and he tucks my hair behind my ear. "So fucking pretty."

I blink open my eyes. He's still watching me.

"So are you."

"Handsome, Double D. I'm handsome."

"That as well."

He smiles that gorgeous smile of his before bringing his lips to mine again. "I like you," he says, his lips brushing over mine.

And honestly, his words surprise me.

"I like you too," I tell him quietly.

"I don't like many people."

"So, I'm one of the lucky ones then."

"Obviously. But so am I. You're like no one I've ever met before."

I don't know what else to say. I only know how it makes me feel, and it's scary. Everything about this moment is scary. Because I know he doesn't mean it in the way my heart wants to take it.

But thankfully, he kisses me again and again, and then I feel his dick starting to thicken and harden inside me, so I stop thinking and instead just feel the things he does to my body.

twenty

WEST

"THIS PLACE IS INCREDIBLE!" Dillon wanders over to where the sun loungers, daybed, and wicker umbrellas are set up, checking out the small island that we've just been dropped at.

The boat left us with a picnic basket for lunch, and the guys said they'll be back later on today to set up for the gourmet torchlit dinner we'll be having before they take us back to the island. So, I've got a full day with her here, all alone.

Whatever will we do?

"I don't even know what I was expecting," she says, dropping her bag on one of the sun loungers. "But it wasn't this. It's so perfect. I can't believe I was considering not even coming. So glad you said you'd come with me."

"Me too. And you should let me pay for half of this."

She gives me the same look she gives me every time I mention it. "It was already paid for ages ago. And I asked you to come with me, so technically, you're my guest, and guests don't pay."

I have money to burn. I know that she doesn't. So, I wish she'd stop being stubborn and let me give her some money for this.

Guess I'll just have to pay her back in some other way.

"What should we do first?" She turns to me, hands going to her hips. "Explore the island a little? Swim? Sunbathe?"

"I vote we fuck."

She playfully rolls her eyes. "We had sex earlier."

She means, when we woke up. That was a few hours ago. *When did a few hours become a long time in between bouts of sex? Since her.*

She fiddles with her cell phone, and then music starts to play. She puts her cell down on the day bed and peels off the dress she's wearing, leaving her in a barely there red bikini. She walks over the sand and into the shallow lagoon, and I watch her. It's hard to not stare at her all of the time, but in that bikini … impossible. Her tits spilling out of it. Her long, dark hair falling down her back. Face free of makeup. Just suntan lotion on her skin, making it glisten.

She's fucking gorgeous. And it bugs me that she has no clue just how beautiful she is.

I'm also starting to realize that I'll miss fucking her when I go home. But not just fucking her. I'll miss hanging with her. She's fun. And adorably weird. I even fucking like her competitiveness and inability to lose. It's cute.

Totally out of character for me. I don't know if it's this place fucking with my head, filling it with hearts and flowers, or if it's the dopamine in my brain from all the sex I've been having.

Don't get me wrong; I have a lot of sex back home. I've never wanted for some ass. But I've never had as much sex in such a short period of time as I've been having with her.

There's not a whole lot to do here but fuck, eat, drink, and sleep. But I honestly think, no matter where we were, I'd have a hard time keeping my dick out of her.

Dillon turns to face me, singing along to the song, some chick crooning about being "Drunk in Love." She starts swaying her hips in time to the music, and I watch her for a while, but it gets to the point where I can't *not* go over to her.

I walk into the water and stop a few feet away. Something raw and animalistic crawls inside me.

"Take your bikini off."

She stops dancing. "What?"

"I said, take your bikini off."

"Now?"

"Yes, now."

She glances around, her teeth sinking into her bottom lip. I want that lip in my mouth. Then around my cock.

"What if someone sees?"

I chuckle darkly. "There is literally only you and me here. The only things that are gonna see you naked are the fish. Maybe the occasional bird."

I wait a beat, watching her. I can see her chest starting to rise and fall with excitement. That telltale flush climbs up her chest. And I know she's into this. I wouldn't push it if she wasn't.

She reaches back and unclasps the bikini top, freeing my favorite tits from their confines. Then, she hooks her fingers into her bikini bottoms and pushes them down her legs, stepping out of them.

I hold my hand out for her bikini. She tosses it over to me. I catch it and then throw it onto the beach.

I hook my fingers into my swim shorts and shove them down. Those get thrown to the beach too.

Her eyes go to my hard dick. I was hard the moment she started dancing in the water.

I'm always fucking hard around her. I feel like a teenager again, walking around with a permanent boner.

Her gaze comes back to me, and she arches her brow, as if to say, *Now what?*

"Touch your tits."

There's no question from her, and I fucking love that. She trusts herself with me, and that turns me on something fierce.

She cups her tits with those dainty hands and starts to play with her nipples. My dick starts to throb, so I wrap my hand around it and give it a firm squeeze.

I see Dillon's eyes go straight to my hand, and then they lift to mine. Desire pools in her eyes.

"Touch your pussy," I say to her. My voice sounds raw. "I want to see you fuck yourself with your fingers."

There's a little hesitation in her movement this time, and I wonder if this is the first time she's done this in front of someone before.

I really fucking hope it is.

With her teeth digging into her bottom lip, she slides a hand down over her flat stomach and between her legs. She parts her legs a little and pushes a finger inside herself.

The throb in my dick is getting insistent. I slowly start to jack myself off, watching her finger herself.

"Fuck, that's hot, Dillon. You're fucking hot."

Hazy eyes meet mine. Little hot gasps are coming from her mouth as she works herself up. "I need you, West. I need you to fuck me."

Who am I to deny her?

Still working my dick with my hand, I walk across the space between, stopping right in front of her.

Reaching out, I wrap my fingers around her wrist and lift her hand from her pussy to my mouth. Curling my hand around hers, I part my lips and wrap them around her fingers, sucking her juices off them.

Fuck, she tastes good.

Her eyes are wide and needy.

She needs my cock inside her now.

First things first though. Letting her hand fall from my mouth, I slide my hands around her hips and kiss her. Just because I fucking can.

You won't be able to in three days. She'll be back in England, and you'll be home.

She loops her arms around my neck, pushing up onto her tiptoes, getting closer to me, and my mouth slants over hers. She tastes of the strawberries and syrup she had on her waffles at breakfast.

She sucks on my tongue, and I know it's because she can taste herself on me.

Fuck, I'm so hot for her.

"I want you," she whispers into my mouth.

"You have me." And in this moment, she does.

Grabbing her ass, I haul her up, and she wraps her legs around me.

My dick is trapped between our bodies, leaking pre-cum against her. I need inside her now.

"Fuck," I groan, pressing my forehead to hers.

"What?" she gasps.

"I left the condoms in my shorts." Which are on the fucking beach. I'm gonna have to go get them. "Wait a sec. I'll grab one."

"Unless …"

I tilt my head back, staring at her. "Unless what?"

Her cheeks start to redden under her tanned skin. "I mean, we don't have to. Actually, forget it. Go get the condoms. I'll wait here."

"Are you suggesting we fuck without a condom?"

She glances away from me, so I grab her chin and force her eyes back to mine.

"Is that what you want?"

"I'm clean," she whispers. "I had a test done before I came here. With the … cheating and … you know, I figured I should get checked. And I'm on the pill."

"I'm always clean." *I never fuck without a condom. Ever.* "I have regular tests. Last was a week before I came here, and you're the only person I've had sex with since." Like I need to clarify this.

Am I actually considering this?

Yeah, I guess I am.

I want to know what she feels like. Maybe I'm losing my fucking mind.

"So …" She chews on her lip.

"So … we're doing this?"

Her eyes lift to mine. "Only if you're sure."

"I'm sure. Are you sure?"

She smiles. "I'm sure."

Fuck. I'm about to go bareback for the first time in my life. It's like losing my virginity all over again. Actually, I sound like I'm losing my virginity all over again.

Well, fuck.

"Have you ever … before?" she asks me in a whispered voice.

I shake my head.

"Me neither. Why does it feel like a big deal?"

I look at her. "Because it is." It's a huge fucking deal. I'm about to stick my dick inside her without a safety net.

"We don't have to," she says quickly, and when she says that, that's when I know I definitely want to.

"I know we don't. But I want to. With you." Then, I kiss her. And I don't stop kissing her, even when I lift her body up and slowly lower her onto my cock.

"Fuck," I hiss against her mouth as her tight heat covers my bare dick, taking me deep inside her body.

Hands on her ass, I lift her up and then back down, fucking her tight little body with my cock.

And it feels amazing.

One of her hands is on my shoulder, nails biting into my skin. The other is tangled up in my hair.

I swallow all of her breathy moans, feeling like I'm going to lose my mind any fucking second now because nothing has ever felt this good.

I feel the tightening in my balls and that telltale tingle at the base of my spine, and now, I'm gonna come. Honestly, it's a fucking miracle that I've lasted this long. But I won't come without her.

"I'm not gonna last. You feel too good," I pant.

"You say that like it's a bad thing."

"It will be if you don't come in the next few seconds. Are you close, or do you need me to get you there?"

"I'm close," she whimpers, breathless.

"Actually …" I lower down to my knees in the shallow water because I have a feeling when I come, it's gonna be big and I'm gonna have a hard time staying upright. "That's better. If I black out when I come, I won't drop you."

Dillon is now straddling me, and she starts riding me like a champ. I have to bite the inside of my cheeks to stop from coming. I need her to come now. I slide one hand to her pussy and start rubbing her clit with my fingers, and I slap her ass with my other hand.

She gasps but doesn't stop fucking me.

"Again," she moans.

I slap her ass again.

She throws her head back and starts coming hard.

Thank. Fuck.

I let go. And I start coming inside her with a guttural roar.

Fuck. Me.

That was … insane.

That's it. I'm never fucking with a condom again. Okay, so that's probably not smart. But who needs smart when it can feel like that?

Dillon slumps against my chest, her head landing on my shoulder.

"Jesus," she says against my skin, muffled under all that hair of hers.

"Yeah," I say because it's all I've got at the moment.

I stay sitting here with her because I don't want to move.

My real life is chaotic and stressful. But here, with her … it's not. I've never felt as content and at peace as I am when I'm inside her.

I honestly have no fucking clue what to do with that knowledge.

"West?"

"Hmm?"

She lifts her head, pushing her hair back from her face. She rests her elbow on my shoulder and puts her chin in her hand. I'm reminded of the first night I met her, when she put her elbow on the bar and missed placing her chin on her hand. The memory makes me chuckle.

"What?" She gives me a curious look.

"Nothing. What were you gonna say?"

"Well, I was just thinking … what if someone is watching us via one of those satellites up there? You know, the ones that governments have up there."

Laughter rumbles through my chest. *Pretty sure we'd be safe even if they were.* "We both just came like motherfuckers, and *that's* what you're thinking about right now?"

She giggles. "Sorry. I was just thinking."

I tease her, but I like the way her mind works.

I press a kiss to her jaw. "Relax. No one saw us."

"Okay." She lets out a soft sigh.

And then I count down in my head.

Three …

Two …

One …

"But just to answer my question, hypothetically, do you think it's possible?"

I laugh because it's funny. She's funny. But it's also scary how fucking well I already know her.

"Double D, I think that if there were a remote possibility that government satellites were trained on this exact spot at this very moment in time, then I'd say whoever was watching got one hell of a show."

"True. And it's not like it's gonna end up on some porn website. Although it is illegal to have sex in public. But I don't know if us being here constitutes as public because there's only you and me—"

"Dillon."

"What?"

I kiss her. Not to shut her up. But because I have to. Because, fuck … I like her.

Really like her.

She's different. Dillon is the realest person I've ever met.

And I've just realized that I might not be ready to let her go just yet. I might not do forever. But I could do a little longer with her.

Now, I just need to figure out how to make that happen. Or if it's even actually a good idea.

Because if I ask her to come back to the real world with me, even for a short time, then I'm gonna have to tell her who I actually am. Or more to the point, who my father is.

twenty-one

DILLON

"CHEERS." I CHINK MY beer bottle against West's before taking a drink.

It's our second to last night here, and we're sitting out on the jetty, watching the sun descend below the horizon. The sky is a gorgeous hue of pinks and blues.

I move my feet around in the warm water, watching it swirl around my legs.

I'm trying not to get sad that my time with West is fast coming to an end. I don't want to waste the couple of days that I have left with him feeling sad, so I'm trying my best to remain upbeat.

"Can you believe our time here is almost over? It's flown by."

"I know. I guess time really does fly when you're having fun fucking."

"Pretty sure that's not the saying."

"No? It should be though."

"Tomorrow is our last full day before we fly home."

West leaves just before me. His flight is in the morning. Mine in the afternoon.

"What should we do?"

"Fuck." He grins at me, lifting his brows.

"I never would've guessed you'd say that."

"I like to mix things up. Stay unpredictable."

Laughing softly, I stare at his profile. "If I forget to say this tomorrow, thanks for making my honeymoon memorable."

He glances at me out of the corner of his eye, a grin touching his lips. "You're welcome."

A fish swims toward us. I lift my feet out of the water, and West chuckles.

"It won't eat you, you know."

"I know. I just don't want it touching my feet. Fish feel weird." I lower my feet back into the water when the coast is clear. "I wonder if fish think that we feel weird," I muse, putting my bottle to my lips.

"I don't think fish think at all."

"They have brains, right?"

"Yeah. But animals are programmed to think about two things—food and sex."

"Just like you." I laugh. "And also me. Actually, you're more of the sex thinker, and I'm the food thinker."

"And that's why we make the perfect team."

My heart swoops and dives. *He doesn't mean it that way. Stop getting carried away.*

West has a swig of his beer, and I stare down at his feet in the water next to mine. So much bigger than my size fives.

"What shoe size do you take? Your feet are massive."

"And you're just realizing this now?"

"Yep. So, what size are you?"

"I'm a fourteen."

"Are your sizes the same as my sizes?"

"What? Are we just making sizes up now?"

"No, your country and my country have different sizes. Well, I think they do. I've seen it on labels when I bought clothes before. UK and US sizing—also European, but that's not relevant here."

"Is any of it relevant?"

"Ooh, I should look it up." I pull my phone from the back pocket of my shorts and open Google. I tap in the search bar and type *US and UK shoe sizes*.

A bunch of websites come up. I click on the first one.

"Oh, hey, so this is weird. So, men's shoe sizes have a difference of a half-size, and for women, it's two sizes. So, you're a fourteen, which is a thirteen and a half in the UK. I'm a five in the UK, and I'd be a seven in the US."

"Huh. Yeah. That is weird. And boring as fuck."

"Piss off." I playfully nudge his arm with mine, and he chuckles.

"So, what're your plans when you get home?" he asks me, taking another drink of beer. "Aside from Googling useless facts and boring people with them."

Cry over never seeing you again. Hate my life a little bit. Get a job I don't want, so I can pay the bills. Find an apartment to rent.

I give him a look. "Well, I'll keep doing that, of course."

"Of course."

"I don't know … look for a job, I guess." I blow out a breath. "I just really wish I didn't have to go back home. At least, not yet anyway. I'm nowhere near ready to have to breathe the same air as my mother and the prick."

"So, don't go home."

I laugh. "Did you hit your head? It's not like I have a choice."

"There's always a choice. You could extend your vacation."

"This place is expensive. And I don't think I'd be able to just stay. You have to prebook and shit. I mean, I could afford another week. I do have money in savings. But it's the money my grandparents left me. I figured I'd use it to buy a house one day. I don't want to waste it."

Also, being here without you would be boring. I'd be sad as fuck that you weren't here, and I'd probably just spend my time moping. But of course, I don't say that.

"What about going somewhere else?" he says.

"Like where?"

"The US."

My heart sputters to a stop. I turn my head, and he's staring at me.

"Baltimore, to be more specific," he adds.

My mouth starts to feel dry. I have trouble swallowing.

"You can speak anytime now, if you want." He's smiling, but his voice sounds different.

"I, um … um … you mean, go there … with … you?"

He glances down to the water before looking back at me. "I can't offer you more than I already have. I don't do relationships, and that won't ever change. But I do know that I'm not quite ready to stop what we've been doing either. You could come to the States with me. Stay at my place for a while. And when you're ready to go back home, you can."

Go with him to America? Is he really saying this right now, or am I hallucinating? I did have seafood at dinner. Maybe it was a dodgy prawn that did it.

"You could even spend time writing. I know it's what you really want to do with your life. Maybe the change of scenery would even inspire a best seller for you."

He's got a point. I could write a book while I'm there. I'd have all the time to write. And going there wouldn't be a waste of money; it'd be like an investment in my career.

And then there's him. I'd get more time with him.

Yes, I have feelings for him. A crush. And going with him would just prolong things. Meaning it would hurt more when I eventually left.

But either way, it's going to hurt when I part from him.

So, why not go to America with him, enjoy myself, and then deal with the aftermath later?

Oh my God. Am I really going to do this?

I think I am.

"So, you're suggesting I go with you to Baltimore, stay at your place, and we keep …" I point my finger between us.

"Fucking."

"Yes."

"Yes, Double D. We'd keep fucking. Nothing would change, except our location. Which would happen to be my apartment. I'd go to training during the day. You could write. I'd come home, and we'd fuck."

Well … hells bells. I didn't want to go home, but I sure as heck wasn't expecting this. For him to say this.

Maybe he likes me. I mean, I know he likes me. But maybe he *likes me*, likes me.

Stop.

And there I am, getting carried away with myself. See, this is why it wouldn't be a good idea.

"So, hypothetically, if I did come to Baltimore and I stayed with you, then I'd expect to pay my way. Like rent or something."

"Hypothetically, that would be a no."

"Then, I won't go." I'm an independent woman who pays her way in life.

"So, you're considering it?" He rests his chin on his shoulder, and his eyes are dancing.

I bite my lip and shrug. "Maybe."

"Okay, what if I changed the hypothetical no to a yes? Would your maybe change to a yes?"

Would it?

Am I really, seriously considering this?

Holy shit, I really am. I'm gonna say yes.

Just like I did the night he put the first offer to me. I tell myself I'm gonna say no, but it's always a yes when it comes down to it.

"I don't know. Change it and find out."

A smile tugs at his lips. "It's done. I accept your terms to paying rent or whatever. So, will you come?"

I feel a flutter of happiness float through my chest. That can only be a good thing. Right?

"Yes." I smile. "I'll come."

His smile widens. "Good." Then, his smile disappears, and his eyes turn a little serious. "Now, there's something I need to tell you."

That flutter of happiness I was feeling? Yeah, it's dropped into the pit of my stomach.

"Like?"

"Well, it's just that …"

"Oh my God! You're married, aren't you?"

I knew he was too good to be true. Hot guys like him do not fall into my lap that easily.

"I've already told you that I'm not married. And really, if I were, would I have asked you to come stay at my place?"

"You might be one of those Pygmies!"

"Not sure what a short African tribesperson has to do with this, but no."

"Not Pygmy! I meant, polygamist! You've got a bunch of wives back home, haven't you?"

He coughs out a laugh. "No, definitely not. I couldn't handle one fucking wife, let alone two."

"So, what is it?"

"Well, if you'd let me tell—"

"Are you in a cult? I saw this documentary about this actress who was a part of this cult! I think she's in jail now though. But is that it? Are you in a cult?"

"Dillon."

"What?"

"I'm not in a cult or a Pygmy, and I haven't married multiple times."

"Then, what is it?" My heart is almost beating out of my chest. I'm so nervous about what he's about to tell me. I can't take any more disappointment in my life.

He glances away from me, out over the water. "Well, it's not about me as such. It's more about my dad. Who he is." He takes a breath and looks back at me. "My dad is the president."

twenty-two

WEST

"DILLON, ARE YOU OKAY?"

She hasn't said anything since I told her about my dad. That was a good minute ago, and a minute is a long time to have someone staring at you. Without blinking. She's starting to look a little scary. I know she's freaking out because she thinks it's a big deal. But it's really not. Not to me anyway. And it's not like she's even from the States, so really, it shouldn't freak her out this much.

"Dillon."

Her big blue eyes blink at me. "I'm sorry, what? For a moment there, I thought you said your dad is the president. But that would be crazy because—"

"He is the president."

"Of America?"

"Yes."

"The United States of America?"

"Uh-huh."

"As in the president of the United States of America? Lives in the White House? Leader of the free world? That president?"

"That would be the one."

"And he's your dad, as in …"

"He provided the sperm that helped make me."

"Gotcha."

Silence stretches out between us. Which is definitely not normal.

"I know you're freaking out. But really, it's not a big deal. It's just something you need to know now that you're coming to the States with me."

"I'm not freaking out," she squawks.

"Your voice has gone high, like really high-pitched."

"It hasn't," she squeaks. She looks away and clears her throat. "It hasn't," she repeats in a deeper voice, sounding nothing like herself.

It's actually quite funny. I'd laugh if I didn't think it might push her over the edge.

"So, um … why didn't you tell me who your dad was before?"

"Because it wasn't relevant."

Accusatory eyes come back to me. "But what if I'd gone home and then found out via the news or something? You might not think it's a big deal. But a heads-up would have been nice. Especially after all the time we've spent together."

She's got a point. I blow out a breath. She went from smiling to annoyed in the space of a few minutes. That doesn't make me feel good at all.

"You're right. I should have said something."

"Yeah, you should have." She's really pissed off. Her eyes look all fiery. It's actually kind of a turn-on when she gets mad. "Imagine if I kept from you that my mum were … I don't know … Elvis." She throws her hands in the air.

"Well, that would be weird as fuck because he's been dead for over forty years. And also, he was a dude."

"You know what I meant! I meant, someone famous. Important or whatever. Stop being a dick." She climbs up to her feet, standing on the jetty.

I stand, too, putting myself in her path. "I'm not trying to be a dick."

I so did not see this coming. I thought she might be a bit weird about it. But not mad.

She folds her arms over her chest. "Well, you are being one."

"Can I ask … why are you mad?"

Her eyes fix on mine. "Because I told you all of my important shit. About my mum and Tim and everything. And you clearly told me nothing of importance."

"You know that's not true." Now, I'm mad.

"I know you told me about your mom." She bites her lip and looks away. "But you kept from me who your dad was. I wondered why you would clam up whenever I asked about your dad. I just figured you two weren't close."

I step up to her and take her chin in my hand, forcing her eyes to mine. "We're not close. Yes, he's the president. And, yes, he's my dad. The former, he's excellent at. The latter, not so much."

He was an absent father and a cheating dirtbag of a husband to my mom up until the day she died, but that's not something Dillon needs to know.

Those gorgeous eyes blink up at me. I brush my thumb over her cheek.

"Him being the president has nothing to do with who I am."

"But it does have an impact on your life, I'm guessing."

"Sometimes." *Most of the fucking time.*

"And you don't live in the White House, right? Because you said you live in Baltimore—unless that was a lie." Her eyes narrow. "Because if it was a lie and you do live there,

I'm telling you right now, I'm not staying in the White House."

I bark out a laugh. "Most people would kill to go stay in the White House."

"Well, I wouldn't. I'm sure it's amazing and everything. It'd be a really nice place to visit. Like Buckingham Palace. But stay there? Nah, thanks. I wouldn't be able to cope with the pressure. I mean, you'd have to look good and dress nice twenty-four/seven. And then there'd be all those agents there, walking around with guns. I'd never be able to relax. No, when I'm home, I just like to chill and wear my PJs."

"Sorry to tell you this, but my apartment has a no-clothes policy."

Her brow lifts. "That right?"

"Mmhmm."

"Do you have security? What are they called?"

"I talk about nakedness. And you ask about security. Should I be worried, Double D?"

She gives me an unamused look.

"They're called Secret Service agents, and yeah, I do."

Her eyes scan the area, like she's expecting someone to leap out of the water.

"But not here. I don't technically have to have them by law. Because I'm an adult, it's my choice. But I have them back home because there are some nutjobs with guns and being the president's son makes me a target. They're not on my ass all the time. They stay at a safe distance, so I can still have some sort of normality in my life. But I came here alone without them. I just needed a break."

"From?"

I sigh and drop my hand from her face. "There was a story in the press. It broke the week before I came here."

"What story? I didn't see anything. But then again, I was caught up in crying into my wine bottle over my mum sleeping with my fiancé, so there is that."

I stare at her in wonder as to how anyone could hurt her. *You could. You are an Oakley after all. Hurting women is in your DNA.*

"You didn't kill someone, did you? I can forgive anything but that. Unless they deserved it. Oh, and hurting animals. I hate people who hurt animals."

"No to the murder. And I love animals." I exhale. "It was stupid. Just a short video clip from when I was back in my senior year of high school. I was seventeen and still messed up over my mom's death and angry with the world. I thought I knew it all. My dad was a senator then. Anyway, I was filmed snorting coke off the stomach of some chick I went to high school with. The clip just surfaced now. Some idiot had probably discovered they had it and sold it for big bucks. My dad is running for reelection, so he was pissed off. Not that I give a shit what he thinks. But I got heat from my coach and team bosses. It's not a good look for them when one of their players is on the news for snorting coke at a party when he was a teenager. They didn't suspend me." *Not that they would. The son of the president brings in way too much revenue for them to lose.* "But we're in the off-season at the moment, so they told me to lay low. I wanted to get away. So, I booked a plane ticket here." *And I'm so fucking glad that I did.*

"You don't still do coke now, do you?" she asks quietly.

"No. I barely did it back then. I was just a stupid kid, trying stuff out."

She blows out a breath. "This is really nuts."

"The drug stuff or president stuff?"

"President stuff."

"Things are only as big as you make them."

She stares up at me. "Your dad holds the access codes to nuclear bombs that could start World War Three. Or quite possibly end our world altogether."

A chuckle escapes me. "I guess that is kind of big now that you mention it. Although I don't think he has any plans to use those codes, if that helps."

"Shut up."

"So … Double D, are you still coming to Baltimore with me?"

She lets out a soft sigh. "Will you stop calling me Double D if I do?"

"Um …" I pretend to think it over. "No."

"Figures."

"But I'll give you lots of orgasms to make up for it." I run my knuckles down her cheek and brush my lips over hers.

"How many are we talking?" she whispers.

"So many that you'll lose count."

She lets out a sweet breath that I take inside of me. "Guess I'll have to still come then."

"Yes, you will."

twenty-three

DILLON

I WALK INSIDE WEST'S apartment, pulling my smaller suitcase in behind me, him following me with his own case and my larger case. He travels a lot lighter than I do, and it's a good thing I took a lot of things with me now that I'm having an extended holiday. In America. With West.

I can hardly believe I'm here! Someone, pinch me.

A few weeks ago, I was miserable and heartbroken, heading on my honeymoon alone. And now, I'm in America with a beautiful man who I get to have sex with.

I might also have a teeny-tiny crush on him. But it'll be fine.

I'll be fine.

I just need to enjoy this. Him. Here.

When I called Aunt Jenny to tell her, she thought I was winding her up at first, especially when I told her who West's dad was. When I convinced her that I actually wasn't, she got all concerned auntie on me. I mean, I'm in a different country with a man I've known for two weeks. Even though it feels like I've known West for so much longer.

I guess when you spend nearly all day, every day with someone for two weeks, it's going to feel that way.

It's like speed-dating on crack. I guess that's why holiday romances can feel so intense between two people. Maybe that's why West asked me to come here. He told me that he wasn't ready to end what we're doing, but it's not like he said he wants anything more from me either. Not like that would be a possibility. He lives here, and I live in the UK. Long distance rarely, if ever, lasts. But that's not what he wants anyway. He's been clear from the start that relationships aren't for him.

Anyway, after I reassured Aunt Jenny that West was a trustworthy guy—that being the president's son, it wasn't like he was a psycho killer—and I agreed to text her every day to check in and call often as well as give her West's address, she chilled out and got excited on my behalf about my going to America.

Also, it's not like I'll be here forever. We haven't actually discussed how long I'm staying for, but I figure we'll just play it by ear.

I guess I'll go home when we get sick of each other. Not that I imagine ever getting sick of West. But I'm sure I'll start to drive him nuts after a while, especially as it's his place I'm staying in and he is used to living alone.

The thought of going back home and not seeing West again causes an ache in my chest, which I squash down.

Focus on the now. The happy. I'm here with him, and everything is fabulous.

Although it was a little bit weird when we arrived at the airport and two Secret Service agents were waiting for us. Well, him. They drove us from the airport to West's apartment building. I asked West if they just go home now, but he said no. Protection is twenty-four/seven—the guys work on rotation, two at a time—so they'll hang around.

I didn't know what *hang around* meant, and I didn't bother to ask.

I'm just glad they're not in the apartment with us because that would be weird.

"Your apartment is gorgeous." I turn to him, smiling.

"Want the tour?"

"Duh." I chuckle. "Of course I do."

"Well, this is the living room, kitchen, and dining room."

It's all open plan. I've never seen an apartment this big. To be honest, you could fit both floors of my childhood home into this one room. It's so light and airy with a high ceiling and light wooden floor. There's a wall of windows with a gorgeous view of the city and glass doors that lead onto a large balcony. There's a sleek, modern black kitchen with a center island, a dark wood dining table, and cream chairs. The biggest flat screen TV I have ever seen hangs on the wall, and sitting before it are a big U-shaped dark gray sofa with a cream rug and a dark wood coffee table.

"It's really nice, West."

"Wanna see the bedrooms?" He winks at me. On anyone else, it'd be cheesy as fuck. On him … soooo hot.

I give him an innocent look and flutter my lashes. "Of course."

Taking me by the hand, he tugs me along toward the living room area and a door that sits on the same wall as the TV.

"This is the guest room." He leads me inside.

It's a decent-sized room, decorated in cream, with cream carpet and white bedding. I would literally be afraid to stay in this room in case I spilled anything.

"It has its own walk-in closet and beyond that a bathroom," he tells me.

"Fancy."

"I do try."

"So, is this where I'm staying?"

He grins at me, showing teeth. "No. You're staying with me."

He tugs me back out of the guest room, across the living space to the door across the way, and into an even bigger bedroom. "This is my room. Where you're sleeping. And having sex. With me."

"You said *having sex*. Not fucking." I slap a hand to my chest. "I am shooketh."

He chuckles. "Sorry, correction: fucking."

I walk into his bedroom. It smells of him. That masculine, sexy scent of his, which if bottled, it would sell for hundreds at a time.

The floor is a thick, soft gray carpet that your toes just sink into. The walls are painted dark gray. It kind of reminds me of the color of his eyes. There's a TV hanging on the wall in here, too, across from his bed, which is huge. A gorgeous dark wood frame, which I imagine cost a fortune, is made up with dark gray bedding. So many pillows that I can't even count them.

"That's a lot of pillows," I comment.

"I like my comfort."

"You know, this might just be the biggest bed that I've ever seen in my life." I walk over to it, brushing my hand over the soft bedding.

"I'm a big guy. I need a big bed. It's comfy as fuck too," he says.

Then, the next thing I know, he's tackling me down on it.

"Ah!" I laugh as we both land on the bed with a soft thud.

West rolls over on top of me. I stare up at him, him grinning down at me, and I run my hands through his hair.

"If you wanted me on your bed, you only had to ask."

"I thought that would be more fun."

I smile. "It was."

He presses a kiss to my inner wrist. "You look good on my bed."

"You look good up there."

"I feel good up here."

He leans down and brushes his lips over mine, kissing me, making me shiver. He slides his tongue into my mouth, making me moan.

And then my stomach rumbles loudly.

West chuckles into my mouth. "Hungry?"

"I'm always hungry."

"True." He pulls back and shifts to his side, so he's lying beside me on the bed. "Wanna order in and chill out here? Or go out to eat?"

"Order in, please," I say, and then a yawn escapes me.

"Tired?"

"Yeah, sorry."

"Don't be. I am, too, to be honest. The time zone difference messes with your body. How about we order food? Chinese sound good?"

"Perfect."

"Then, we can shower while we wait for it to arrive. Together, obviously."

"Obviously."

"Just doing my bit for the environment, trying to save water."

"You're too good for this world."

He gives a *what can you do* shrug, and I can't help but laugh.

"After we're done saving water, we can eat Chinese in bed and watch a movie, if you want. And then fuck, if you're not too tired," I suggest.

"I'm never too tired to do that with you."

"Talking of doing that with me, I have a question."

"Will I want to answer it?" He smirks.

"I hope so."

"Okay, hit me with it."

"So, I know on the island, we were exclusively sleeping together. But now that we're here—and I know this is an extended trip for me and this is your home—and with us not using condoms since the desert island trip, I just want to know … if … you know …"

His fingers take hold of my chin, and he turns my head to him and stares into my eyes. "I'm only having sex with you. No one else."

"You said sex again. Not fucking." I grin.

He gives me a serious look. "I'm only fucking you, Double D." Then, he presses a kiss to my lips. "And the same goes for you. It's only my dick that you get to play with."

"You mean, I came all the way here, and I only get to have sex with you when there are all these gorgeous American men to be had? Bummer."

I waggle my eyebrows at him, and he playfully narrows his eyes.

"Need me to remind you what my dick can do to you?"

"Maybe … I mean, it was a long flight here. I might have forgotten."

His hand goes to his zipper, and he tugs it down. "Well then, let me give you a recap."

twenty-four

DILLON

WEST HAS A FEW days before he has to go back training, so he's taking me out to do some sightseeing. He asked if there was anything specific that I wanted to do, but considering I don't know much about Baltimore, I wasn't sure, so I said I'd leave it up to him.

We're in his car, which is a black Range Rover, destination unknown. He said he wanted to surprise me. He's wearing a ball cap. I have a feeling he wears a ball cap a lot when he's out. I'm not sure I like it. I can't see his hair, and I happen to really like his hair.

His Secret Service guards are following us in a black car. It's weird, having people following you and guarding you. Not that they're guarding me, but I'd like to think that if some wacko with a gun tried to shoot me, they'd do something about it.

It's kind of cool if you think about it. First time in America, and I have government security. Well, West's security, but still, it's cool as hell.

Although I kind of get the impression that West isn't so keen on the security. Not the guys. He seems to like them well enough. Just the whole *people following him around* thing. I sense that it bugs the shit out of him.

"Question."

"Will I want to answer?"

"Possibly."

"Hit me."

"Literally?"

He slides me a look before looking back to the road. "Funny."

"I know."

"So, are you gonna ask me or not?"

"Oh yeah. Do you dislike the security? Not Nick and Aiden, just having to have them?"

"You're on a first-name basis with the agents?"

"Of course. Aren't you?"

"Well, yeah, but they've been guarding me for the last four years. You've been here two days. Do you make friends with everyone?"

I roll my eyes. "Not everyone. But it'd be rude not to know the names of the men who are guarding your life."

"Guarding my life sounds a little dramatic."

"Well, what would you say they do?"

He goes silent a moment. "Follow me around in case someone decides to make an attempt on my life."

"That's the same thing!" I laugh.

He slides me another look, his expression impish. "Nuh-uh."

I shake my head, exasperated. "So, back to my question. I get the impression you're not so keen on it."

"I'm not. When I was a teenager, we used to have security with my dad being a senator back then. It was annoying, them following me around. I couldn't do anything."

"You managed to go to a party and snort coke."

He chuckles. "True. But they were around a lot. When I got older, I figured I had freedom from all of that. Then, my dad got himself elected president, and here we are. I fought the security at first, but the threats that came in couldn't be ignored, so I had to accept the way it is. But hopefully for not much longer."

"How long has your dad been president for?"

"He's three years into his first term."

"They serve for four years, right? And can do up to two terms?"

"Someone knows her American politics."

"I really don't. Just that. You said he's running for a second term, right?"

West sighs. "Yeah. If he gets elected again, I'll have to live with this for four more years, and then I'll be free." He goes quiet for a moment. "I feel like shit for thinking this because all things aside, he is a great president, but I really don't want him to get elected for another term. I want my life back. Once I'm out of the public eye, the security will go, and I can just get back to playing ball without all of his political shit following me around. I'll be talked about for my football again and not the fact that I'm his son. I'm twenty-seven; I'm at my peak. If he leaves the White House this next election, I'll have my good years left, where I can really make my mark as a ball player and not the president's son. If he gets reelected, I'll be nearly thirty-two when he's out of the White House, and I'll be heading for retirement a few years later."

My heart squeezes painfully for him. For once, I actually don't know what to say. So, instead of words, I slide my hand into his, link our fingers, and give his hand a squeeze. For a moment, he stares down at our entwined hands, like he's never seen me hold his hand before.

Which is weird because we've held hands tons of times before.

But not like this. In a comforting way.

Not wanting to freak him out, I slide my hand out of his with the pretense of getting something out of my bag.

I'm still rummaging around in it, looking for the fake thing, when he says, "We're here."

He pulls into a parking spot outside this huge gray stone building and turns off the engine. Unclipping my seat belt, I get out of the car. I notice the black car belonging to the Secret Service agents pulling up behind the Range Rover.

I stare up at the building. Above the door, engraved into the stone, it says *Peabody Institute.*

West meets me on the pavement.

"You know, where I'm from, institute means a place where the mentally ill go." I slide my eyes to his. "I know I act a little crazy. Even talk crazy sometimes. But please tell me that you've not brought me to a mental institution." I'm only half-joking.

"No." He laughs. "It's not that kind of institution. This is one I think you'll like."

Taking me by the hand, he tugs me forward, and I follow him up the steps. He pushes the door open and leads me inside.

And holy mother of God.

My heart actually stops with true happiness.

I step a little farther inside, my hands pressed to my chest. "It's a library."

But it's like no library I've ever seen. It's huge. I count up five stories high. All filled with shelves that are loaded with books.

There is a heaven after all, and I'm standing right in the entrance of it.

"You like it?" West steps behind me, a hand sliding to my waist.

"I love it," I breathe, unable to take my eyes off it. I can't stop staring. It's just so beautiful. "You literally couldn't have brought me to a better place."

I can practically feel his smile.

"Well, I figured a writer would want to see the library that we have here."

I turn so that I'm facing him. "This isn't a library. It's paradise. And you are frigging awesome." I plant a kiss on his lips before I whirl back around. "I've never seen anything like this. When I was a kid, I used to spend a lot of time in my local library, but it was nothing like this. The whole library could fit in the reception area here."

His fingers sweep my hair aside and brush over my neck. "Such a little book nerd."

"I wear that badge with pride."

"Lucky for you, I like nerds."

I glance back at him. "Lucky for you, I like okayish-looking American football players."

"You can just call it football, you know. And okayish-looking?" He lifts a brow.

"Fine. Better than okayish. And, no, I can't just call it football. Because football is a game played with a round ball and said ball is kicked around by the feet. *You* carry the ball."

"You know, we kick the ball sometimes too."

"Still not football. More like rugby. Except you guys wear all that protective equipment and rugby players don't."

"It's nothing like rugby. It's football."

"Beg to differ. You know, if you weren't *so* much older than me—"

"Four years, Double D. I'm hardly your sugar daddy in this scenario."

"And if I'd lived in America and we'd gone to school together," I continue, ignoring him, "you'd have been the hot football player, and I'd have been the book nerd who you didn't give the time of day to."

"You sure about that?"

"That you wouldn't have given me the time of day? Yep."

He stares down at me, the ball cap shading his eyes. "You look anything like you do now when you were at school?"

"Nope. I had braces and a bad haircut."

"Then, yeah, you're right. I wouldn't have looked at you twice."

"Ass," I murmur, bumping mine back into his hips.

He hisses, gripping hold of my hip. His lips come to my ear. "Do that again, and I'll find a dark corner to fuck you in."

A thrill runs through me. "I bet there're a lot of dark corners in this library. But what about Nick and Aiden?"

"I don't want to fuck them."

That makes me laugh. "I meant, they have eyes on you at all times."

"Not *all* the time."

Well then …

"Let's go exploring then. Let me see all of the books and pick them up and smell them and—"

"Smell them?" He looks mildly disturbed.

"It's a book-nerd thing. Books have a smell to them, new and old. Especially old. They smell of history."

"Book-smelling? Well, that's killed my hard-on."

I snort and then smother the laugh with my hand. "Sorry."

"Come on," he grumbles, tugging on my hand, leading me into the library. "Let's go and look around, so you can smell some musty, old books."

twenty-five

WEST

"YOU TAKING A NAP over here?"

"Fuck off, Brooks." I chuckle as he takes a seat on the bench next to me. "Just having a water break."

Kai Brooks is our resident quarterback and the closest thing I have to a best friend. We joined the team at the same time. He's good people. All of the guys are. We're lucky to have a great team of people around us. It can be hard, having friends when your old man runs the fucking country. It's hard to know who's real or kissing your ass because of him. But with these guys, I know they're real. First off, I knew most of them before my dad became president. And none of them kiss my ass. But they always have my back on and off the field. Especially Brooks.

He picks up a bottle of water from the cooler in front of us and chugs some back. "Coach is running us pretty hard today."

"No kidding. Did someone piss him off?" I look out over some of the guys still out on the field, sweat dripping from them.

First day back training, and he's had us running drills for the last hour straight. I'm in shape; I keep up with my gym time, even when I'm not here at our training facility—and all the sex I've been having with Dillon counts as some serious workouts—but even I'm feeling it today.

I crack open another bottle of water and down half of it.

"Probably Knox," Brooks says, referring to our right guard, who also sidelines as a comedian. "How was the trip?" he asks.

"Yeah, it was good. Beautiful place." Beautiful women vacation there. Well, woman. Namely one—Dillon.

"I've always wanted to go. Really need to get my ass out there."

"You do. It's a fuck of a journey, but the reefs alone make it worth it."

"You go diving while you were there?"

"Yeah. Did a night dive too. Was cool as fuck."

"Sounds it." He drains his water and crumples the plastic bottle in his hand. "What else is there to do there, aside from diving?" There's a tone to his voice that tells me this is leading somewhere, and I'm pretty sure I know exactly where.

"Not much. Good place to relax."

"What was the pussy like there?"

"It was mostly couples."

There's a beat of silence, and then he says, "Heard you brought a souvenir back with you. Dark hair, hot …"

I slide him a look. "Where'd you hear that?"

"Miles."

Roman Miles is the tight end and team gossiper.

"Miles needs to watch more ESPN and less E!"

Brooks chuckles. "So, it's not true?"

"I didn't say that …" I put the bottle to my lips and drain off the last of the water as he laughs.

"No shit! I thought Miles was talking bullshit. Didn't sound like something you'd do—meet some chick on vacay and bring her back here with you. So, is it serious?"

I give him a look. "Fuck no."

"But she came back here with you. She's English, right?"

Fuck me. How much does the press already know? See, this is what I get for not reading the news. Maybe I should start watching E!, like Miles.

"Yeah, she's from the UK. But she's only here on an extended vacation. She wasn't ready to go back home after her vacation was up." And I wasn't ready to stop seeing or screwing her. "So, I invited her to come stay with me for a while. No big deal." I shrug and toss my empty water bottle into the nearby trash can.

"Does she know that?"

"What?"

"That it's no big deal."

I glance at him. "She knows."

"And she's okay with it?"

"Yeah."

"You sure? Because in my experience, sometimes, women say they're fine with things when in fact they're really not."

"That's not the case with Dillon. She and I are on the same page. We're just having some fun."

Yeah, I asked her to come here with me, but it was only because I wasn't ready to stop fucking her. Not because I want a relationship with her.

She's staying in your place, sleeping in your bed. That's about as relationshippy as it gets.

But it's not forever. It's only temporary. And temporary I can do.

I might like Dillon. More than I've ever liked any woman. But I also have nothing to offer her. I can't be in a relationship and then risk hurting someone the way my father hurt my mom time and time again. I like women. Fucking love them. Or more to the point, I love fucking them. And what if I were in a relationship with Dillon and my head got turned and I ended up hurting her? I would never cheat on her, like my father did to my mother. But I would have to end things with her, and that would hurt her. The last thing I ever want to do is hurt Dillon. Not like that. She's been hurt enough.

Although I've not looked at or thought about any other woman since I met her.

It's been three weeks, man. That doesn't mean anything.

It's fucking nuts that it's only been three weeks since I met her. It feels like so much longer.

"So, do I get to meet this Dillon?"

"No."

He laughs. "You ashamed of her or something?"

"Quite the opposite. I just don't trust you." I smirk.

Brooks is an all-American good ol' boy from Texas. Women love his Southern accent, baby blues, and pretty-boy face, and I know for a fact that Dillon would. Not that I think she'd do anything with him. I'm just not willing to put it to the test. I want to keep her to myself while I have her.

"I'm wounded." He slaps a hand to his chest.

"Shut up, pretty boy."

"Says Mr. Eligible Bachelor, three years running."

Yeah, since my dad got the presidency.

"Fuck off," I mumble.

"Hey, ladies!" Coach Ackerman yells before Brooks and I can get into a sparring contest. "You okay over there? Need a massage? A mani-pedi?"

Todd Ackerman has been head coach here for years. He's the reason I'm on the team. The reason all of us are. He's a great coach and man, but he takes no prisoners when it comes to the team and what's best for it.

"I could take a massage, if you're offering, Coach," Brooks quips.

"Shut the fuck up, Brooks, and get your ass back on this field! You as well, Oakley! Vacation's over!"

Laughing, we both get up from the bench and jog back onto the field.

It's good to be back out here, with the guys. But I'm also eager to get back home to Dillon.

Just so I can fuck her, obviously.

No other reason.

twenty-six

DILLON

I STARE AT THE blank Word document in front of me. The cursor blinking at me.

What am I going to write about?

I have some ideas saved, but they're on my laptop back home. I'm using West's laptop that he's kindly lent to me.

He went to training early this morning. Said he'd be back home later this afternoon, so I have all this free time to write.

I can do this.

I pick my coffee cup up and take a sip. *God, that's good.*

West has this fancy built-in coffee machine that he had to teach me how to use. The coffee is divine. I could live with this coffee machine and be the happiest gal in the universe.

The lifeblood of any writer is coffee. And wine. Also snacks.

I currently have coffee and snacks. The snacks are Haribos because they remind me of being on the island. The wine will come later. I have to be a sensible adult and drink after five. Unless the writing goes shit, and then I'm cracking open a bottle early. That's when I pull out the *it's five o'clock somewhere* line to make myself feel better about drinking in the early afternoon.

Maybe I should have a mid-morning mimosa. Might get the creativity flowing. I could pretend I'm still in the Maldives.

No. Don't be a lush. Coffee now. Alcohol maybe later.

Okay, definitely later.

But now, words.

What to write?

What to write?

Nothing. I literally have nothing. I now have all this free time to write, and I have nothing to write. *Bloody typical.*

I can't waste this time that I have though. Because at some point, I will have to go home. I can't stay here forever. Even though I would love to.

Yes, my crush on West is still thriving. Maybe growing a little.

Okay, a lot. But I have it under control. Kind of.

I open my notepad and pick up my pen. West bought them for me yesterday. It was kind of sweet. Okay, a lot sweet.

He ordered them on Amazon. Did you know they have same-day delivery with Prime in America? Yeah, me neither. I wonder if we have that back home. I have Prime, but my deliveries come next day. I feel so cheated.

Anyway, we were talking about my writing, which was when he offered to lend me his laptop so I didn't have to buy a new one to work on. He has a MacBook. Like top-of-the-range MacBook. I have a shitty laptop back home that cost me two hundred quid. I feel so swish right now, using his MacBook. Also, I am nervous as fuck, having liquids around it. Not enough to stop me from drinking coffee though. Or wine later, of course.

Anyway, back to the notepad. He said he had a surprise for me and pulled out an Amazon box from behind his back, and I opened it up to find this notepad, pen, and a mug. Which is what I'm drinking my coffee out of. All of them with funny quotes on it.

Apparently, another thing I told him when I was drunk was my love of coffee mugs with funny quotes on them.

On the front of the mug, it says, *And then God said, "Let there be sexy people." So, he made writers. And West Oakley.*

I have a feeling that he added the last part at the bottom. It's cheesy as fuck, and I love it.

The notepad says, *Please do not annoy the writer. She might put you in a book and kill you.*

And the pen's quote says, *Fuck off. I'm busy.*

Honestly, they are the best gifts I've ever received. I love them.

And I really should use them. Meaning, *Write something, woman!*

I stare at the blank page. Sigh. Put the pen down and take a sip of my coffee. Then, grab a handful of Haribos out of the bag, shove them in my mouth, and start chewing.

I stare out the window for a little while. Get up and walk around. Do some stretches. Consider putting the television on and then talk myself out of it because I really do need to write.

Sit back down and stare at the blinking cursor.

Pick my coffee up and drain it.

Then, I go make another coffee and get some crisps—or chips, as they call them here. Pour half the bag into a bowl so that I don't eat them all and take them and my fresh coffee back to the table and sit down.

The document is still blank. The cursor is still blinking at me.

For Christ's sake, why is this hard?! I love writing, and I'm a good writer.

I can do this.

Grabbing my phone, I select the Music app and put some songs on at random. "Cruel Summer" by Bananarama starts to play. I love this song. Hearing it play gives me a warm feeling in my chest, and for some reason, it makes me think of West and being in the Maldives with him. Maybe I heard it playing when I was there with him.

Holding on to that warm feeling, I close my eyes and try to think of some of the ideas that I wrote on my laptop back home. I shift through them in my mind, but nothing sticks. Maybe it's because I'm still in the holiday mood. This song definitely has me feeling that way.

Ooh. Maybe I should write a book where the heroine is on holiday, like I just was.

Maybe she meets a guy while she's there. Like I met West.

They hook up. Have lots of sex. Like West and I did …

Wait.

Holy shit. I think I have it.

No, I don't think. I definitely do have it.

My mind starts to spin with ideas. My heart beating with the excitement of a new story.

I think I can do this. I really do.

Then, I blink open my eyes, press my fingers to the keys, and start typing.

twenty-seven

DILLON

"HONEY, I'M HOME." HE'S all freshly showered after coming back from training.

My eyes flick to the clock on West's laptop. It's after four p.m. Bloody hell, I've been writing pretty much all day without a break.

That's never happened to me before.

I notice that my hands are aching. But it's a good kind of ache. The *I achieved something today* ache.

Feeling happy to see him, I pop out of my seat, run over to him, and jump into his arms. He catches me with an *oomph*, my legs going around his waist, his hands cupping my butt. My fingers thread into his hair, and I plant a kiss on his lips. He moans and dives into the kiss without hesitation.

When our mouths break apart, we're both breathing heavier.

"Hey." I smile at him.

"Hey yourself." He gives my butt a squeeze.

"I wrote today," I tell him, unable to contain my excitement.

"That's great."

"Like, I wrote all day! I was struggling at first, but then I got this idea, and bam! I couldn't stop writing."

While I've been saying all of this, West has carried me into the kitchen. He sets me down on the countertop, goes to the fridge, and gets a bottle of water.

"Want anything?" he asks me.

"No, I'm good."

I watch him twist the cap off the bottle and then take a drink. Is it weird that I'm getting turned on from watching the way his throat works when he swallows?

"How was training?" I ask when he lowers the bottle from his mouth.

"Brutal. Coach had us running drills for hours. I'm tired. Even my ass muscles ache."

"Aw, poor baby." I pout. "No sex for you tonight then."

His eyes snap up to mine. "I said I was tired, Double D. Not dead."

I laugh softly. "I can give you a massage if you want?"

"I want."

"But before the massage, I need to ask you something. Well, run something by you."

"How about massage while you run something by me?"

"Deal."

I hop off the counter and follow West to the sofa. He sits down, and I move to sit next to him. He's obviously not happy with this seating arrangement because he picks me up and moves me to sit in his lap, facing him. Then, he takes hold of my hands and places them on his shoulders. He's tired, yet he still has the strength and energy to pick me up and move me around. I wish I had that kind of energy left when I was tired. When I'm tired, I struggle to pick up the remote control to turn the television on.

I start to massage his shoulders, and he groans, laying his head back against the sofa and closing his eyes.

"This pressure okay?" I ask as I knead his muscles with my fingers.

"Perfect."

I run my fingers up his neck, pull the tie from his hair, and then slide my fingers into the dirty-blond strands, massaging his scalp.

"That feels good," he groans.

"So, this thing I need to ask you …"

"Uh-huh?"

"Well, my book idea, the one I've spent all day plotting out and writing?" I feel a frisson of excitement inside me at the mere thought. "It's kind of about me and you."

"Okay."

"Okay, as in a questioning okay? Or okay as in, yes, that's okay?"

"Okay, as in a questioning okay."

"Don't you think it's crazy that there are variations of meanings for the same word in the English language? I honestly love it though. Words, I mean. I just love words and writing and—"

"Dillon."

"Oh. Right. So, yeah, the book is like fiction based on fact. I was thinking about us—you know, how we met—and then I thought, *Why don't I write a story about us?* Well, not about us. Write the story of how we met. You know, what took me to the island, how we agreed to start hooking up, and my coming here for an extended holiday. But not use our names or any details about you and me, or my mum and Tim, just use the basis of our meeting for the story. I started the first chapter from when I found out that Tim and my mum were having an affair and how I went on my honeymoon, alone. But instead of it being me, my character will have another name—one I haven't decided on. And so will Tim and Mum, but actually, in the story, she won't be the heroine's mum; she'll be her sister. So, like, changing it up, you know." I move my hands from his hair, tracing patterns over his cheekbones and jaw, giving his face a little mini massage, like I've had in the past when I had a facial. Then, I move my hands down to his chest and start massaging his pectoral muscles.

His eyes are still closed, and he's quiet. I wonder if he's fallen asleep.

"West, are you still with me?"

"I'm here."

"Okay, so of course, you'll be in the book but not as you. You'll be the hot guy who my heroine meets on holiday, and I'll write about her coming to America with him. All of our stuff, but I won't write the actual intimate things that have happened between us."

"You mean, the sex we've had."

"Yep."

"I don't mind you writing about that." He pops open an eye and grins.

"I'm sure you don't. And of course, the characters will have sex, just not exactly like we've had."

"And continue to have." He closes his eyes but slides his hands up my thighs, his fingers going dangerously close to deterring my thoughts toward actual sex instead of talking to him about writing the fictional sex.

"So, basically, I want to check that it's okay with you that I loosely use our time together for the basis of my book?"

"What, will my fictional name be in the book?"

"Oh. Huh. Well, I don't know yet. I haven't gotten around to choosing names for any of the characters yet."

"Just putting it out there, but I think King is a great name."

"King?"

"Of sex."

"Of course." I roll my eyes. "I'll take it into consideration." I move my hands up to his biceps, working the muscles there. "So, does that mean you're okay with me writing the book?"

"Sure. You're not using my name, so it's fine with me. In truth, I wouldn't care if you did use my real name." He lifts that big shoulder of his. "It's my team that would take issue with it. And my father."

"I get that. And like I said, it's fiction loosely based on reality." I move my hands lower to his abs and start rubbing them. "Thanks for being cool about this. Gah! It's so exciting. Also, I think I have the title for the book, but I wanted to check with you. I'm thinking of calling it *The Two-Week Stand*. You know, what we initially called our fling."

"You were the one who called it that, not me."

"Oh yeah, I did, didn't I?"

"Yep. And I like it. I think it's a cool name for a book. Not that I know much about romance books. So, when it's finished, will I get to read it?"

"You'd wanna read it?" I'm genuinely surprised.

The only person in my life who has ever asked to read my books is my aunt Jenny. But he's asking to read it when it's done, and my heart is going all soft in his direction.

He opens his eyes, looking kind of sleepy and gorgeous. "Course I would. I need to make sure you do my dick and fucking skills justice."

I poke him in the side, making him jump.

"I wanna read it because you're writing it."

"And for the sex scenes."

"Well, obviously."

I start massaging his shoulders again.

"So, while we're on the subject of favors, I have one to ask myself."

My hands pause on his shoulders. "Okay."

"Well"—he sighs—"I have a party that I have to go to in a few weeks."

"Okay."

"And I was wondering if you'd come with me."

"You're asking me to go to a party with you?"

"Yep."

My chest fills with happiness. "Of course I'll go with you." I start massaging him again.

"Cool."

"Whose party is it?"

"Well, it's my stepmom's fiftieth birthday."

"Your stepmom. As in the First Lady?"

"Yes …"

"And where is this party going to be held?"

"At their house."

My hands freeze again. Actually, my whole body freezes, stiffening. "You mean, the White House?"

"Uh-huh."

"You're asking me to go to the fiftieth birthday party of the First Lady of the United States at the White House?"

"Your voice sounds all squeaky."

"Of course it's squeaky!" I squeak. "It's the White House! The president and First Lady! It's a lot."

"It's really not. They're just people."

"To you!"

Shit! What am I gonna wear? I'm gonna have to go shopping. And also Google what one should wear to a party at the White House.

"You can't back out of going with me, Double D. You already said you'd go."

I stop freaking out and look at him. Really look at him. His brow is tense.

"I'm not backing out." I soften my voice. "Should I take it that you're not keen on the thought of going?"

His shoulders lift under my hands. "I just know how it'll go—that's all."

"How will it go?" I ask the question carefully.

Another shrug. "My dad will find some way to tell me what a disappointment I am to him, and I'll retaliate with some shit from the past."

"So, why go to the party?"

"Because it's expected. And I like Catherine. She's a decent person. She just married a dick."

I know he has a difficult relationship with his dad. But that's the most he's ever opened up to me about it. He's usually quite evasive when it comes to his father.

I'm not really sure what to say. I just know that I want to make him feel better. So, I do one thing that I know always makes him feel better. I lean in and press my lips to his, kissing him.

As I go to move back from the kiss when it comes to an end, West's arms band around me, keeping me close.

"You know, I was just thinking that you're probably going to need some inspiration for all those sex scenes you're gonna be writing."

I lift a brow. "I won't write the actual sex we've had," I remind him.

"I never said write the actual sex. I said inspiration to help you write it."

I see the look in his eyes, which screams sex, and my lower belly coils with anticipation.

"Oh, yeah, I could definitely do with the inspiration." I'm not gonna need to watch porn for any sex-scene inspiration while I've got him here to give me plenty.

"Wanna get started on that inspiration now?"

I bite my lower lip. "Uh-huh."

West slides his hand up my back and grabs a handful of my hair. He guides my head down to his, but he doesn't kiss me on the mouth. Instead, his lips land on my neck, and he starts to suck on that magical spot he found, which sends bolts of lust straight to my clit, making me moan.

"You like that?" he murmurs against my skin.

"So much." *I like you too. Way too much.*

Fuck, where did that thought come from?

He moves me so that I'm lying on my back on the huge sofa, and he's now lying between my legs.

We start kissing, and he's moving his hips, rubbing his hard cock, which is encased in his sweatpants, against my clit, which is trapped beneath panties and leggings. But even through all this material, it feels good as hell.

"I need you inside me." My chest is dancing up and down with excitement.

"I know I said inspirational fuck but quickie now. Long, inspirational fuck later."

When West says quickie, he means no foreplay. Not that this will be quick. The man doesn't know the meaning of the word.

Not that I'm complaining, of course.

He sits up, divesting himself of his clothes, while I quickly pull off my leggings, panties, T-shirt, and bra.

Then, we're both naked, and he's back on me. Skin to skin. And nothing has felt better in my life than being naked with this man.

He kisses my mouth while he slides inside me.

When he's to the hilt, he pauses. Stops kissing me. Just stares into my eyes.

My heart starts to thrum in my chest.

I feel like something changes in this moment. I don't know exactly what. But something.

He starts to move, slowly fucking me, but doesn't take his eyes from mine.

"I like you," he says in a rough, quiet voice.

My mouth dries. I lick my lips. "I like you too."

Our eyes stay locked on each other's, and with his slow thrusts and words ringing in my ears and the intensity of the moment, I start to feel a pressure on my chest.

Like the feelings that I have for him—the ones I've been hiding, locking away—are breaking down the door and forcing their way out.

It's too much. I'm feeling too much for him. And if I keep looking into his eyes, he's going to see exactly how I feel.

He's going to know that I'm falling for him.
Fuck.
I'm falling for him.

twenty-eight

WEST

"WEST, I'M SO HAPPY you're here. It's been too long since we last saw you." Catherine kisses me on the cheek.

"Happy birthday, Catherine."

We're at the White House for my stepmom's birthday. She's having a gathering of family and close friends to celebrate.

"Thank you." Her eyes immediately go to Dillon, who's standing at my side.

"Catherine, this is Dillon."

"Hi, ma'am. Mrs. First Lady," Dillon stumbles. "God, sorry. I'm so nervous. Happy birthday."

She puts out her hand to shake, but Catherine leans in and hugs her and kisses her cheek.

My stepmom is a wonderful woman. Too good for my dad. Just like my mom was.

"It's so lovely to meet you, Dillon. You're from England. Whereabouts?"

"East Yorkshire."

"I've been to England but only London. I've heard that Yorkshire is beautiful."

"Yes, it is." Dillon sounds so formal that it makes me want to laugh.

My father strides over, deciding to honor us with his presence. "Weston." He sticks his hand out for me to shake.

No hugs from the old man. I can't remember a time when he ever hugged me.

I take him in. It's been a while since I last saw him in the flesh. He has more gray in his hair than he did before. I hate to admit it, but I do look like him. Staring at him is like looking at myself in the future. Except I can't even imagine having his clean-cut hair and wearing a suit every day. The one I have on tonight feels like it's choking me. Although I did like the way Dillon reacted when she saw me wearing it, and her eyes said that she had definite plans on removing it from me tonight.

"Dad." I release his hand and watch as his eyes slide to Dillon. "This is my friend Dillon," I tell him. I don't know why I felt the need to call her *my friend* to him. Even after all these years, I'm still subconsciously choosing my words with him so as not to get the third degree over my life choices and how they'll affect him. "Dillon, this is my father, President Mitch Oakley."

"Hi, Mr. President. Gosh, it's so wonderful to meet you."

My father says nothing, his eyes doing that probing thing he does when he sees a potential threat. Dillon is a beautiful woman. That fact does not escape him. But even he will overlook beauty if it's a perceived threat to his political ratings.

Maybe bringing Dillon with me tonight was a mistake.

With a few simple words, my father has the ability to make people feel like a bug he's about to squish under his Ferragamos. Probably part of what makes him a great president.

I don't want him to make Dillon feel shitty. I have to take his crap. She doesn't.

"Dillon is from England, Mitch," Catherine imparts happily. "Isn't that wonderful?"

"Hmm. So, what brought you to our country, Dillon?"

No *hello* or *nice to meet you.*

God, he's an ass at times.

"Oh, erm …" Dillon's eyes nervously shoot to mine. "Holiday. Sorry, vacation. I'm here on vacation."

She's so nervous. I just want to pick her up and carry her out of here.

"How did you two meet?" he asks me.

I hold his stare. He's checking to see if I've brought home another scandal for the press to run a story about. He's not worried for my sake, but his own.

"On vacation." I'm not making this easy for him.

His eyes go to Dillon. "So, you were on vacation first in the Maldives and now America?"

Dillon swallows. "Yes, sir. I, um … I was on vacation first in the Maldives. But when West suggested I come to America after my vacation ended there, I thought it would be a good place to get inspiration for my new book. I'm a writer. Author. I write books."

"What type of books do you write?" Catherine asks Dillon. "Will I know them?"

"Oh no." Dillon laughs softly. "I'm not well known at all. I self-publish my books. I write romance."

"Oh, how wonderful!" Catherine beams at her. "I love romance books. Come with me, and we'll get a glass of champagne and talk all things romance and books."

She threads her arm through Dillon's and leads her off, and I'm thankful to Catherine for whisking her away from the awkwardness of this conversation. I watch them go for a few seconds before turning back to my father.

"So, you brought home some random girl that you met on vacation?"

"No, I invited a friend to come stay with me for a little while. I'm surprised you didn't already know about Dillon."

He gives me a look. "Of course I knew. I just didn't expect you to bring your latest fling with you here to Catherine's birthday party."

"She's a friend."

"Whom you've known for a few weeks. I'm assuming you're screwing her. Do you really think bringing some hook-up back home with you was a good idea after the reason you went on the vacation in the first place?"

It's hilarious that he's giving me a hard time about having a fling when this man spent all of his married life to my mother—and maybe his married life to Catherine—fucking anything with a pulse.

I clench my jaw. "I went on vacation because of a video of something that I did when I was a kid."

"You were seventeen and snorting coke off a random girl's stomach."

"Seventeen. Ergo a kid."

"I had a job when I was seventeen. Not partying and stuffing drugs up my nose."

"I was hurting over Mom's death. I made a bad choice. I'm not proud of it."

"Your mother had been dead for two years at that point. You can't use her passing as an excuse for everything."

I feel all the old hurt come rushing back, angering the fuck out of me. "It's not an excuse, but not everyone could get over her death in point-three seconds after she died, like you," I hiss.

His jaw clenches. "I mourned your mother."

I laugh humorlessly. "Yeah, fucking your assistant must've really helped you to deal with the grief."

"Is that why you do this shit? Bring some random girl you picked up on vacation here, just to get back at me for the past?"

"Believe it or not, *Mr. President*, not everything is about you."

"Hi … um, I'm really sorry to interrupt." It's Dillon, and my eyes close on a sigh. There's no way that she didn't hear what he just said. "Catherine, um, I mean, the First Lady got taken away to greet some guests who had just arrived and she asked me if I would send you over," she says to my dad.

My dad stares at me a beat. "We'll talk later," he says to me and then looks at Dillon. "Enjoy your evening."

Dillon watches him stride away before she looks back at me.

"Any chance you didn't hear any of that?"

She gives me an awkward smile. "He's not keen on me, huh? I mean, I get it. It's fine."

"This really is a case of *it's not you, it's me*." I reach out and take hold of her hand, tugging her a little closer. "My father looks at my choices in life not as how they'll affect me, but how they'll affect his approval ratings."

Nothing I've ever done—or will do—is good enough for him. It's always been this way, and it only got worse when he realized that I wouldn't be going into politics and headed into the NFL instead.

It's funny. Any other parent would be over the fucking moon that their only son got drafted into the NFL but not my father. He sees it as a disappointment.

She blinks up at me. "Did he really"—she lowers her voice—"do what you said … after your mum died?"

I sigh and nod. I also got the privilege of walking in and seeing him fucking her over his desk. My mother's body was barely even cold. But then it shouldn't have come as a surprise. He screwed anything with a pulse in all the years that they were married, so her death wasn't going to slow him down.

"So … your full name is Weston?" She bites down on a smile.

I know she's changing the subject, trying to lighten the mood, and I could kiss her for it.

"Where did you think West came from?"

"The compass." Her lip breaks free from her teeth and becomes a grin. "Weston," she repeats, musing. "Hmm … I like it. I think I'm gonna call you that from now on."

"Please don't."

"Well, seeing as you asked so nicely, like I did all the times I asked you not to call me Double D and you did … then I'm definitely gonna keep calling you Weston, *Weston.*"

It's my turn to grin. I move a little closer to her and lower my voice. "Have I told you how utterly fuckable you look tonight?"

Her breath catches. "You might have mentioned it once or twice."

She's wearing a full-length red dress, which her tits look amazing in. It has a slit up the leg to her thigh, which gives me easy access, and she has on these gold heels that have straps around the ankles, which make her legs look even longer. Her hair is down and curled, and I'm dying to get my hands in it. Preferably when my cock is either in her mouth or pussy. I'm not fussy; I'll take whatever I can get from her.

An idea comes to me. "You want a tour?"

She blinks up at me. Just looking at her is making my dick hard. "Of the White House?"

I was thinking more my cock, but we'll go with that for now.

"Yeah."

She stares at me for a beat, and then understanding floods her eyes.

Yeah, baby, I want to fuck you right now.

She bites the corner of her lip. Her breathing gets a little faster. "Okay," she says softly.

Taking her by the hand, I lead her out of the room filled with people and out into the large hallway. The Secret Service agents stationed in the hall acknowledge our presence.

"I'm taking my guest on a tour," I tell them.

"No problem, sir." One of them nods. "Enjoy your tour, miss."

"I will. Thank you."

We walk down the hallway. Her heels clicking on the floor. Just the sound of them … the thought of fucking her in those heels has my feet moving faster. She doesn't complain though.

I stop at the first door I come to and open it up, checking inside. *Empty. Perfect.*

I lead her inside and shut the door behind us. The room is already lit by the lights in the glass display cases, so I don't bother turning the light on.

I watch her walk into the room, looking at the items in the display case. I go and sit down on the round banquette bench in the middle of the room, just watching her.

She's a fucking goddess.

I've known a lot of women in my time. None like her though. She is something else entirely. And I'm going to fuck her right here, right now.

She moves from one display case to the next, her fingertips pressing against the glass. "These look old."

"They are."

"Surely not as old as you?" She turns her head, resting her chin on her shoulder, and grins at me.

I raise a brow. "Just for that, I'm going to spank you."

"That so?"

"Mmhmm."

"And what if I don't want to be spanked?"

"I'm sure you'll be agreeable to it when you're riding my cock."

She turns to face me and leans back against the glass. "Such a dirty mouth."

"Makes you wet though, doesn't it? I bet your panties are already soaked, and I haven't touched you."

"Wouldn't you like to know?"

"I'm going to know." I spread my legs and beckon her with my finger. "Come here."

She holds out on me for a few beats, but then she's walking toward me. She stops between my legs and stares down at me, brow raised, as if to say, *I'm here. Now, what are you going to do with me?*

Oh, baby, I'm going to do a lot with you.

I slide my hand up her thigh, but my fingers don't meet bare skin.

"You're wearing pantyhose." I frown.

"I was coming to the White House. I wasn't coming here with bare legs."

So proper yet so fucking dirty. Gripping the flimsy fabric, I rip it from her leg and then do the same to the other.

"Feel better?" She's trying to act like she's pissed off, but the flush on her chest tells me otherwise.

"Much."

Then, I slip my hand between her legs and press my palm to her panties. "Soaked, like I thought."

She leans forward and presses her hand against my cock. "Hard, like I thought."

Fuck, she's hot.

Her brow is raised. Both of our chests are rising and falling.

Then, we're kissing. Hard and fast.

I grip the backs of her thighs and lift her onto my lap, so she's straddling me.

"I'm gonna fuck you so hard." I yank down the front of her dress and capture her nipple with my teeth.

"Are you sure this is a good idea?" she pants.

"The best one I've ever had."

"What if someone comes in?"

"No one's coming." *Except for us.* "Get my cock out."

Fingers fumble with my belt and zipper while I suck on her tit. When her hand wraps around my dick, it's like fucking heaven.

She starts jacking me off. I yank her panties to the side and plunge two fingers inside her.

I catch her moan with my mouth. I don't think anyone will hear, but I'm also not willing to test that theory. I want to fuck my girl, and nothing is going to stop me.

My girl.

Well, that's a new thought.

Dillon's head falls back, and she starts riding my hand. "Jesus … West, keep doing that, and I'm gonna come."

I pull my fingers from her pussy, and she lets out a moan of frustration. I get a possessive kind of satisfaction, knowing how much she wants me … needs me in this moment. Even if only to make her come.

"Why did you stop?" she huffs.

"Because I need to be inside you when you come." I grip the elastic of her thong and snap it, tearing it from her body. Then, I shove the panties in the inside pocket of my jacket.

She raises a brow. "You're keeping them?"

"Souvenir. Now, climb up on my dick." I slap her ass. "And ride me hard."

"So fucking bossy," she mutters but does as I asked.

She rises up onto her knees. I hold out my dick, and she slides down on him. Her sweet, soaked pussy grips my dick like she owns him.

Maybe she does.

When she's full of me, her ass pressed to my lap, she shudders over me.

Our eyes meet. Her blues so wide. So trusting. So needy. I cup her face with my hand and glide my thumb over her lips. Lips that are painted red. I want that lipstick all over my mouth. Grabbing a handful of her hair, I tug her mouth down to mine and kiss her.

Her tongue sweeps over mine, and this sudden, intense urgency to have her, to be even closer to her, hits me out of nowhere.

It's like a thirst. A hunger I need to sate.

I need more of her. All of her.

What's happening to me?

I feel dizzy. Hot. Needy.

I tug my tie loose and unbutton the top of my shirt. "Fuck me," I groan into her mouth. "I need you to fuck me."

She rides me hard, but nothing feels enough right now. I feel insane. Like I could fuck her forever and I'd never get close to getting everything I want from her.

All my senses are filled with her. The sounds she makes. The way she smells … the way she touches me.

She's taking over me. I feel out of control.

What the fuck is wrong with me right now?

Maybe I just need the control. I need to be the one fucking her.

Shifting forward, holding on to her, I take us down to the floor. I shove my pants down my ass, and I start fucking her hard. My hands planted on either side of her head on the floor, I pound into her over and over.

When she starts to come, she bites her lip to contain the curse and cries that I know she wants to make. I watch her come. Her eyes slam shut, ecstasy covering her features, and nothing has ever looked more beautiful in this moment than her.

Nothing has ever been more beautiful than her.

I feel this tightening in my chest and that fucking dizziness again.

What the fuck is going on?

Maybe I'm having a heart attack.

Well, what a way to go.

West Oakley, player for the Ravens, dies from heart attack while fucking his girl.

There I go again with this my girl *shit.*

Dillon isn't mine. I don't have a girl. And I don't want one.

I move my hips again, but I don't go hard this time. My movements are slower. I bring my mouth to hers and kiss her. Her fingers slide into my hair, pulling the tie from it. My hair falls around my face.

"Come for me," she whispers.

I increase my tempo a bit but not much.

If someone were looking in from the outside, they might say I was making love to her right now. But I'm not. Because I don't love her.

Fuck, my head is messed up tonight. It's the fight with my dad. Seeing him always messes with me.

Shutting my eyes, I bury my head into her neck and start to fuck her again. Hard. And harder.

Her arms come around me, holding on.

The sound of my skin slapping hers and the feel of her tight, wet pussy gripping my cock drive me exactly where I need to be.

When I'm done emptying myself inside of her, I lift my head, needing her mouth.

Our eyes meet before our lips do, and something happens in this moment. I don't know what. But there's something.

Shutting down whatever it is, I kiss her, and I keep kissing her until we can't stay there any longer and we're forced to clean up and rejoin the party.

But I'm off-kilter all night. Like something isn't right.

And it isn't until I'm lying in my bed later that night with Dillon's body curled around mine that I realize what's wrong with me.

I have feelings for her.

I'm starting to feel things for her. Real things. And I can't because I can't be the man she needs. That she deserves.

I know that I need to end this thing between us. For both our sakes. But selfishly, I'm not ready to do it yet.

I just need a little more time with her.
Then, I'll end things with her.

twenty-nine

DILLON

I TYPE, *THE END*. And sit back in my chair.

Holy shitting noodles. It's finished. *The Two-Week Stand* is officially done.

Well, not officially done. There will be edits and rewrites. But the first rough draft is complete.

Halle-bloody-lujah.

I can't believe I finished a book in four frigging weeks. Who knew I could write one so quickly? Not me! I guess when you have tons of free time and the story is already there in your head because you've lived almost all of it, then it's easier to do. The only changes I had to make were names and sex scenes, but who doesn't love coming up with a good sex scene, right? And also, I had to write the ending from scratch because, obviously, West and I haven't had our ending. Yet.

And maybe we won't. It's not something either of us has discussed. Currently, we're acting like we're in a relationship but under the guise of still having a fling.

Things are amazing between us. We had one weird day. It was the day after the party at the White House. He was a little cold toward me. I did worry that he was going to say that things had come to an end for us. But the next day, he was back to being his normal self, so I put it down to him feeling off after spending time with his dad.

I've really fallen hard for the guy. I can't remember ever feeling like this for anyone else.

I know. Stupid. But also inevitable. It'd be hard not to fall for him.

Sometimes, he looks at me, and I think he feels the same. Especially when he's inside me. But it could just be wishful thinking on my part. And I'm too afraid to ask in case the answer I get isn't the one I want to hear.

It's kind of like, you know, in the movies when someone's tied to a guillotine and their head is under the blade and the rope that's holding it up, stopping it from falling, is slowly fraying. And the person who's there to save you is caught up, fighting the bad guy, and you're just lying there, praying the rope doesn't reach the last strand and the blade doesn't drop.

Well, I'm the person on the guillotine. The fraying rope holding the blade is my time here. And West … well, he's either the villain or the hero of the story, depending on how things go.

I do know that I will at some point have to leave America. I'm not actually sure how long I can legally stay in the country without having to go home. I guess that's something I need to find out.

The thought of leaving West makes me want to throw up, so I try not to think about it too much. Meaning I worry about it every single day.

But today is not that day because I've finished my book and it's party time!

I push my chair back and go into the bedroom, where West is watching a game tape.

He's lying there on the bed, shirtless, wearing just a pair of shorts. The remote is in his hand, resting on his chest.

Gorgeous. I have to hold back a sigh of appreciation.

"Hey," I say.

He hits pause on the remote and looks at me. "Hey yourself."

"So, I have news." I'm almost bouncing on my toes with excitement to tell him. "I finished my book."

He sits up. "You did? That's amazing!"

He opens his arms up for a hug, which obviously, I'm all in for. I practically jump into his lap.

"You wrote that book quick. I mean, that is quick, right?"

I ease back a little, so I can look at him. "Yeah. Really quick. It just poured out of me. I mean, I knew the bones of the story." I indicate my finger between him and me. "So, that helped immensely, and I had a lot of free time to write that I didn't used to have before. So, yeah, it's done. This is just the first draft, and it needs to be edited and stuff." I pause and bite my lip. "But I was wondering if you wanted to read it. I know you said before that you'd want to read it, and I would totally love it if you did. But you don't have to. No pressure at all."

"Dillon."

"Yeah?"

"I want to read it."

I smile, and I know it's goofy as fuck. I probably have hearts in my eyes right now. "I know you're busy at the moment, so whenever is fine."

"I want to read it now."

"Really?"

"Really." He smiles, and my insides melt like ice cream in the sun.

It's official. I love this man.

Oh, of course you do, you fucking idiot. You've been in love with him for ages.

The fact that you can't tell him how you feel and that you have zero bloody clue how he feels about you is the problem.

"Okay. Let me grab your laptop." I climb off the bed. "You can read it straight from the laptop if you want. Unless you'd prefer me to print it out, which I can do."

"Laptop is fine."

"Cool. Well, I'll just go get it."

I practically skip out of the room and over to the dining table to get his laptop. I don't skip back for the obvious reason—that knowing me, I'd probably fall and break his laptop.

He's still sitting where I left him when I come back to the bedroom.

I hand over his laptop. "It's right there on the screen. Actually, it's at the end, so you'll need to go to the beginning." I lean around the laptop and scroll the document to the top. "There, it's ready."

Then, I just stand there, next to him.

"Are you gonna stay and watch me read or …"

"Christ! No! I'll go make coffee or something. Then, I'll watch some TV. You want any coffee?"

"No, I'm good."

"Cool." I start to back away toward the door. "So, I'll just be out there, keeping busy."

"Okay."

"Want me to close the door?"

"Sure."

I shut the bedroom door behind me and slap my hand to my forehead, wishing I weren't such a moron. Then, I walk into the kitchen to make myself some coffee.

thirty

DILLON

I'M CURLED UP ON the sofa, just finishing my second cup of coffee, when I hear the bedroom door click open.

Shit. That was fast. I quickly glance at the clock. It's not even been an hour yet. Forty minutes at the most.

Oh God, he hates it, doesn't he? I mean, it's not been long, so he couldn't have read that much—unless he's a speed-reader. Even then, there's no way he could have finished a seventy-thousand-word book in that time. But then he doesn't have to read the whole book to hate it. Just the first part. Or maybe he's just taking a break, and I need to stop freaking out.

I sit up straight, put my coffee cup down, and smile at him. "Hey. All okay?"

He stays near the doorway, and I notice that he's wearing a shirt now.

Oh, maybe he has to go out somewhere, and that's why he stopped reading. Okay, I can relax now.

"You going out somewhere?" I ask him.

"No." He shoves his hands into the pockets of his shorts. "I read the ending, Dillon."

"Oh, um, okay." I laugh, but it sounds awkward to my own ears because I now have this off feeling in the pit of my stomach.

His voice sounded as stale as yesterday's bread, and the only time he calls me Dillon is when he's inside of me or annoyed with me. And he's definitely not inside me at the moment.

"So … did you hate it? Because it's fine if you did. I'm not sensitive. At all." I'm totally sensitive when it comes to my work, but he doesn't need to know that.

"Is that how you see this going?" He points at me and then himself. "Me declaring my undying love for you and proposing? Us getting married and having some fucking happily ever after?"

"What?" That off feeling in my stomach turns into worry. I push up from the sofa, getting to my feet. "No, of course not."

"You sure about that?" His expression is closed off. His jaw tight. He looks … resigned.

And that tightens the strings of worry inside me.

"Of course I'm sure. Just because I wrote the ending of the story that way doesn't mean anything. It's just a story."

"About us."

"Loosely based on us."

"I read the beginning before I skipped to the ending. Everything about it—how we met, et cetera—is exactly as it was."

"You knew I was going to do that! But I can't finish the story with a sad ending. People won't want to read that. But writing it isn't a reflection of what I'm hoping for." *But it is. If I'm really honest, it's all I want.*

"You're telling me, that ending is purely fiction?"

"It is fiction when it hasn't happened."

He exhales a sigh, and the empty, desolate sound sets off an ache deep inside of me. Like I can hear all of his thoughts in that one breath, and none of them are good.

"What I read in there, that wasn't an ending. It was the start of something, and we will have an ending, Dillon." He pauses. "And I think that ending should be now."

Even when you know something is coming, it doesn't make the impact of it hurt any less. It's like a physical blow to the body. And the hurt from his words is cutting through my skin and climbing into my blood and bones.

I stare at him, feeling lost, my heart racing with panic. There's no air in my lungs. Like someone is standing on my chest, crushing the life out of me.

He doesn't want this anymore.

Doesn't want *me*.

Isn't that the story of my life?

The unwanted child.

The unwanted fiancée.

Now, the unwanted fling.

Pain runs through my veins like poison.

I could argue with him. But what would be the point? I do want him. I want to be with him. And it would only delay the inevitable. Just because my heart was hoping for different … well, that's on me, not him. The only person I have to blame is myself. Yes, at times, this felt like we were in a relationship. And there were signs that maybe he wanted more. Moments when I thought he might feel the same as I do.

But he doesn't. I'm not what he wants.

"Okay." My bottom lip trembles. I press my lips together and swallow past the burning ache that's climbing its way up my throat. My insides are crumbling under the earthquake of devastation that I'm feeling. "I'll … do I have time to look for a flight back home, or do you want me to leave right now?"

"Jesus, Dillon." He shakes his head. "I'm a lot of things, but I'm not fucking heartless."

It's right there on the tip of my tongue—to ask if he's sure about that. But that'd be a shitty thing to say. West never promised me anything. He was clear from the start. It's not his fault that I fell in love with him. That's on me.

"I didn't say … I just …" I wrap my arms over my stomach, needing to hold on to something and all I have is myself. "I'll look for a flight now." I pick my phone up from where I left it on the sofa. But I'm not sure where to go. I don't want to stand here and look for a flight while the reason my heart is breaking is standing right there in front of me. "I'll pack my things while I look." I walk past him and to the bedroom, and it's a stupid move on my part because his scent hits me straight in the solar plexus.

Closing the door, I sit down on the edge of the bed and pull up Google. I start searching for a flight back home. Preferably the cheapest possible.

My hands are shaking. My legs too.

It's okay, Dillon. It's gonna be okay.

I find a flight that leaves early tomorrow morning with two changes in Vienna and Frankfurt, but they'll get me to Manchester, and it's cheap. It's not like I'm in any rush to get back to England. I have nothing to go home to.

Tears well in my eyes.

I press the heels of my hands to my eyes to stop them from falling.

I'm okay. I've gotten through worse.

Sucking in a breath, I go to West's closet. I ignore all of his clothes hanging there, and I pull my two cases out from where they were stored. I open them both up, laying them on the floor. I pull my clothes from the hangers and drop them into the largest case. I get my underwear from the drawer he gave me to use. Then, I go to the bathroom, get my things from there, and drop them in the smaller case.

I close my cases up, and I sit back on my heels. A tear hits my leg.

Stop. No crying. Not here.

I wipe my face dry with my hands and then order an Uber from my phone.

Standing, I shove my phone in my back pocket and pull my cases upright. I get my bag from beside the bed. Remembering my phone charger, I unplug it and shove it in my bag, and then I hang it off my shoulder.

I glance around West's room, making sure I've not forgotten anything else. But all I see are the times when I lay in his bed with him, his arms wrapped tight around me.

God, this hurts.

So much.

I stand there, breathing in and out, fighting down the hurt and pain and panic that all want to be free to wreck me.

I've got this. I just need to get out of here.

Grabbing hold of my cases, I drag them out of his bedroom.

West is standing by the window, staring out. He turns when he hears me. His eyes go down to my cases and then up to me. There's no emotion there. Not even a flicker.

"I got a flight," I say, hating how raw and croaky my voice sounds.

"For tonight?"

I hate even more how normal his voice sounds. This isn't affecting him at all.

"Early tomorrow morning, but I'll just get a room at the airport hotel." I don't actually know if there is one, but if not, I'll just hang out around the airport. I don't see myself getting much sleep tonight anyway.

"No, just stay here tonight, and I'll drive you to the airport in the morning."

"It's fine, honestly."

There's no way I can stay here tonight. Knowing that he no longer wants me. I don't think I could bear to be under the same roof as him and not be with him.

"It's best if I go."

"Can I drive you to the airport?"

"No, it's fine. I've got an Uber coming."

"Can I at least help you with your bags?"

"No. I got them." My words are short because I need this over with. I need to get out of here.

"Okay." He rakes a hand through his hair, and I feel a pang of pain in my chest, knowing that I'll never get to touch him that way again.

My throat is burning, and tears are threatening my eyes again. I need to leave.

Dragging my cases to the front door, I leave them there. I go to the small closet where my shoes and jacket are and put them on.

I turn back to West. He hasn't moved. He's still standing in the same spot. And my heart aches so fucking much.

"So … I guess this is good-bye."

He says nothing, and I fidget on the spot, wanting more than anything to stay but knowing that I have to leave.

I open the door and drag my cases out into the hall. West still hasn't moved, hasn't said anything.

I take a step back into the apartment. "I just wanted …" My voice breaks, and I clear my throat. "I wanted to say thank you."

His brow furrows. It's the first real sign of emotion I've seen in him since he walked out of his bedroom and ended us. "You're thanking me?"

"For inviting me to stay here with you. It's been"— *everything*—"nice."

"Nice," he echoes.

My phone vibrates in my pocket. I get it out and look at the screen. "So, um … my Uber is here." It's time to go. My insides start to rattle as the reality of the situation takes hold.

This is the last time I'll ever see him. Ever speak to him.

I stare at him, desperately trying to soak up the last remnants of him that I'll ever have, imprinting him into my memory. Wanting him to come over to me. Say something, anything. Even if it's good-bye. But even more, I wish that he'd tell me he made a mistake. That he doesn't want me to go.

He does nothing.

I take a step back as disappointment cuts through me, and I reach for the door handle to close it.

"Dillon."

My heart pauses at the sound of my name. I look over at him. "Yes?"

He stares at me for what feels like an eternity. Then, he looks away. "Have a safe flight."

"Have a safe flight." Those four words crush the small fragments that remain of my heart to dust and make my eyes sting with tears that I can't stop.

Turning from him, I shut the door. The thunk of it closing is so final.

The end.

thirty-one

DILLON

TIME SLOWS DOWN WHEN your heart is hurting. The days drag on. I've been home for three days. It's been four days since I walked out of West's apartment. It feels like it's been longer.

Not seeing him is agony of the worst kind. I miss him so much. I spent nearly seven weeks with him. The first two of them solidly. I got so used to being with him that not having him around is strange. And shitty. So very fucking shitty.

When I got to the airport after the Uber driver dropped me off, I ended up wandering around and sitting in the airport all night until my flight boarded in the early morning. I was sleep-deprived and emotional. My journey back was hella long with the two stops and plane changes, and looking back now, it wasn't the best idea I've ever had. Being stuck on a plane with nothing but my thoughts for company for long periods of time was torturous. But I hadn't exactly been thinking straight when I booked that flight.

I just keep thinking if I hadn't asked him to read the book, maybe I would still be there with him right now. Maybe if I'd never written the book at all, things would be different. But I guess it was always destined to end at some point. West and I had an end date stamped on us, but it was only him who was privy to the exact date and time.

The funny—or not so funny—thing is, I don't even have a copy of *The Two-Week Stand*. I wrote it on West's laptop, and stupidly, I never emailed it to myself as a backup. I wasn't even thinking about that when I left his apartment. It wasn't until I got home that I realized it. And I can't bring myself to text him and ask for him to send it to me.

I haven't heard a thing from him. Not even a text to check that I got home okay.

Not that I expected him to. Just hoped. But I guess when West is done with someone, he really is done.

So, after all of that, I have nothing. I don't have West, and I don't have my book.

Maybe that book was a curse anyway. I mean, West read some of it and dumped me. Not dumped me. You can't be dumped if you're not in a relationship.

He just … put a stop to us.

Actually, you know what? He did break up with me. I don't give a shit what he might think or say, but for those seven weeks, we were in a relationship. He might not be grown up enough to admit it, but I am. And when he read that ending and saw that possible future with me, he got scared—okay, those are Aunt Jenny's words. She thinks he maybe has unresolved issues from his mum dying and finds it hard to get close to people. Maybe he's scared of losing them like he lost her. I didn't tell her about his difficult relationship with his dad. I trust Aunt Jenny implicitly, but that's West's private business and not mine to share. I only told her about his mum dying because it's public knowledge. You can literally Google him, and it's there in detail.

And I get what she's saying, but who the hell doesn't have issues? My dad died when I was a baby, and my mother screwed my fiancé. You don't get any more messed up than that! And I was there, ready to be with West.

But whatever.

Actually, no. *Screw him!*

So, I think I might have reached the anger stage of my grieving over our breakup.

Aunt Jenny says there are five stages to a breakup— denial, anger, bargaining, depression, and acceptance. They're supposed to go in that order, but mine have been all over the place, and I skipped a couple. I haven't had denial— probably because my relationship with West wasn't conventional. Weirdly, acceptance that it was over came first. I didn't try bargaining with him because I knew it was a lost cause and that his mind was made up. I've been dealing with the depression since I left his apartment, and now, apparently, I'm angry.

Thank God Aunt Jenny has gone to the shops to get us some more Prosecco because I could really do with a drink right now. She's also grabbing takeaway while she's out because she says I haven't been eating enough, and she's right. Maybe now that I'm feeling angry with West instead of just sad, I might feel like eating more.

I'm staying at Aunt Jenny's until I can get a job and a place sorted—you know, because of the whole having nowhere to live due to giving up my apartment to move in with the prick I was supposed to marry. Now, that definitely feels like eons ago. So much has happened since then. I can't believe I even considered marrying the prick. What was I thinking? Clearly, I wasn't.

I hear a knock on the front door. Jenny might have forgotten her key, but she hasn't been gone that long either, and we're not expecting anyone else.

I've been hiding myself away here. I've not even told my friends that I'm home yet. I'm just not up for peopling quite yet. Aunt Jenny told me that I made it into the local newspaper and that there was also a small segment in the nationals. I guess an unknown girl from Hull being seen with the American president's son would make news. Thankfully, people don't seem to know that I'm home, or if they do, they haven't figured out where I'm staying, and as I'm not going to be seen with West anymore, the story should die a quick death.

If only my heart would. At first, I did wonder if a heart was irreparable after being broken twice in a short period of time, but it's hanging in there, feeling all the hurt and pain and loneliness of missing West and the general shittiness that is my life. I'm just hoping this newfound anger will sort me out.

I get up from the sofa and make my way into the hallway and to the front door.

On my way there, I have these few seconds of stupidness where I think it might be West. That he's come to see me. Even though, deep down, I know it won't be him, my stupid heart still reaches for that notion, even with knowing I'll be left disappointed when I find out that it's not him.

I reach the door, push up onto my tiptoes, and look through the peephole. It's not West.

Pain and anger hit my chest like a punch—not because of the disappointment, but because of who's standing on the other side of the door.

I yank the door open and stare at the woman who gave me life. "What are you doing here?" I snap.

She smiles. "It's nice to see you too, darling."

"I know you're not here to see Jenny, so I'm guessing you're here to see me. How'd you know I was here?"

"I bumped into Phil at the pub last night. He said you were here. Said he saw you arriving the other day."

Phil is Aunt Jenny's next-door neighbor and someone my mother used to see years ago, before she got bored and tossed him aside for someone else. I should have considered that he might have seen me getting here the other day and told her. She has her fucking spies everywhere.

Still, I don't know why she's here. Or maybe I do.

"So, you waited until Jenny went out to stop by."

She shrugs her slender shoulders. "I was out and happened to see her pass by in my car, heading toward the supermarket, so I thought I'd take the opportunity to come see you."

"Ever think that I don't want to see you?"

"Now, don't be like that, darling."

"You slept with my fiancé!" I yell at her. I can feel all the old hurt and anger seeping up inside of me.

"Don't shout, Dillon. And you're still upset about that?" She waves a hand like it was nothing. Like my feelings are nothing. "Tim and I aren't together anymore. And honestly, sweetheart, I did you a favor. Better you knew what he was like before you tied yourself to him."

I stare at her, flabbergasted. I shouldn't be surprised by what she's saying because she's been doing it all of my life. Making herself out to be the hero in the story when she's actually the villain. But still, it stuns me to hear her say it.

I think it's in this moment that I realize what a true narcissist my mother actually is.

"Are you going to let me inside, or am I going to stand on the doorstep all night?"

I take a deep breath, clenching my jaw. "You slept with my fiancé. For months. Behind my back. You broke my fucking heart. I don't see that as you doing me a favor. So, no, Mum, you're not coming inside because I don't want you here. I don't want you in my life, period."

"You want me to say I'm sorry? Fine, I'm sorry."

"Wow." I press my hand to my chest. "If there was a medal to be won for shittiest apology ever, you would win. Hands down."

She huffs out a sigh, sounding irritated. "There's no need to be sarcastic. It all worked out for the best. You went off to the Maldives and met that gorgeous man there. I mean, the president's son, Dillon. I guess I did teach you well after all. Is he here?" She glances over my shoulder. "West, is it? Phil only said he saw you arrive but no man. But I figured you wouldn't be leaving a guy like that alone. I know I wouldn't."

And there it is. That's why she's here. Either she's set her sights on West—or higher—or she thinks there's some sort of payday to be made from this.

It's a sad, sorry kind of feeling to not even be disappointed at this point. Deep down, the instant I saw her through the peephole, I ultimately knew that she wasn't here for me. There was some other reason, something to do with her own selfish wants and needs.

And West was her target.

Well, she's missed out on that one. She's four days and about four thousand miles too late. Which gives me a weird sense of satisfaction.

Although it is a singular kind of pain to know that you're not loved by the one person who should love you. But I also get some clarity. Because the way she treats me has nothing to do with me or the person I am. It's all her.

Maybe something happened in her childhood that made her this way, and she carried it through to adulthood and never cared to make the change in herself when I came along. Or maybe she was just made this way. That I'll never know. But I know for damn sure that I am nothing like her, nor will I ever be the mother she is—or lacked to be—if I have a child of my own. My child will know every single day how much they are loved and wanted and that they are the only thing that matters.

I stare at her for what feels like the longest time, knowing this will be the last time I see her. Does it hurt? Of course. But it's also freeing. Knowing I'll never have to deal with her shitty treatment of me again.

I'm making the decision to cut her off to make my life better, and I know, ultimately, I'll be happier for it.

"We're done, Mum. You and me. I don't want to see you or speak to you again."

It's her turn to stare at me. "Are you being serious?" Her tone sounds angry.

I knew this was the way it would go. If she doesn't get her way, she turns nasty.

"Yes. I can't keep letting you hurt me over and over and looking the other way in hopes that you'll stop one day. I'm done."

"You always were an ungrateful little cow, Dillon. I should have aborted you when I had the chance."

Yes, that hurts. But it's not something I haven't heard come from her cruel mouth in the past.

"Good-bye, Mum."

I start to shut the door, but she stops it with her hand.

"You think now that you've got your fancy boyfriend, you're better than me, eh? Well, you're not! You're trash. And don't come running back to me when it all goes to hell, which it will because you screw up everything you touch."

If you wondered where my lack of confidence and self-loathing came from, well, it's from right there. From words like that, which I've heard my whole life.

"Let go of the door," I tell her calmly. I won't fight with her. I won't stoop to her level.

"You don't get to get rid of me that easily. I'm owed, Dillon, for all the years of my life that I lost, having you hanging on to me, dragging me down!"

"Not today, Satan."

I didn't see Aunt Jenny coming up the path. But I can't say that I'm not relieved to see her here.

My mum whirls around at the sound of Jenny's voice. "Oh, here she is. The warden at the gate. Why don't you just fuck off and mind your own business, Jenny?"

"Dillon is my business, and you're literally standing at my house, you dumb bitch. Now, get off my property, or I'll drag your cheap, skanky arse off myself." Aunt Jenny lowers the bags in her hands to the ground.

My mum lets out a mocking laugh. "You lay one finger on me, you fugly bitch, and I'll sue your fat arse for assault, and I would have a hell of a time spending your money." She puts her hands on her hips. "So, yeah, do it. Drag me off here."

I'm standing here, watching them in a standoff. I don't know what makes me think of it, but all I know is I want her gone, and I don't want Aunt Jenny to do something stupid and have my mother sue her because I know she would.

I quickly walk back into the living room while they're still yelling at each other, and I pick up the full cold cup of coffee that I didn't drink earlier off the coffee table. I walk back to the front door with it and pour it all over my mother's head.

She screams and whirls around at me. "You stupid little bitch! What the fuck did you do that for?"

"I was doing you a favor." I shrug. "Your hair looks dry, and I've heard cold coffee is good for it." Obviously, I've never heard that, but it felt good to pour a drink over her. Also, her vanity won't allow her to stay here, looking like that. It was the best and easiest way to get her to leave.

Aunt Jenny laughs while I just stare calmly at my mum, though my hand is trembling around the mug.

"I could sue you for this, you know?" she screeches at me.

I shrug my shoulders again and allow a smile this time. "So, sue me."

She glares at me for a moment. "This isn't over." She points a finger at me before she turns on her heels and stomps off.

I don't doubt for a second that it's not over. It'll take a while before she fully gets the message. But if I keep ignoring her, she'll eventually get it, and I'll finally be free of her and the hold she's had over me my whole life.

"That was awesome." Jenny picks the bags up and comes inside.

I shut the door behind her and take one of the bags from her hand.

"And a long time coming."

"I guess." I shrug for the third time in minutes. Guess I've turned back into a teenager.

Jenny stops in front of me, and then she reaches out and touches my arm, her kind eyes staring into mine. "Awesomeness aside, are you okay?"

"No." I give a sad smile. "But I will be."

"Yeah, you will." She wraps her free arm around me and hugs me, the safe, sweet, familiar scent of her Angel perfume soothing me.

Even though I'm being hugged by one of my favorite people in the whole world, I can't help but wish that it were West here, hugging me.

thirty-two

WEST

"YOU WANTED TO SEE me, Coach?" I stick my head in the open door of his office.

"Yeah. Take a seat, West."

West. He never calls me West. Always Oakley. This can't be good. I have this momentary panic that I'm gonna be traded.

Shit.

My heart starts to beat rapidly. I've been off my game this week in training. I know I have.

I knew letting Dillon go would be hard. I just didn't realize it'd be this hard. I'm not sleeping properly. She's everywhere in my apartment, like a ghost. I can still fucking smell her there. Every time I close my eyes, all I see are her tear-filled eyes. I hurt her. I fucking loathed hurting her, but I knew it had to be done. I can't be the man she deserves. If we were together, I'd just end up hurting her, way more than I did last week.

And ultimately, nothing really ever lasts. People hurt each other. They leave. They die.

I walk into his office, closing the door behind me, and take the seat across from him at his desk.

"You want something to drink?" Coach asks me.

He's offering me a drink. I'm so done. Fuck, I don't want to get traded. This place is my home. These guys are my family. Shit, Coach Ackerman has been more of a father to me than my own father ever has been.

I lost Dillon. I can't lose them too.

But you didn't have to lose Dillon. You chose to push her away. It's your fault that you're both miserable.

"Water." I clear my croaky throat. "Water would be great."

Coach goes over to the fridge he has in his office and pulls out a bottle of water. He hands it to me and then takes a seat at his desk.

In the silence, I unscrew the cap from the water bottle and take a drink. He doesn't start talking until I put the bottle down on his desk.

"How do you think training went for you today?"

"Good." *Shit.* I screwed up at every turn. He knows this, so I don't know why I'm lying. I sigh and slump in my seat. "Shit. I was shit."

"Yeah, kid, you were."

He doesn't mince words. It's what makes him a great coach. He won't pussyfoot around with his players. You're screwing up? He tells you. I'm just hoping my last week's performance isn't giving him a reason to push me out the door. He might like me. We might get along great. He cares for his players and their well-being. But the team's success comes first and foremost to him. And if my game is on the downslope—which it is—when it should be better because I'm in my prime right now, he's gonna worry about that. I'm just praying that a week's worth of fuckups hasn't changed his view on my playing ability. I know the higher-ups like the revenue that my name brings in, but if Coach wants me gone, then I'm gone.

If I get out of this office with my ass intact and my name still on the roster, I swear to God that I'll figure my shit out. I won't let my private life interfere with my game anymore.

This is what I get for getting too close to Dillon. I have no one to blame for the way I'm feeling right now or the way I made her feel. It's all on me.

"Look, West." He leans forward and rests his arms on his desk, linking his hands. "I'm not one to beat around the bush, so I'm just gonna say it."

Fuck. This is it.

"You need to get that girl back."

Huh. What?'

"I'm probably crossing some line here, but this needs saying. You're a good player, West. You've always been a good player. Reliable. You train and work hard. But I knew there was more in you, a greatness that you were holding back. I tried to get it out of you for years, and I'd see glimpses of it on the field. You'd pull some amazing shit out of nowhere, and then I wouldn't see it for another four or five games. That greatness, those moments … they're the only reason I've kept your ass on this team. Mainly because I figured, one day, you'd let go of whatever shit had been holding you back, and you'd explode onto the scene like you were always meant to. But honestly, lately, I was starting to get doubtful. Then, that shit in the press happened. Not your finest moment, but we've had worse than a player snorting a little coke at a party when he was a punk kid.

"You went away on that trip, and when you came back, it was like a switch had been flipped inside of you. You came on the field, and you were fucking here. That's why I pushed you all so hard that first day. Because you were flying and I wanted to see what was gonna come out of you.

"You fucking showed up that day, Oakley. And every day after that. Your game was at the level it was always meant to be. The rest of the team and I were pissing our pants for the season to start and to get you out there. Because if you kept going that way, then no one and nothing would stop you."

I know I was playing better after I got back. I felt better. Sure, Coach and the team were passing me praise, in line with where I was fucking up, but nothing that seemed out of the ordinary. I had no idea that I had been playing at my peak best.

"That all stopped a week ago. When your girl went home. And, yes, I know she left. I keep track of my boys' private lives. What happens out there affects what happens here." He taps his finger on the desk. "It's not a fucking coincidence that she left and your performance took a nosedive into the shit pit. You ain't even good anymore, kid. I've got rookies out there who can outplay you with their eyes shut."

"Gee, thanks, Coach."

"It's the truth, and you know it. You want your ass kissed? Then, get yourself to DC and spend some time listening to those bullshitting politicians because you sure ain't gonna get your ego groomed in here. Your daddy could be Jesus himself, and I'd still be saying the same things that I'm saying now. And that girl was good for you, Oakley. I don't know what you did to fuck it up—and I know you fucked it up because aside from the game, the one other thing us ballplayers are good at is fucking up our lives." He lets out a sigh.

"Your head's not in the game, Oakley, and I need it back before the season starts. I need the West Oakley who came back and showed us what he's actually made of. Now, I'm not here to tell you how to run your life. But something's gotta change. From what I'm seeing, that girl, she was a good look on you, and she made you happy. You came to the game better than ever. All those stresses and worries that you'd been carrying around left. I know it can't be easy, having your daddy sitting in the White House. But when something makes you as happy as I saw that girl make you, then a man would have to be a damn fool to let that go."

thirty-three

DILLON

THE COFFEE SHOP IS busy, and the line is long. It's midday on a busy Saturday. I've only been working here a week.

The day after the confrontation with my mum, I decided to drag my arse out of the house and back into the land of the living, and I saw the sign in the window that they were hiring. I'd gone to get a coffee and come back with a job. It's not forever, but the pay's okay, and the hours are good. It'll do me until I figure out what I'm actually going to do with my life.

This isn't my first busy day. Every day is busy here. People like their coffee. I do too.

I'm only taking the orders and working the till. I'm not making the coffee, thankfully; otherwise, the line would be even longer. I'm slow as shit.

I only get to make the coffee when the shop is quiet— to help me practice and hopefully get quicker.

I'm just glad to have a job and not be moping around Aunt Jenny's house. And a job means, I'm earning money, so I can look at getting my own place soon. I keep throwing around the idea in my head of investing the money my grandparents left me and buying my own place, so I don't keep paying rent, but something in my head stops me every time I have the thought of putting actual roots down here.

It's weird that the thought of marrying Tim didn't feel as much of a commitment as buying a house does.

If I didn't already know that I was never meant to be with that guy, then that would tell me.

I heard from an old colleague that Tim is with some other poor, unsuspecting girl who'd started work there. I could send her a message and tell her what he's like, but she probably wouldn't believe me. I know I wouldn't have in the beginning.

My mum hasn't been back around or in touch with me since I poured my coffee on her. I still can't believe I did that. Kind of funny that it was coffee that I poured on her, and then I got a job in a coffee shop. Some kind of weird irony or even maybe a joke in there.

I do feel sad that I no longer have a mum. But really, did I ever have one in her? No.

I have Aunt Jenny and my friends, and that's enough for me right now.

I'll start work on a new book soon. I was thinking I might write something outside of romance. Maybe crime. Or a good thriller. Get all my residual inner anger with my mum and West out in a book. Kill a few fictional characters to soothe my soul.

Do I still miss West? Of course I do. I miss him as much as I did last week, if not more. But I'm sure the ache of waking up every morning and remembering he's not there and the loneliness of climbing into bed at night and not having him to hold on to … well, it will get easier. It has to.

I'm sure at some point, my memories of him will fade.

Honestly, the thought of forgetting what he looks and sounds like scares me because memories are all I have. Along with the photos that I took of us and him on my phone, which I really need to get around to deleting or I'll never begin the process of moving on.

That's it. Tonight, when I get home from work, I'll delete them all from my phone.

I'll also pick up a bottle of wine on my way home to help me get through the process. Maybe two bottles. I'm not working tomorrow, so why the hell not?

"That'll be four pounds and eighty pence," I say to the woman I'm currently serving.

She gets her credit card from her purse, so I select Card Payment on the touchscreen till. The receipt prints off with her order details, which I line up on the counter for my colleague Shannon, who's busy making everyone's orders, and then I hand over the payment receipt to the woman.

"If you could just wait over to the side, your order will be with you soon," I tell her.

"What can I get you?" I turn my attention to the next customer, who's just moved up to the counter.

And my heart nearly falls out of my chest. Actually, I think it might have because I can't feel it beating in there anymore. I press a hand over it to check.

"Wh-wha-what are you doing here?" I stammer, staring into the face of the man who, the last time I saw, was telling me to *have a safe flight*.

"Hey, Double D," West rasps in that voice of his that I've missed so much.

Goose bumps explode all over my arms.

He places his hands on the counter and leans in a little closer. I get a whiff of his scent, and longing explodes in my chest.

"How've you been?" he asks in a soft voice.

Two weeks of silence, and that's what he asks me. How the hell does he think I've been doing since he tossed me out of his life? Shit. I've been shit.

And he's standing here in a black T-shirt and blue jeans, his hair hidden under a ball cap, looking beautiful.

In this moment, I think I actually hate him.

The longing that was in my chest is shoved out and replaced with anger. "Why are you here?"

"Can we talk?"

"No. I'm working."

"When's your break?"

"In an hour."

"Can we talk then?"

"I don't know."

"Dillon, please. I just want ten minutes of your time. That's all I'm asking."

I stare at him for a moment, weakening in his presence. "Okay. Ten minutes. But you'll have to wait until I'm on my break."

He smiles. "I'll wait, and I'll have a coffee while I do. You know how I take it."

I fix my jaw. "I've forgotten." Yes, I'm being childish and stubborn, but he doesn't get to just turn up here, unannounced, at my place of work and ask to talk.

"Americano with milk," he says softly.

"Medium or large?"

"Large, please."

"Takeaway or staying in?"

"Staying," he says, giving me a pointed look.

He's staying here the whole hour? I was hoping he'd go and come back. *For fuck's sake. How am I supposed to get through the next hour with him here?*

I ring his order through on the screen, my damn hand shaking the whole time.

"That'll be two ninety-five," I tell him without looking at him.

Using his Apple Pay on his watch—the fancy bastard—he pays for his coffee.

I print off both receipts, sliding one along the counter to Shannon and handing his to him, ensuring not to touch him.

"Wait over to the side, and your coffee will be ready soon," I tell him before moving on to the next customer.

I can't concentrate, knowing he's standing there. I can feel him watching me. But I refuse to look at him.

I almost breathe a sigh of relief when his coffee's ready and he goes and takes a seat, but he selects a table across from the counter, right in my eyeline.

The next hour is absolute torture. I can feel his eyes on me the whole time. Every time I chance a glance at him, he's watching me.

I don't even know why he's here. He could be here to beg for my forgiveness and ask me to get back with him. Which I absolutely will not do.

Yeah, sure you won't.

Or maybe he's here because he feels guilty about how we ended and he wants to apologize and then go home. Although traveling four thousand miles to apologize does seem a little excessive when he could have just called.

I just wish I knew what he wanted. I'm driving myself nuts here. I could ask one of the girls to cover, so I could take my break early. But I don't want to rush for him. I want to make him wait even if it means torturing myself in the process.

Finally. After what seems like an eternity, even though I've been busy this past hour, it's time for my break.

I grab my bottle of water from under the counter, and on shaky legs, I walk over to him, my heart taking the back door exit. My mouth dries, and I can no longer feel my legs shaking. I'm assuming they've gone numb.

I slide into the chair across from him. Setting my bottle on the table, I curl my hands around it. "You have ten minutes," I tell him. "But first, I have a question."

His look is wary. "Okay."

"How did you know where to find me?"

"I know people in high places."

I love and hate the smile that touches his lips in equal measure. So, I give him an unimpressed look.

He shifts in his seat. "I asked one of my Secret Service guys to locate your aunt Jenny's address. I went there, and she told me you were here."

I'll be having words with Aunt Jenny later. The traitor.

"Fine. Your ten minutes starts now."

He sits forward in his chair, pushing his empty coffee cup to the side, bringing him closer to me. "I love you," he says, flooring me.

Those words are like a bomb. Dropped in the middle of the table.

I feel them hit my chest, like a mixture of shrapnel and Cupid's tiny fucking love arrows.

My heart inflates.

My brain cries out in confusion.

"I'm sorry, what?"

"I love you, Dillon. I'm in love with you. And I'm sorry that I fucked up. I know I'm probably getting all of this wrong, just blurting out that I love you like that, but it's the truth."

My insides are trembling with shock. "And, uh"—I lick my dry lips—"when did you, um, realize that you love me? Was it before or after you broke up with me?"

"After."

"What, like a day? A week? A week and six days? What exactly made you realize? Because I'm a little confused that you've turned up here out of the blue after two weeks of no contact and you're telling me that you love me when the last time I saw you, you were telling me that we would have an ending, that there would be no start of something for us. Pretty much, you told me that you had zero feelings for me at all."

"I had feelings for you. I just didn't understand them, and honestly, when I started to a little, they scared the shit out of me. Then, I read the end of your book. All I could see was you and me together like that, and I panicked."

"If the thought of you and me together causes you to panic, then you shouldn't be here, West, telling me that you love me."

"That's the point. It did scare me. But it doesn't now. I've had time to think things over, and I talked with Coach. He helped slap some sense into me."

"Literally?"

"No."

"Shame."

"Dillon, when we started out, I said that I would never lie to you. But I did—the moment that I told you that we had to end. I didn't want that. But I thought it was the only option. I knew then that I had feelings for you, but I told myself that I was no good for you. That I couldn't be the man you deserved. I'm not good at this stuff. I've never even had a relationship. You were my first."

He's acknowledging that what we had was a relationship. That's a start. It also helps to melt some of the ice in my chest.

"This isn't an excuse, but my dad cheated on my mother throughout the course of their marriage, and I saw what it did to her. It broke her down piece by piece until there was nothing left. I know this isn't rational, but at one point, I even thought that her tumor came from the stress he'd put on her in their marriage."

"Why didn't she ever leave?"

He shrugs. "I don't know. Love maybe. Dependency. I never asked her. All I knew was that I would never become the man my father was even if that meant not having a relationship to avoid hurting someone. With you, I knew I'd eventually do whatever was necessary to push you from my life, even knowing it would hurt us both."

"You're not your dad." I lower my voice.

"You're not your mom, but it doesn't stop you from worrying that you could be."

He's got me there. No matter how much I try and tell myself that I'm nothing like her, that I never will be, that fear is always there, lingering. What if I turn into her without even realizing, and then once I'm there, it's too late to turn back and undo the damage?

"So, what's changed? What's different now?"

"I can't live without you. I tried for two weeks, and it fucking sucks. I can't function. I barely sleep. My game is shit. I'm just shit without you."

I look down at the table and scratch my nail over the wood. "And what is it that you want from me?"

"A chance. Just like you gave me … well, my character in the book when he fucked up toward the end."

My eyes flick to his. "You read it all?"

"Yeah. It's really fucking good, Dillon. I don't know much about romance, but I know ours was really fucking epic. Until I messed it up."

I press my lips together. "I don't know."

"Please, Dillon. I'm not above begging. If I have to get down on my knees here and make a total ass of myself, I will."

He starts to slide off his chair, but I grab his arm, stopping him.

"That won't be necessary," I hiss.

"So, you forgive me?" His eyes light up.

I feel that ache in my chest again. "I forgive you. But …"

"Don't *but* me."

"West, when you broke up with me, it gutted me, but after being home a while and thinking over things …" I let out a sad sigh. "We would have broken up at some point anyway. I live here, and your life is in America. Long distance never works. Not long-term."

300

"If I could stay here with you, I would. But my job is in America."

"You'd live in Hull?"

I'm shocked, but also I just couldn't see West here. The thought of him living in my little corner of the world makes me want to laugh. Everything about him is too … big for Hull. And I'm pretty sure his dad would have a coronary if his son lived here.

"If I could." He reaches his hand over the table and takes hold of mine, and I let him. The feel of his skin on mine is everything that I've been missing. "Dillon, do you love me?"

Do I love him?

Is the sky blue? Do birds sing in the morning?

"Yes," I whisper. "I love you."

Relief covers his face. It's crazy to me that he even considered that I might not.

"Then, come back to America with me."

"I can't. I just got this job. I can't just quit and come to the States with you."

"Why not?"

"Because … well, because eventually, I would have to come back home. I can't stay in America forever. I only get a limited time there, and I can't quit this job because I'd have to come back here and then get another, meaning—"

"Dillon." He leans over the table and presses his lips to mine.

He kisses me, and everything just disappears. All the hurt I felt, the anger, and the disappointment. Nothing seems to matter anymore now that he's here and kissing me.

"Sorry," he whispers, moving back. "But I couldn't wait any longer to kiss you."

"It's fine," I breathe. "Feel free to shut me up that way anytime."

A smile touches his lips. "Noted. Now, back to you coming to the States with me."

"I can't—"

He holds up a hand, cutting me off. "You can apply for a work visa."

"But I don't have a job in the States. Duh."

He laughs a deep, husky sound, and it makes my stomach swoop and dive, like there's a flock of birds in there.

"God, I've missed you. And you're right. You don't currently have a job in the States, but you do potentially have an American publisher."

"I'm sorry, what now?"

He gives me a nervous look. "Okay, so don't be mad, but I might have given *The Two-Week Stand* to an editor friend of my teammate's for her to read, and she loved it. She wants to set up a meeting with you to talk about them publishing it."

"You … what? I'm … what?"

He laughs a low, toe-curling sound. "Her name is Addison. She gave me her number for you to call her."

"A publisher … wants to publish my book? For real?"

"For real." He smiles.

And I can't even be mad that he went and gave my unedited book to an editor to read because he said that she loves it.

She loves it.

Oh. My. Fucking. God.

"So, if you get this deal—which you will because you're a fucking awesome writer—then you'll have work ties to the US because of your publisher."

"And I'll be able to stay there. With you."

He cups my face with his hand. "Yeah, babe, with me."

So, my choices are to stay in Hull, working at this coffee shop, or go live in America with the man I love and have my book published, living out my dream?

Hmm. It's a tough one.

"I'll be paying rent this time," I tell him firmly.

When he got me to the States last time, he wouldn't take any money from me for rent. The only thing I could do to contribute was buy groceries, and he wasn't even keen on that.

A smile lights up his face. "I'll do whatever it takes to get you back home with me."

Home. With West. Now, that sounds pretty damn good.

"I love you, Double D. Pretty sure I have since the moment you stumbled into the bar on the island."

"You fell in love with me *that* night?" I give him a dubious look.

"Okay, well, maybe not *that* exact night. It was probably the night when you let me stick my dick in you for the first time."

"So romantic." I roll my eyes.

"I'm not. But for you, I'll try."

And that there is the most romantic thing he could have said. My eyes start to fill with tears.

"Shit, I upset you. I'm sorry." His eyes are bright with worry.

"No, they're good tears, I promise. I'm just … happy—that's all."

"Thank fuck. And I promise you, I plan on spending the rest of forever trying to make you happy."

Forever.

Who would've thought that my two-week stand would turn into forever? Definitely not me. But here we are.

I take West's hand in mine and squeeze it. "I promise to make you happy too."

"You already do, Double D. You have since the moment you came into the bar and sat on the stool next to me. I might not have loved you then, but you've been making me happy since the moment we met."

That makes me smile. "You too."

He lifts a brow. "You don't remember that night."

"Semantics. I might not remember, but I know that you made me happy, for sure. Just because my brain is shit and—"

"Dillon."

"What?"

He kisses me again. "I love you," he says against my lips.

Smiling, my heart full of everything that I feel for him, I whisper, "I love you too, West."

epilogue

WEST

"Beer and a Long Island iced tea," I tell the bartender.

Dillon and I are back on the island where we first met three years ago. I'm sitting in the bar, on the exact stool my bored ass was sitting on when I first laid eyes on her. Only I'm not bored this time. I'm actually nervous as fuck.

I've just ordered the same damn drinks we both had on that first meeting. The bartender is the same guy who served me all those years ago. He actually remembers us. Well, he remembers Dillon and how drunk she was that night.

Although, drunk or sober, my girl is unforgettable.

And, yes, even though Dillon was wasted that night and remembers very little about it, I remember everything. That night changed my life. She changed my life.

These last three years with her have been amazing. Just being with her, living with her, loving her … it's so effortless. We fit together. We make each other happy. We make each other better. Well, she makes me better. Dillon was already awesome as fuck.

In the last few years that we've been together, my game has only improved. Coach was right when he said Dillon made a difference in my game. Because she makes me happy. When I'm happy, I play at my best.

I can't believe that I ever thought I didn't need someone. That I didn't need *her*. Dillon is my whole life. Every decision I make, I make with her in mind.

Dillon's career is soaring, and I'm so fucking proud of her. She's released three books in the time we've been together, including *The Two-Week Stand*, which absolutely flew off the shelves. It became an overnight best seller, landing on a bunch of lists, one being *The New York Times*. Dillon absolutely freaked when she got the news. We had a big celebration that night. The books Dillon has written since *The Two-Week Stand* have all been a part of a series following on from it but about different characters, which, of course, are fictional. We've never told anyone that the book is based on our first meeting. That's something we want to keep private between the two of us.

Dillon has been working so hard recently; we both have. She just finished up writing the first book in a new series, so I brought her here on vacation for a bit of R&R. But that's not the only reason I brought her.

Today is actually the third anniversary to the day when we first met.

She's back at the villa, showering, getting ready for dinner. Yes, it's the villa that I stayed in when I was first here.

It was the place where we spent our first night together. Even if I did sleep on the chaise and Dillon was in the bed. It was also the place where we had sex for the first time.

That villa holds a lot of special memories.

Seems I've turned into a sentimental fucking sap. But I'm in love, so sue me.

I told Dillon I'd meet her at the bar after she finished getting ready. She's been known to take her time in getting dressed up. But that's not the reason I came out first. I'd wait for-fucking-ever for Dillon.

I wanted to be here, so I'd be sitting here, waiting for her. Like I had that first night. Not that I knew then that I was waiting for her. Or maybe I was always waiting for her, but I didn't fucking know it.

Although, tonight, I'd like it if she made an appearance sooner rather than later because I'm starting to sweat like a bitch and it has nothing to do with the heat.

I take a drink of beer and then check my watch. She shouldn't be much longer.

I glance around the bar. There are a few people here. Not too many—thank fuck. I might like an audience when I'm on the field with a ball in my hands, but generally, I'm a private person.

Not that I'm afforded that while my dad is still in office. He got elected for a second term. It wasn't the happiest of days for me. I was pleased for my country. But selfishly, I was more than ready to get my privacy and life back. Although when he was reelected, it was a fuck of a lot easier since I had Dillon in my life. She has a way of making me feel okay about everything.

Mostly when she's naked.

But there isn't much longer left, and then his presidency will be over. Then, I'll be free from the constraints of being the president's son. Although my life has been overshadowed by his presidency, there was definitely a change when my game improved and I was kicking major ass on the field. I was being talked about more for my game than for who my father was. And the fact that I was finally dating someone definitely caught the press's interest. So, when I'm mentioned in the news now, it's more for my sport or my relationship with the best-selling author of *The Two-Week Stand*.

A flash of red catches my eye, and I turn my head to see my girl walking into the bar.

My heart speeds up in my chest. It never gets old, looking at her. I get the same reaction now as I did when I saw her walking through the bar three years ago. Granted, she's not stumbling on drunk legs this time. She's sashaying confidently toward me, and she's wearing my favorite red dress. It's short, showing off her gorgeous legs. It hugs her tits, giving good cleavage. What's not to like about it?

Well, apart from when other men stare at her in it, which is currently happening right now. That pisses me off. Jealousy—another thing I didn't know I could feel until Dillon.

Dillon is beautiful, so men are going to ogle her. Doesn't mean I have to like it. But I love the fact that it's me she's with and no one else. And I intend to be with her until we're old and wrinkly with one foot in the grave.

Reaching me, she slides in between the stool and presses her hand to my chest. "Hey, handsome."

She kisses me on the lips. When she goes to move back, I cup her face and kiss her deeper, sliding my tongue into her mouth, loving the soft moan she makes, which, of course, shoots straight to my dick.

Down, boy. There'll be time for that later.

When I release her, she's breathing a little harder, her face and chest flushed. "Get a room." She grins, sliding her cute ass onto the stool next to me.

"Got one—with the hottest girl on the island," I respond.

"Oh yeah?" She picks up her drink and takes a sip from the straw. "Do I know her?"

I love it when we play little games like this.

But I have a feeling that the way I thought this moment was going to happen—the one I've been planning out in my head for months—is not at all going to go the way I thought it would.

But from the moment I met Dillon, nothing has gone as I planned. That's what I love about us. Our life together is constantly full of surprises.

"Probably not. And you probably shouldn't sit here either. Or kiss me for that matter. She gets real jealous. Like crazy-mad jealous. She'd totally kick your ass."

She raises a brow, chewing on her straw. "She sounds awesome."

"She is." I bring my bottle to my lips and take a drink. "I actually met her on this island. Three years ago today in fact."

When I look at her, her eyes have softened. "That so? Well, happy anniversary."

She tilts her glass in my direction, and I tap it with my bottle.

"Yeah … and please don't tell her this because it's a surprise." I lean a little closer, lowering my voice. "But I brought her here to ask her to marry me. I plan on proposing tonight."

She gasps, and her eyes widen.

She blinks a few times.

Her throat works on a swallow.

And my heart is fucking racing.

I turn in my seat toward her and pull the ring box from my pocket.

Then, I slide off my chair, getting to my feet, and crack open the box. "What do you think of the ring? You think she'll like it? I had it specially designed with her in mind. Red's her color."

The ring is a red trillion cut diamond, surrounded by small diamonds, set in a platinum band. It cost a fucking fortune, but she is beyond worth it.

Dillon swallows and moistens her lips with her tongue, her eyes fixed on the ring in my hand. "I, uh … I think she'll love it."

Her eyes lift to mine. I see love and happiness swimming in them, and my heart thumps.

"She's a lucky girl."

"I think so." I grin, and she laughs softly, nudging me with her knee. "But in all honesty, I'm the lucky one. She changed my life. Changed me for the better."

She sniffles. "I'm betting she thinks the same things about you."

I stare at her a beat. Staring into those eyes that first captivated me and never let me go. And I never want them to let me go.

"So … do you think there might be a chance that she'll say yes to marrying me?"

"Oh, I think there's a one thousand percent chance that she'll say yes."

"A thousand percent, huh?"

"Yep."

"Dillon?"

"What?"

"Will you marry me?"

A smile and then, "Yes. A thousand percent yes."

I slide the ring on her finger, and then I kiss her.

"I love you," I say against her lips, my hands cupping her face.

"Love you too."

I kiss her again, and then I keep kissing her.

Because I plan on spending the rest of my life kissing her.

Dillon and I might have started out as a two-week stand, but we're forever now.

A real happily ever after.

OTHER BOOKS BY SAMANTHA TOWLE

STAND-ALONE NOVELS

CONTEMPORARY ROMANCE
Under Her

Sacking the Quarterback (BookShots Flames/James Patterson)

The Ending I Want

When I Was Yours

Trouble

ROMANTIC SUSPENSE
River Wild
Unsuitable

PSYCHOLOGICAL THRILLER
Dead Pretty

SAMANTHA TOWLE

CONTEMPORARY ROMANCE BOOK SERIES

THE GODS SERIES
Ruin
Rush

THE WARDROBE SERIES
Wardrobe Malfunction
Breaking Hollywood

THE REVVED SERIES
Revved
Revived

THE STORM SERIES
The Mighty Storm
Wethering the Storm
Taming the Storm
The Storm
Finding Storm

PARANORMAL ROMANCE NOVELS
The Bringer

THE ALEXANDRA JONES SERIES
First Bitten
Original Sin

acknowledgments

MY HUSBAND AND CHILDREN. There are no other three people in this world that I would want to be stuck in a house with amid a global pandemic; we're three lockdowns in, but we still continue to laugh and have the best time. I know living with a writer isn't easy. Yet you all still love me. And I love you three like I didn't even know possible. Infinity and beyond, my darlings.

My Ungodly Hour Team. I owe the completion of this book to the three of you. Tash, for the yelling and sprints. Vic, for the blurbs and teasers. Elle, for the words of encouragement. You three girls are the bomb. I literally can't write a book without you all now.

My Venga Girls. What would I do without you all? It's the best feeling to be mates with a bunch of women who share my weird sense of humor!

My Wether Girls. Our group continues to grow but remains the exact same. In there, I am surrounded by wonderful, supportive women, and it warms my heart to see and helps to restore my faith in the human race daily. I've needed that reminder even more so this past year.

My editor, Jovana. You put up with my flaky last-minute ways, taking it all in stride. I honestly couldn't do this without you. So, don't ever leave me. Please.

My agent, Lauren Abramo. I'm so lucky to have you. You handle my weird writer ways. My change of plans. Take the worry and stress that I'm feeling away with a few calming words. I get to see my books in stores, in foreign print, and hear them on audio because of you. You are fabulous. So, you can't leave me either. Please. Also, a big thank-you to Kemi Faderin for handling my foreign deals and keeping everything in line.

My cover designer, Najla Qamber. Your help with this cover has been so greatly appreciated. From the last-minute cover change to the rush on teasers and promo material, you and your team have been amazing! I owe you.

Thank you to each and every member of the blogging world, who work tirelessly to help promote books, without ask or complaint. We authors couldn't do it without you. You are truly appreciated.

And as always, to you, the reader. You are the reason I get to live my dream. And stay home and work in my Oodie! Thank you from the bottom of my heart.

about the author

SAMANTHA TOWLE IS A *New York Times*, *USA Today*, and *Wall Street Journal* best-selling author.

A native of Hull, she lives in East Yorkshire with her husband, their son and daughter, and three large furbabies.

She is the author of contemporary romances (The Storm Series, The Revved Series, The Wardrobe Series, The Gods Series) and stand-alones (*Trouble*, *When I Was Yours*, *The Ending I Want*, *Unsuitable*, *Under Her*, *River Wild*, *Dead Pretty*, and *Sacking the Quarterback*, which was written with James Patterson). She has also written paranormal romances (*The Bringer* and The Alexandra Jones Series). With over a million books sold, her titles have appeared on countless best-seller lists and are currently translated into ten languages.

Sign up for Samantha's newsletter for news on upcoming books: https://samanthatowle.co.uk/newsletter-sign-up

Join her reader group for daily man candy pics, exclusive teasers, and general fun: www.facebook.com/groups/1435904113345546

Like her author page to keep in the know: www.facebook.com/samtowlewrites

Follow her on Instagram for random pics and the occasional photo of her: www.instagram.com/samtowlewrites

Pinterest for her book boards: www.pinterest.co.uk/samtowle

Also Twitter to see the complete nonsense she posts: https://twitter.com/samtowlewrites

And lastly, Bookbub, just because: www.bookbub.com/authors/samantha-towle

Printed in Great Britain
by Amazon

79479712R00183